THE CHESS MURDERS

CW00516509

MURDERS

THE SECOND LORD KIT ASTON MYSTERY

THE CHESS BOARD MURDERS

THE SECOND LORD KIT ASTON MYSTERY

JACK MURRAY

Kit Aston Series
The Affair of the Christmas Card Killer
The Chess Board Murders
The Phantom
The Frisco Falcon
The Medium Murders
The Bluebeard Club
The Tangier Tajine
The Empire Theatre Murders
The French Diplomat Affair (novella)
Haymaker's Last Fight (novelette)

Agatha Aston Series
Black-Eyed Nick
The Witchfinder General Murders
The Christmas Murder Mystery

DI Jellicoe Series
A Time to Kill
The Bus Stop
Trio
Dolce Vita Murders

Danny Shaw / Manfred Brehme WWII Series
The Shadow of War
Crusader
El Alamein

ISBN: 9798513845669
Imprint: Independently published

For Monica, Lavinia, Anne and our angel baby, Edward

Prologue

Petrograd, Russia: 30th December 1916

Oswald Rayner gazed at the semi-conscious man lying at his feet. Calmly, he removed a Webley Service revolver from his overcoat pocket, aimed at the man's head and fired one shot. The bullet entered the forehead, ending the life of Grigori Rasputin.

Prince Felix Yusupov looked on. He betrayed little emotion at what he'd just witnessed. Instead, he merely nodded to Rayner. Kneeling, Rayner gazed without pity at the dead man. He lifted Rasputin's lifeless arm, pulled back the sleeve of his coat and checked for a pulse. The former adviser to the Tsarina had proved a little more durable than Yusupov had anticipated. Rayner was keen to make sure he really was dead. Satisfied his mission was accomplished, he rose and pocketed his revolver. A half-smile appeared on his face.

'Look on the bright side, Grigori Yefimovich, it would've been an awful hangover,' said Rayner, eyeing the corpse.

Yusupov rolled his eyes and said sardonically, 'Good to see such respect for the dead Oswald.' His English was perfect.

Rayner smiled and replied in Russian, 'I'm sure you gave the poison respectfully Felix.'

This made Yusupov grin. The smile turned to laughter when Rayner added, 'And the bullet was delivered with such affection.'

'I think, Oswald, you should take your leave. I'm not sure how much it would be appreciated if His Majesty's Government were found taking an active role in the politics of Mother Russia.'

'Perish the thought old chap,' replied Rayner wryly, before adding, 'Are you certain you don't want some help in moving our friend, here, into the river?'

'We can manage, Oswald. Time to make an exit,' said Yusupov with one eye on the street. He seemed on edge again and could not hide his nerves.

'Hopefully not pursued by a Russian bear,' smiled Rayner.

The two old friends embraced. Then Rayner walked away from his companion and the lifeless body of Rasputin without looking back.

Yusupov regarded the dead body again before turning to the car parked some way behind him. He signalled for help and then lit a cigarette. The cigarette helped settle him. It had been a traumatic night.

Killing someone in cold blood was a new experience for him. He hoped one he would never have to repeat. This was not because he felt that a moral line had been crossed. Far from it, the rightness of his action was clear to him. Rasputin was a malign influence on his country; a danger who was better off dead. His distress stemmed from Rasputin's ungentlemanly refusal to die at the first time of asking. This necessitated more violent measures. His hand went to his neck as he

2

remembered how the poisoned man had come back to life suddenly and attempted to strangle him. He shuddered involuntarily. It was over. Or so he expected.

One unwelcome thought lingered like the last guest at a party. If this were an example of the Russian peasantry given a glimpse of real power, what would the rest of the country be like? Were the millions of illiterates, uneducated animals living and dying in filth, as strong as this man? What would happen when they decided enough was enough? This was too depressing to contemplate. He fought to empty his mind from such thinking. However, this would be a temporary respite. The fear would never go away. For him, his friends and for people of his class, the future was more uncertain than he could ever remember.

His associates walked up to him, and they set to work moving the body towards the River Nevka.

*

The journey back to his apartment took Rayner twenty minutes. His chief concern was ensuring he wasn't followed. There was no reason his presence should have aroused suspicion, yet the worry remained. Rayner had to be careful. Russia was an ally against Germany albeit an unreliable one. He was a British agent operating within its borders. Close friends, like Yusupov, were aware of his role, but it was not something that Britain wanted other members of the Russian elite to know. Rayner intended keeping it that way.

Arriving back at his apartment, he found three men already there. All three looked up as he entered. If he was surprised to see them, Rayner kept it to himself. They looked at Rayner expectantly.

3

'How is our mad monk?' asked the seated man. He was the oldest of the three. His hair greying at the sides; he wouldn't see sixty again. The ruddy complexion suggested someone who was seconds away from exploding, even when he was relaxed.

Rayner nodded confirmation. 'Yes Ratcliff, we're free of that particular problem.' He took off his hat and coat. Underneath he wore several layers of clothing. It was very cold outside and only marginally warmer inside.

The other seated man spoke, 'Any complications?' His dark hair was brushed off his forehead. A trim moustache made him seem older than his thirty-five years.

'Sadly, yes. I had to apply the coup de grace, so to speak,' admitted Rayner.

The two men looked at one another. This was not good news. The idea of the British secret service being implicated in the murder of a Russian citizen had the potential to create many problems for Britain, not the least of which was the exit of Russia from the War.

'Nobody saw me, if that's what you're worried about, and we all know Felix can be trusted.'

The second man spoke again, 'Felix might talk. If not now, then sometime in the future. We have to think beyond the here and the now.'

'True, but he and I go back a long way. I trust him, Cornell.'

Cornell nodded but remained grim. Ratcliff looked down into his empty cup. This was unforeseen. The silence was heavy in the air; Rayner expected Ratcliff to explode any moment. He was not known for his self-control. Finally, he looked up. He was angry but, thankfully, in control.

4

'That damned fool Yusupov. Why couldn't he do what he said he would do. How difficult can it be?' Ratcliff thumped the table. 'Colin's right, this could come back to haunt us.'

'What are you suggesting, Ratcliff?' said Rayner.

Ratcliff glared up at Rayner, 'Don't worry, I'm not suggesting we add to our body count. One execution is quite enough for the moment.'

Finally, the third man spoke. He was the youngest of the three. His fair-haired flopped down from his forehead and he brushed it back.

'You do see that Yusupov only has to mention this to one other person, and we have a big problem. We wouldn't like it if Russia started killing people in England; even people we don't like.'

He was standing by the window smoking a cigarette. His tone was nonchalant, but the message was clear and unarguable. Rayner poured himself a drink and sat down. Their main problem had been dealt with, but it risked creating another in its place. Which was worse? Embarrassment for Britain or seeing Russia pull out of the War because of the increasing influence of Rasputin on policy? Rayner was clear on this answer. Before he could speak, Ratcliff, almost reading his mind, responded to the younger man.

'I think "C" won't be happy at the way it was done, but he won't shed any tears for Rasputin. Hundreds of thousands of lives have been saved by his death.'

The young man nodded coolly and removed the cigarette that hung magically on his lower lip. He mouthed the words, "cock up" to Ratcliff. Fire burned in the older man's eyes for a moment and then he shook his head. It wasn't worth it. Not tonight.

Ratcliff turned to Rayner, "Might be best if you went to Stockholm for a while.'

Rayner nodded in agreement. This made sense. He was also relieved that Ratcliff had seen sense. Cornell seemed to calm down too. The tension slowly left the room. Seen through the lens of the lives that would be saved by the death of Rasputin, it seemed pointless to worry about how it had come about.

Cornell refilled his own cup with vodka and Ratcliff's. They clinked cups. The young man, noticeably, did not join the celebration. Instead, he returned to gazing at the street below. He liked staying by the window, endlessly fascinated by the people scampering around in the cold.

'Will you tell Hoare?' asked Ratcliff.

Rayner laughed at this. Soon he was joined in the laughter by the other two men. Samuel Hoare was in overall charge of the British Secret Service mission in Russia, but he had not been privy to this operation or any run by this little group.

'Only that our chap is dead. It's too late now to tell him what we knew, never mind our involvement. Remember, this came directly from "C". We shouldn't worry.'

Rayner glanced at Ratcliff. He had a faraway look in his eyes. Cornell noticed this also but remained silent. It was late. Britain had saved Russia from itself. The mad monk was dead.

What could possibly go wrong?

Part 1: Opening Moves

1

London: 1ˢᵗ January 1920

Sheldon's was an exclusive club in London, which valued
privacy, exclusivity and yet more, privacy. In fact, so exclusive
and private was Sheldon's, it would have been famous for its
privacy had it chosen to publicise what set it apart. Instead, its
reputation had grown hand in hand with its unashamed desire
not to intrude, in any way, on public consciousness.

Club members were asked not to mention it on their
inevitable listing in Who's Who. One unfortunate civil servant
had made just such a mistake before the war. The Boer War.
He was forced to resign. Even now, members still spoke of
this to the occasional new member who arrived. The chap
ended up in India, apparently.

There were two routes to membership at Sheldon's. One
was family: if your father was a member then any male
offspring was automatically granted membership from the age
of twenty-one. New, old blood would arrive year after year
ensuring a changing changelessness to the demography of the
club.

The only other channel was money. Sheldon's was almost
entirely funded by the generosity of new members. They were
required to pay an enormous entrance fee to enjoy the right

not to tell the world that they were a member of an exclusive private club.

Lord Oliver "Olly" Lake sat alone in the corner of the library in Sheldon's. He was by the window overlooking the park. Like his father and his grandfather before him, he was a member of Sheldon's by birth right. This was his favourite armchair. Cigar-brown, made from the softest of aniline leather, Olly Lake ardently wished he could sink into its luxury and escape the world he hated.

Outside his window the world chuntered on. In the park, people were walking this way and that. Young men, young women, mothers, old people walked, talked, sat, and ate all before him in his front row seat. He wondered why people bothered. There wasn't really any point to it all. If he'd had the energy, he would have popped into the park himself and shared this wisdom. Without looking around, he picked up his surprisingly heavy Waterford cut-glass whisky tumbler and held it in the air, moving it left and right. Within seconds, silently, invisibly it was refilled.

A drunkard he sat, detesting himself and the world around him. Down below, he spied a beautiful young girl walking through the park accompanied by her mother and current beau. She walked with an effortless, slender grace. Her dark hair was tied at the back, her head was held high, not through conceit, but because she still had a purpose, and the passion to pursue it.

She would learn, thought Lake. Passion was good until it became obsession. When you're so consumed by something that you can no longer think of anything else, then obsession, not indifference, becomes the negation of passion. And Olly

Lake was in the grip of an obsession so strong even alcohol could not tear it from his mind.

A few members strolled past Lake. A swift glance down at him, a shake of their heads and they walked on. Few sought his company now; even fewer were sought by him. The War, they said. No one was sure exactly. He'd been decorated at Marne, wounded at Neuve Chapelle, promoted at Ypres, then he had disappeared. Some said it was hush, hush intelligence. No one was sure.

A drunkard he sat, not yet thirty, wishing he had the courage not to reach thirty-one. Lake rose from his seat with some difficulty. He made an inelegant departure from the library swaying left and right. A few members looked up as he made his unsteady progress. They saw a tall man, fair-haired with blue eyes that were once clear but now filled with hatred.

Once he had been a good-looking man. They had been proud to be seen with him. His was a vintage year for the club. He had joined at the same time as his friend, Kit Aston. Older members had been aware of standards slipping for many years. Their arrival had rejuvenated the club. No longer.

Gripping the stair handrails tightly, Olly Lake somehow made it to the bottom without accident and marched, eyes straight ahead, out into the night air. He descended the steps of the club and stumbled straight into a burly man.

'Watch where you're going you damned fool,' slurred Lake. His eyes struggled to focus on the man he had bumped into, but he was unquestionably large. His hat was pulled down low over his forehead but the eyes he investigated were of a type instantly recognizable to Lake, even in his diminished state.

10

Seconds later, he was being hustled into the back of a waiting car. Struggling was useless such was the strength of the man who had accosted him. Lake fell asleep in the back of the car within seconds. Nearby another drunk, lying on the street, looked on. He laughed bitterly.

The doorman of the club also witnessed the scene. He shook his head in disgust. Lord Lake had really descended to the depths.

Lake slept fitfully although it was not a long car journey. His head screamed in a protest that was two parts nausea, and five parts excruciating pain. As soon as he was taken out of the car, he threw up prodigiously on the street. He looked up to his tormentor in the heavens.

'Are you happy?' he asked, ignoring the stares of the people passing by.

Bending over, he was ill once more.

'That feels better,' he lied.

He remained bent double for another few minutes. 'I hope this is worth it,' he said to the man standing over him. He looked up at the big man. 'Not sure I can walk so well, old boy.'

Moments later he was being half-carried up a flight of stairs and then into a large apartment. He was deposited into a dark room and heard a door locking. He was dimly aware of another person in the room, lying on a bed. He heard a voice coming from the other bed.

'You too?'

Seconds later Lord Olly Lake passed out.

-

They sat outdoors in front of the teahouse in the Summer Garden. At the bandstand, a small orchestra was playing

11

Tchaikovsky. Around them, people laughed; some danced. Children played hide, and seek, in the long grass or bushes as their mothers sat chatting to friends. July in St Petersburg was hot: Kit, Olly and Kristina were happy to have shade, but the mood was otherwise sombre.

Olly looked at Kristina and marvelled, once more, at his luck to have met someone so beautiful, and his misfortune to fall in love with her. Her boiling blond hair was tied back in with a blue rag, she had a half-smile that never left her face. His eyes never left hers. He wanted to run away to the middle of Russia and hide her away from the fever. This wasn't a fever of the body. It was a fever of the mind. Russia was burning up with revolution, whether from the anarchists or from the liberals or from the generals, like Kornilov, it was all the same.

She held his hand tightly for he needed her courage. His was failing. He feared no one yet, since the moment he had met her, fear was his constant and unwelcome companion. The sun broke through the leaves of the tree and shone directly into his eyes. It was blinding. He held his hands up to shield himself from the light.

*

'Ah,' said a voice. 'You're awake.'

The voice. He knew it from somewhere. Lake tried to focus but the light shining directly above, blinded his eyes. He could make out two men in the room with him through the blur. They were shadows initially as his eyes tried to overcome a combination of alcohol, nausea, and tiredness.

His throat was parched. He was lying on a bed in a room that had probably never been decorated. Brickwork showed through the plaster. There was no other furniture aside from the second bed, a chamber pot, thankfully empty, and a

12

bedside table with a lamp. He could almost imagine rats the size of small dogs scuttling around the room as he sat on the bed, welcoming death.

'No rooms left at the Ritz, then?' he asked sardonically.

In a moment, the light was turned off and there was darkness. A table lamp was switched on. His eyes adjusted more easily in a light less harsh. He looked up at the two men. One was built on an impressive scale; the other was smaller and more malevolent looking. Lake turned towards the other bed. It was now empty. He raised his eyebrows by way of a question. The bigger of the two men motioned with his head. Lake guessed the other man was now in a different room.

Lake was beginning to feel the full force of his hangover now. Never again, he thought. He realised he was still dressed in his tuxedo. The smell of it was overpowering, a combination of sweat and possibly other fluids that he decided not to think about. It made him feel ill again. Patting his pockets, he realised they were empty now. He groaned.

'I don't suppose there's any chance of a cigarette, chaps? Happy New Year by the way.'

13

2

Belgrave Square, London: 1st January 1920

Kit's apartment was on the first floor. It consisted of a long hallway which led through to four bedrooms, a large living room with an opening that revealed an equally spacious dining room. The décor was a decided rejection of modernism in terms of the furniture and paintings hanging on the wall. No art deco. No Bauhaus. But nor was there, unnecessary, ornamentation. There was a minimalism to the choice of furniture that betrayed a bachelor presence. The only decoration, aside from the furniture were the table lamps, a large globe and several paintings and drawings. An extensive library dominated two of the walls in the living room, floor to ceiling.

Kit and Bright sat down while Miller went to prepare afternoon tea. On the table separating the two leather sofas was an antique chess board. Bright lifted The Times and leafed through the paper while Kit looked at the afternoon post.

'Damn,' said Kit, as one telegram captured his attention.

Bright looked up from the newspaper, 'Something wrong?'

Kit looked down at the telegram again before replying, 'Nothing important. I made a commitment before Christmas which is somewhat inconvenient now.'

'I see. Can't you just bail out? Tell them you've an illness in the family or something.'

'Yes, that might do the trick. I would definitely like to avoid this.'

'Really? Why? Sorry, don't mean to pry,' smiled Bright. He was curious, but equally, he and Kit had only recently become friends. It was not his place to be so inquisitive.

'Nothing secret. A chap called Filip Serov challenged me to a chess match before Christmas. He's over in England on a chess tour and, I suppose, he thinks he should play against this country's foremost players,' smiled Kit. 'Lord only knows why he chose me.'

Bright looked at Kit archly before breaking out into a grin, 'I'd heard of your ability at chess but can't say I've heard of him. It doesn't sound like he'll be opening for Middlesex any time soon.'

Kit laughed and shook his head.

'No, he'd probably denounce cricket as a game invented by the ruling class, played by the ruling class, for the sole entertainment of the ruling class.'

It was Bright's turn to laugh.

'He wouldn't be far wrong, would he? I mean any sport that makes a distinction between "gentlemen" and "players", is sorely in need of a good shake up in my view.'

This made Kit more thoughtful, 'I know. We fought a war this way. Extraordinary when you think of it. Our amateurs came up against German professionals. They came damn close to winning.'

Bright became more serious also, 'Yes. Don't get me wrong, Kit, I'm not going to start quoting Marx, but things are changing.'

15

Returning to the telegram, Kit said, 'Serov has always been a Bolshevik. I met him before the War. We played a couple of games. Even then he was banging on about the bourgeoisie. I didn't think it would improve his temper if I pointed out that I was part of the aristocracy. Nothing so vulgar as the bourgeoisie.'

They both laughed and then were silent for a few moments as they reflected on the remarkable events in Russia over the last few years.

Almost as an afterthought Bright asked, 'Who won?'

Kit smiled, 'Between Serov and me? Honours were even then, but he's a lot better now. I've been otherwise employed these last few years.' Bright and Kit looked at one another and four years passed in a moment. Nothing needed to be said.

Bright looked thoughtful and then suggested, 'If you think he can beat you now maybe it's best you pull out.' Kit looked surprised at this suggestion, so Bright added, 'I mean it. No point in handing the Bolsheviks a propaganda victory.'

'I think you've reached the heart of why he challenged me in the first place. Nothing would please his paymasters more than victory in a chess match against a representative of the elite, and an amateur to boot. To be fair to Filip, he would be confident of beating me. No point in picking a fight with someone who could give you a bloody nose. My word, the symbolism! I'm sure the Bolsheviks would have a lot of fun with that.'

Bright was laughing now.

'Your defeat could herald the world revolution they're so keen on. Imagine.'

This made Kit laugh again and then he stopped himself. Thoughts of Mary came back to him. Sensing his change in

16

mood, and the reason for it, Bright stopped laughing also and gazed sympathetically at his friend.

'She'll be here soon Kit.'

Kit nodded in gratitude but could say nothing. Mary was in Scotland to attend the wedding of a school friend. She was to be one of the bridesmaids. She had been looking forward to it for months, but everything had changed with the death of her grandfather and then meeting Kit again. She had travelled up for Hogmanay with the wedding to take place a week later. She and Kit wrote letters everyday not to mention the frequent telegrams. There was no question, Kit was missing her. His mood had been lifted by the arrival of Bright in the apartment, but he desperately wanted to see Mary again.

'I'll tell him I'm not going to play. He can say what he wants. I won't respond. I'm not turning this into a three-ring circus.'

As he said this, Miller entered the room followed by Sam, Kit's little Jack Russell. Sam hopped up onto Bright's knee.

'He senses weakness,' acknowledged Bright, as Miller put down a tray with tea and some sandwiches.

Kit looked up at Miller, 'Thanks Harry. Has the boy been fed?'

Miller laughed, 'Yes, not that it matters. Even if he's not hungry, he'll target getting more food as a matter of principle.'

Bright laughed also as he fed Sam a bit of the cucumber sandwich, 'Why ever do you say that?'

'Just a feeling Doctor Bright, call it intuition,' said Miller as Sam gobbled down the rest of Bright's sandwich and looked up at the doctor in expectation.

'You have remarkable insight into the canine mind, Harry,' smiled Bright.

17

'Just this little so and so.'

Bright handed Sam his second sandwich, 'Last one, Sam, last one.' Both man and dog knew it wouldn't be.

3

Edinburgh: 1st January 1920

Filip Serov stepped off the gangplank onto the wet, smoke-grey concrete dock, narrowly avoiding the puddle forming rapidly at its base. He glanced up at the leaden sky and the rain falling gently on his face. The temperature was probably around freezing point. He was surprised by how warm it was.

The three-day journey had taken him through the Arctic-cold of Petrograd, through the less-than-tropical Baltic Sea to Stockholm and, ultimately, to Edinburgh. New Year's Day arrived somewhere on the North Sea, apparently, but not for him. It was another two weeks away on his calendar.

He saw a heavy-set man looking at him intently. The man was wearing a tweed overcoat, a scarf and a Homburg pulled down so that only his bespectacled eyes showed, and an impressive, dark moustache flecked with grey. A nod of the head told Serov this was the man who had come to meet him. They walked towards one another. The man spoke perfect, if slightly accented Russia.

'Mr Serov, I presume.'

'Yes, am I addressing Mr Bergmann?'

'Please let us be less formal. I am Georgy,' said Bergmann with a welcoming smile. They shook hands and Serov inspected him further. He was in his fifties, guessed Serov.

The name and the accent suggested that he was from one of the Baltic states. His bearing was military. Serov suspected that he was a part of Cheka, Russia's secret police. It made no difference if he was or was not. This man was part of the Revolution, a revolution that he, Serov, believed in. More importantly for Serov, this man clearly knew their leader, Vladimir Ilyich, or Lenin as the world knew him.

'Filip,' replied Serov smiling in return. He followed Bergmann as he led him out of the port to a waiting car.

Once inside, Filip saw there was a driver. He nodded to him. Bergmann introduced the other man, 'This is my friend and associate Leon Daniels, I may have mentioned him in my correspondence.' The two men shook hands across the seat dividing the driver from the passengers. If Bergmann was heavyset, then Daniels was constructed on a wholly different and even more epic scale. Serov made a mental note not to upset this man although he seemed quite friendly on this first acquaintance. The car quickly sped off into the centre of Edinburgh and Bergmann used the journey to outline the plan for the next few weeks of Serov's stay.

'From tomorrow, we have arranged a series of visits to chess clubs. You will start here in Edinburgh. After this, we will move south towards London. As I may have mentioned, our itinerary will include Manchester, followed by Birmingham, Cheltenham and finally a short period in London. All these cities, except Cheltenham, have a very large number of workers and trade unionists. You will have a chance to meet key leaders of the labour movement as well as play chess against enthusiasts in all of the cities.'

'Excellent. And Aston?' asked Serov.

'Sadly, Aston has not been in contact since before Christmas when he'd suggested that he might be open to a correspondence-based game,' replied Bergmann. He added, 'But don't worry, I have some ideas on persuading him.'

Serov smiled also, 'I'm intrigued.' He desperately wanted to renew his rivalry with the English lord.

'Well, I've suggested to the press that a challenge has been laid down. With some sympathetic journalists, I hasten to add. I suspect pressure may be brought to bear on Aston even if he is reluctant,' said Bergmann with a sly look which suggested Aston would be brought to heel.

Serov nodded grimly, 'Good, I look forward to playing him again.'

'You're sure you can win?'

Serov looked at Bergmann and smiled. This made Bergmann smile also and he answered his own question, 'Forgive me Filip. As you know, a lot rests on the world seeing you take on and defeat the heroes of imperialism such as Aston.'

Serov laughed, 'Just concentrate on getting him to play and gaining the attention of the press. I'll do the rest.'

Bergmann glanced at Daniels but said nothing. He noticed the hint of a raised eyebrow and a smile. For the rest of the short journey, he and Serov chatted amiably about Edinburgh and the people they drove past on the street.

They pulled up at an impressive building on Princes Street. The Old Waverley Hotel rose before the men as they exited the car. Made from Craig Leith sandstone, time had rendered the original tan colour dark. It gave the building a forbidding austere character. Serov liked this. He was a serious person. This was a serious building.

21

'Good choice,' said Serov to Bergmann as they entered the hotel. A doorman stood at the entrance and doffed his top hat. Bergmann nodded back. Daniels followed with his bags. His first impression of a man mountain was proved correct. Bergmann's associate was enormous.

Rather than go to the reception, Bergmann led the two men to the elevator. They went to their second-floor rooms. Bergmann rapped the door and a few moments later, a small man opened the door. Serov felt instinctively that he would not like this man. A brooding insecurity hung over this man like a bad smell. Sly, greedy eyes studied the new arrival. Bergmann spoke in Russian to the little man.

'Fechin, meet our guest, Filip Serov.'

Fechin's handshake was limp which only added to Serov's negative view of his character. Serov consoled himself with the thought that not all the soldiers of the Revolution would be to his liking but at least they were united in fighting for a just cause. Happily, the room was large and elegantly furnished. Serov hoped the other hotels would match the impressive grandeur, and seriousness of the Old Waverley.

Fechin called down for room service while Bergmann, Serov and Daniels sat down to discuss further the plans for the week. Daniels and Fechin were to accompany Serov to each of the locations, but Bergmann would only be able to join periodically. His role would be to keep the momentum going on publicity and prime some of the people Serov would meet over the course of his stay.

Serov was slightly disappointed to hear Bergmann would not be around for large periods of his tour. The thought of time with Fechin did not appeal. Daniels seemed a friendlier sort. Serov detected that he was no more enamoured of the little Russian than he. Bergmann shrewdly guessed the prospect of spending time with Fechin would not be appealing.

'I should mention also that another gentleman will joining our party in Manchester. He sends you, his apologies. His name is Mr Ezeras Kopel. I think the two of you will get on very well.'

Serov nodded and replied, 'Kopel? Is he Latvian also?'

'He is a fellow countryman, but he has lived in Russia for many years. I doubt you'll find anyone more committed or more capable in bringing the Revolution to the rest of the world.'

'I look forward to meeting Mr Kopel.'

This seemed to satisfy Bergmann, who smiled back to Serov. It was clear to Serov that Bergmann was most desirous that he should have a comfortable stay. This was reassuring. The meeting concluded with Bergmann announcing his intention to travel to London on the overnight train. They would meet up again in Manchester two days from now. By then he hoped that Aston would have been persuaded to play the game.

'You should use the next hour or two to take a walk around Edinburgh. It's a beautiful city. The castle is well worth a visit. Leon, perhaps you could accompany Filip.'

Daniels looked at Serov, who made it clear he was more than happy with this arrangement. Turning to Fechin, Bergmann said, 'In the meantime, could you come with me? I have some tasks that need attending to.'

The small Russian followed Bergmann from the room, leaving Daniels and Serov to one another's company.

Serov looked at his companion. Although serious, he felt a kinship with this man. He sensed an integrity in him and Bergmann, which was clearly absent in the other. Men like this had made the Revolution happen. They were brothers in arms against the imperialists. Literally, as he was to find out.

4

Belgrave Square, London: 2nd January 1920

The next morning saw Kit was rereading Mary's letter for the seventh time when he heard a voice at the front door. Then there was silence for a few moments. This turned into a minute then another minute. Finally, Kit called out from the lounge, 'Do I need to come out there with a bucket of cold water?' Laughter followed this. The door opened to reveal a slightly dishevelled Richard Bright and Esther.

'I was showing Esther the art,' explained Richard.

'The art of what?' smiled Kit

'I heard from Henry this morning,' said Esther. 'I gather things are rather tense again between him and Aunt Emily. She's still not accepting that Henry's in love with Jane,' said Esther.

Kit smiled in sympathy. 'You know the change in Henry over that holiday was remarkable.'

Esther thought for a moment and then replied, 'Yes and no. He wasn't always such a gloomy goat. Up until he was thirteen, you wouldn't have said he'd become so morose and moody. Before then he was good fun, and he was always bright. In fact, he was more than bright. He was smart. When Governess Curtis left us, and Jane was sent to the school, it all coincided with his teenage years. Then he lost Uncle Robert.

It wasn't easy for him to adjust. Speaking of it now makes me think, it wasn't such a big change really. I can remember Uncle Robert would sometimes needle him about his lack of interest in sport. But I can tell you, Henry gave it back with interest. He had the beating of Uncle Robert in these verbal duels. Mary even said as much. She thought one of the reasons Uncle Robert backed off Henry in the end was that he knew he was getting bested.'

'Really? I never suspected Henry of being so combative.'

'Oh, he was. Then, particularly after we lost Uncle Robert, that side of him seemed to disappear. Instead of arguing he just went into himself, excluding everyone, except Jane obviously. I think we're seeing the real Henry now and I'm so glad.'

Esther continued, 'It's such a pity, you know. Mary and Henry were such a pair. Occasionally, before Henry became so morose, she and I would treat him and Jane awfully. Nothing cruel. But Henry and Mary would have real flare ups. She enjoyed provoking him. He was a match for her, I can tell you. I think Mary relished the duelling because he was so good at it, too.'

Kit smiled despite the sadness he was feeling, 'I suspect both of you were too conspiratorial ever to fall into disagreement.'

Esther laughed, 'Yes, we were. Always.'

A few minutes later there was another knock at the door. They heard Miller answering followed by the sound of male voices loud and hearty in the corridor.

Surprised, Esther raised her eyebrows in a 'who are they?' manner.

'A Mr Chadderton and a Mr Stevens,' said Miller, entering the room.

Charles 'Chubby' Chadderton and Aldric 'Spunky' Stevens entered the room. Kit and Bright rose immediately.

'Esther, my dear, so sorry it's taken so long,' said Chubby walking over to Esther and giving her a hug.

Bright looked at Kit expectantly but Chubby beat him to it.

'Dr Bright, I'm Charles Chadderton, I've known your two friends longer than they care to mention.'

Bright and Chubby shook hands. The tall man was in no way as large as his name suggested. He was, however, clearly full of good humour and Bright found himself taking an instant liking to the new arrival.

'And I'm Spunky,' said the other man holding out his hand.

A look of amused shock passed over Bright's face and he looked at the innocent face of Kit, who was trying not to laugh. Spunky was like a dastardly villain from a penny blood. An eye patch over one eye and a monocle over the other. It quickly became apparent he was very far from being a scoundrel.

'You're Spunky?' said Esther naively.

Bright nearly choked when he heard this and began coughing. Esther stood up and gave Spunky a peck on the cheek. This brought a caddish smile and colour to his face.

'Thank you for everything you did, Mr Stevens. Richard are you unwell?'

'Fine,' coughed Richard, who was anything but.

Things were never gloomy with Chubby and Spunky around. He was glad to see his two friends. All that was missing was Olly Lake and the gang would be back together again. He wondered where Olly was now. It had been too long. He made a note to himself to see Olly as soon as was possible. Hopefully, by then, Mary would be at his side.

The introductions made, chairs were found for the new arrivals, and they chatted about the recent events. Chubby and Spunky filled in Esther and Bright about their role in helping Kit uncover Strangerson. When they reached the part about breaking into Strangerson's apartment, Spunky halted and glanced at Kit. Receiving nodded confirmation from Kit, he continued with his story. He had a natural story teller's gift for holding the attention of his audience and it was a good story. Adjusting his monocle, he shifted uncomfortably in his seat before continuing.

'We used somewhat nefarious means to uncover Strangerson's connection to the threatening Christmas cards.'

Bright broke in at this point, 'I thought it was the police that searched Strangerson's flat?'

'Oh, they did old boy,' smiled Spunky, 'It's just that we were there first; thought we'd check if there was a typewriter in his flat. No point in sending our flat-footed cousins along on a wild goose chase. Did them a favour if you ask me. Anyway, once we'd established beyond a shadow that this blighter could've typed the cards, we gave Kit the nod and then Inspector Stott organized the rest.'

Bright nodded at this, then said laughing, 'Well, the scoundrel had it coming even if it wasn't quite...'

'Legal?' suggested Chubby with a grin.

'Quite,' agreed Spunky. "Luckily, Inspector Stott suspected nothing.'

'Far from it, Spunky. He knew full well what was happening. He chose not to notice,' smiled Kit. 'A good man, Stott. Wasn't sure at first but he grew on me.'

'Really? Pragmatic goose,' said a surprised Spunky.

'Indeed,' said Kit.

The morning passed quickly as the group chatted about Strangerson's impending trial. All felt confident he would hang. There was little sympathy for Strangerson on this score.

'Will you join us for lunch?' asked Esther.

Neither Chubby nor Spunky were free and they separated outside the apartment. Kit cried off also, preferring to give the couple a little time together. For this, he received a grateful nod from Bright. After dropping off the pair in Leicester Square, Kit and Miller returned to the apartment. As they entered the concierge handed Miller an envelope addressed to Kit.

Kit opened the envelope which contained a short, handwritten note. After a few moments he turned to Miller, 'Seems we'll have to head out again immediately. My former commanding officer wants to meet up. He suggested a rendezvous in St James's Park.'

'Shall I bring Sam? He probably needs a walk. The old boy's been stuck in here all morning.'

'Good idea, Harry. You can both indulge your favourite pastime.'

Miller glanced up with a smile on his face, 'Yes, usually lots of very attractive ladies in the park when it's not raining.'

A moment later, Sam came bursting into the room yelping in delight. He ran around Kit, excitedly.

'Coat on, Sammy-boy. It's a tad chilly out there but at least it's dry.'

29

5

London: 2nd^d January 1920

The overnight train from Edinburgh pulled into Kings Cross. It was still dark as Bergmann disembarked from the train and made his way outside the station. Rather than going to his flat in town, he went directly to a small café near the offices of the Daily Herald on Broadway in London. The cold air stung his face and he decided against sitting outside which he would have preferred. He was immune to cold, but he suspected this might not be the case for the person he was meeting.

He looked across the road at the offices of the Daily Herald. The newspaper was in the vanguard of the labour movement in Britain. Despite its financial struggles, partly brought on by its unpopular anti-war stance between 1914-18, it had managed to survive. This was due to genuinely insightful journalism. It had made revelations of conspicuous consumption by the rich at the Ritz during the War. This was at a time when many were suffering hardship. The paper also campaigned for better conditions and pay for workers. It was at the forefront of the union movement and often providing encouragement for those considering industrial action.

Another major platform for the paper was its support for the Russian Revolution. Through organised rallies and editorials, the Herald built support in Britain for the new government in Russia. The ongoing civil war in Russia also received significant coverage in the paper. With sympathies closer to the Bolsheviks than the White Army, the paper was prominent in campaigning against any armed intervention in the war.

Unsurprisingly, the newspaper was viewed with some alarm by politicians in the two main parties as well as the security services who were keen to monitor its activities and relationships. It felt like a fifth column operating in the country and had been subject to investigation in the past regarding links to the Bolsheviks.

As Bergmann waited, he thought about Billy Peel, the journalist he had been recommended to meet. He was nicknamed "Pit Bull" by his colleagues. Peel exhibited many of the characteristics of the much-maligned canine. Stumpy, ugly, and tenacious as hell, when Peel sank his teeth into a story, he didn't let go until blood appeared. Not only was he aware of his nickname he took great pride in it.

Ambition was the central component of Billy's life. It was the platform upon which his success was built. He could smell a story the way a wine connoisseur could distinguish a good claret.

His beginnings in journalism had not singled him out for greatness. Originally an obituary writer for a local newspaper in Belfast, the Newsletter, he had graduated from this position as his increasingly lurid revelations about the recently deceased resulted, on several occasions, in litigation. Although the paper had won every case, the publicity was not what the editor wanted for the paper.

Peel was moved to a new area for the newspaper: sport. It was hoped that an uncontroversial area such as sport would curb Peel's tendency to create news where none existed. Alas, this was doomed to failure. Peel's revelations that hinted at rampant lesbianism among Ulster's hockey team proved a bitter pill for the editor to swallow as well as for the fathers of the girls involved. The crime desk seemed the next logical place for Peel's unique talent to flourish. His stint here proved short lived as matters in France came to a head.

After the War, Peel stayed in London. He used the contacts of his colleagues to find a home at the Daily Herald. It was with little regret that Peel's former editor bid a final farewell to his sports columnist. There was just a pang of guilt, however, as the editor wondered what sort of havoc Peel would wreak at his new paper.

He didn't have long to wait. Even by the standards of the Daily Herald, Peel was a firebrand. Initially, his wrath was poured upon the army generals who had provided disastrous leadership for the working men of Britain and Ireland. The owners of the Herald loved the passion in Peel's prose and gradually gave him an open brief to write on any subject he pleased. Peel had arrived.

He was going to make the Establishment pay.

*

Peel recognised Bergmann through the café window from the description the Russian had given him. He seemed to be talking with someone, but when he walked inside, he saw that the big Russian was alone.

In person, Peel was every bit as diminutive as his erstwhile canine namesake. A brief handshake was followed by a few

33

words of greeting. A casual observer would not have detected much warmth from either party. Peel went straight to business.

'So, Bergmann, what's the story?'

Bergmann was used to dealing with people in a direct manner himself. Peel seemed similarly inclined. This suited him. He was happy to forego small talk in favour of a briefing on the essentials.

'You're aware that Filip Serov has just arrived in the country?' asked Bergmann.

'Yes, and I could care less. And if I could care less, then I can tell you, my readers will care even less than that. They're trying to survive on pennies from factory owners. Chess? Who gives a ___?'

Bergmann thankfully interrupted Peel before his full eloquence could be shared with the rest of the café which had suddenly become interested in the conversation. Aware of this, Bergmann decided to pay his bill.

'Thank you, my friend. Perhaps we could go to the offices of The Times and continue our conversation, or the rest of the world may know what we're going to talk about.'

Peel smiled ruefully and mumbled a half-hearted apology. The two men rose from the table. Bergmann paid his bill, and they walked along Broadway towards Westminster. The cold slapped the faces of both men. For Bergmann it was quite refreshing, but Peel began to grumble. Despite hailing from Ireland, he was no lover of cold weather.

'Make this quick Bergmann. This may feel like summer in St Petersburg to you, but I'm foundered.'

'Petrograd.'

'Who cares? It's freezing my___.'

34

Once again, Bergmann interrupted Peel, for fear of being treated to an anatomical analogy that conjured up highly unwelcome images.

'I'll be quick, Peel. There are several reasons why the arrival of Serov should be of interest to you. Firstly, he will be playing a series of chess matches up and down the country. These matches will be against the very cream of the bourgeoisie in Britain. And he will beat them all. Secondly, he will be meeting workers and Trade Union representatives on this tour. He will give speeches at meetings__.'

This was more interesting. Peel asked the obvious question.

'He speaks English?'

'Fluently.'

Peel nodded and then added, 'Interviews?'

'Exclusivity, Peel.'

'All right. Anything else?'

'Yes, the part I think you shall find most interesting is the match against Kit Aston.'

'Lord Kit Aston will play a chess match against Serov?'

Bergmann hesitated a moment, 'This is where I may need your help. Aston indicated before Christmas some interest but since then I've heard nothing. This could work to our benefit, however, if you get involved.'

'How?'

'The original idea was that we start the match via telegram correspondence with the end game in London, face to face. The British Chess Federation are very supportive and willing to stage the final leg of the match at Hampton Court. The week or two of correspondence chess would be published in your paper so that by the time Serov is in London, we would have enormous public interest. You can have as much access to Serov as you wish.'

Peel was now interested. Bergmann could see he had hooked his fish and did what all great salesmen do in this situation. He shut up.

'I don't need to live in his underwear,' thought Peel out loud. He chose to ignore Bergmann physically flinching at the idea, 'but it might work. I'll have to run it by George Lansbury.'

'Lansbury?' asked Bergmann.

'My editor.'

'Of course.'

After a few moments, time enough for Peel to have played out how the story could run as well as potential fault lines, he quizzed Bergmann in a way that, for once, impressed the big man and made him grateful that he had selected Peel.

'What if Aston wins? It'll be embarrassing. The ruling class papers will have a field day.'

'He won't. Serov is too good. He'll be world champion one day.'

'What's to stop Aston cheating, getting help? I mean, correspondence chess, that's ridiculous. He can spend hours on this. Why not find other people to help him?'

'Who can Aston turn to? He's one of the best players in your country. What other help will he get? Chess literature is, at best, poor. Even if Aston finds the relevant chess writings, they will only help him through the early moves. The end game is where everything happens. Aston will be alone and exposed by Serov. He will be crushed and the workers in Britain will see how your establishment, your rulers, can be beaten by one of their own.'

36

'Serov comes from a working-class family?'

'Better than that, he grew up in a state orphanage. His parents were executed for agitating against the Tsar. Hanged, I believe. Not the wisest thing for parents of a small child to be doing, of course. He's always been a strong Bolshevik. He started long before the Revolution.'

'I'll emphasise his background then,' nodded Peel, enthusiasm burned in his eyes.

Bergmann smiled inwardly. Peel was now fully on their side. He felt completely confident in the ability of Peel to create mayhem on his behalf. The thought of what Peel was capable of prompted a snigger from Bergmann.

Peel noticed this and said, 'What's so funny?'

Bergmann didn't answer but replied instead, 'I've taken up enough of your time, comrade.' Putting his left arm on Peel's shoulder, he shook his hand, and they parted company.

6

Kit, Miller, and Sam strolled through St James's Park. The rain looked like it was going to hold off a bit longer. It was just the cold they had to contend with. Sam trotted along happily. He was clad in his favourite coat made from Kit's old uniform. It always amused the two men when they saw Sam dressed up and ready for battle.

'If ever a coat was ready made for a dog, it's this,' observed Miller. 'Aggressive so and so.'

Sam growled in reply, sensing Miller was, as usual, making fun of him.

'I'll swear he understands,' was Miller's only comment.

They walked around the lake. Up ahead, they had their first sight of Buckingham Palace. Its bright walls caught a shaft of sunlight and seemed to shine out against the leaden-grey sky and the leafless trees.

'Have you ever been there, sir?' asked Miller.

'Not for a few years,' replied Kit. He didn't need to explain why. 'My family were rarely invited to court. You know my father.'

Miller did know Kit's father. Their relationship was strained. He and Kit rarely spoke. Over recent years, Kit's visits to the family home were increasingly rare. Miller dropped the subject of the Palace, wishing to avoid anything which might pain Kit. As they rounded the lake, Kit saw the meeting place. Ratcliff was not yet there. He handed Miller the lead.

'You take Sam off in the other direction. I'll see you back at the car in an hour or so.'

'Very good, sir,' replied Miller. He led Sam along a different route while Kit headed towards his appointment.

*

Roger Ratcliff viewed Kit as he walked towards the meeting place. He could see his old comrade-in-arms limp as he walked. This caused him to ache inside. So many young lives lost or blighted by the carnage. Kit was one of the lucky ones. He turned and spoke to Colin Cornell.

'Prompt as ever. You can always rely on Kit. Do you want to stay or go? Up to you.'

Ratcliff and Cornell looked at one another. Cornell shrugged and said, 'Probably better if he doesn't know I'm involved.'

This seemed to disappoint Ratcliff, 'I'd love to know why you and he don't get along, Colin.'

'Ask him,' said Cornell turning and walking away.

Ratcliff watched him go before turning and walking down the hill to join Kit, who was gazing out at the lake.

'Kit,' shouted Ratcliff as he neared the seat. Kit looked up and waved.

Kit stood up and turned around. He saw the burly Ratcliff smiling at him.

'Major,' said Kit smiling.

'Roger, Kit. You can call me Roger, now. Thankfully, this damn war is over.'

'This war? I hope we haven't another one looming,' said Kit grimly.

The smile left Ratcliff's face and he took on a grimmer expression. 'Funny you should say that.'

Ratcliff noted the look of shock on Kit's face as he sat down. The two men glanced around the park, a final check before they began to talk.

'I think you know my views on Russia and the risk it poses for Europe. Winston's of a like mind, but the rest of the cabinet and that infernal Welshman continue to put their collective empty heads in the sand.'

'Is this related to the Civil War or has something new cropped up?'

'You're presumably aware of Comintern?' Ratcliff saw Kit nodding so he continued, 'Kit, they're coming after us. No question. Russia has no respect for borders. They view Britain and its empire as their main enemy. They know we've been supporting the White forces with our arms stockpile at Arkhangelsk.'

Kit laughed. 'Well, I'm no lover of the Bolsheviks but we can hardly complain that they don't respect borders when we've been intervening in Russia for years. You know this as well as I do, sir.'

Ratcliff did not smile, 'Their stated aim is world revolution. Britain runs half the planet. Who do you think their biggest target is? It'll be war one day, Kit, mark my words. For now, though, they're happy to stoke up trouble wherever they can. War by proxy. They're doing it in India, they're doing it in Afghanistan, and they'll do it here also.'

'Yes, I was aware of the activities of Manabendra Nath Roy. But he's a fanatic. He can't take on all of India himself even with Russian backing.'

'Doesn't have to. We've tens of thousands of troops out there. What can they do against a nation of three hundred million? He may not be the one who finishes us there, any more than Gandhi, but it's part of a process. This is one thing we don't appreciate, and the Bolsheviks do. Time. It'll do for us in the end. It always does. I should add that Lenin's been arming the Muslims in India for a while now. The Muslims and Bolsheviks forming an alliance is the very stuff of nightmares for Whitehall. Nothing would please him more that Britain being bogged down in a conflict over there.'

'But you're not seriously proposing we fight them, Roger?' Kit was aghast. Ratcliff didn't reply but looked at Kit to confirm this was his view. He looked at Kit shake his head in clear disagreement.

'You may disagree Kit. But we must be ready for anything they do and, yes, if it were up to me, and Winston, I might add, we'd be over there right now finishing them off before it's too late.'

'Are you suggesting they've been active here?'

'Don't be naïve Kit, of course they're active here. They've been fermenting trouble for a couple of years now. There are Russian networks operating here; of that you can be certain. Even before I left the Service, we had them under observation and they certainly pose a threat to our security.'

Ratcliff could see Kit remained sceptical.

'They don't have to arm the workers, Kit, they just need to make them angry enough about inequality. They've various puppets they can use. Trade Unions or newspapers like the Daily Herald will happily relay Bolshevik propaganda all day long. It's only a matter of time before they try to influence an election.'

Kit remained unconvinced. If anything, he was feeling concerned at the fervour with which his former commanding officer was speaking. It was not wholly a surprise. Ratcliff had always been particularly antagonistic to communism. There was a new tone in his former commanding officer that bordered on paranoia.

'You may laugh Kit, but I see a time when Russia is not just trying to manipulate public opinion. It's only a short step from there to owning politicians within the Labour Party.'

'We know a bit about that, sir,' pointed out Kit.

'Clearly, we've done similar,' acknowledged Ratcliff.

'But we're British,' Kit did not try to withhold the sardonic note in his voice. Thankfully, it made Ratcliff smile. Although he often disagreed with the major, he recognised Ratcliff was a passionate defender of his country although not beyond using unscrupulous methods. In addition, Ratcliff was always willing to listen to counter arguments. There had been many occasions in Russia when Kit had needed Ratcliff's support in restraining the more aggressive tendencies of other undercover British operatives. Ratcliff and he would never be close friends, but they had developed a mutual regard and trust.

'Yes Kit. But look, I'm sure you're not interested in hearing me rehash old arguments. You had enough of that in nineteen seventeen. The reason why I wanted to meet you is regarding Mr Serov.'

Kit shot Ratcliff a look. 'How on earth did you hear about this?'

'I had word of this probably a long time before you did, Kit. I'm told the idea's been circling around various departments in the Bolshevik government for a while now. I understand it was the Propaganda people who were the most positive.'

This satisfied Kit. Although he had spent barely a year in Russia, he knew how seriously the Bolsheviks treated news coverage of the Revolution. Their approach was based on identifying heroes who would project a positive face for communism to the nation and the world. It was not enough just to highlight "the little man", the fight for hearts and minds also had to be waged with the intelligentsia. In this regard, Serov would fit the bill. His Bolshevik credentials were unimpeachable. He was good looking, probably a genius, yet he retained a common touch that would make him attractive to people from all walks of life. As Kit thought about it, he realised why the British Secret Service would be interested.

Ratcliff eyed Kit closely. He could see how Kit quickly understood the ramifications of their conversation. Gently, he asked, 'I was wondering what you intended doing?'

'I can't play,' replied Kit.

This seemed to disappoint Ratcliff, although Kit could not be sure. The face of Ratcliff usually portrayed two emotions: good-humoured calm or rage. There was not a lot in between. Travel between the two emotions took place at an unhealthy velocity that was as bad for Ratcliff's blood pressure as it was unwelcome to those on the receiving end.

'Well of course, it's your concern but may I ask why?'

At this point Kit was rather stumped for an answer that did not sound a little like a child wanting to be excused rugger because it was a little wet outside.

'I've been rather busy these last few years as you know,' pointed out Kit. 'My game is not quite what it once was.' This didn't sound as bad as he'd expected. Then Kit asked Ratcliff why he was interested.

'I'm in no position to tell you anything now, Kit. It was more of a request,' replied Ratcliff.

'You wanted me to play the match?'

'Yes.'

'Even though you must know that Serov has every chance of winning. I'm not quite the player I was. Clearly, Serov will have had more recent match practice than I. He'll be very focused on the game. I won't be, as you may imagine.'

Ratcliff smiled, but there seemed to be sadness in the smile.

'I hope you won't be offended, Kit, but I wasn't expecting you to win. In fact, I fully expect the Russians to try and make capital, so to speak, out of your probable defeat in the press and elsewhere.'

'So why on earth would I play?'

'There's a lot of interest in this game, as I said. It goes all the way to the top. We could use your participation as a bargaining chip to have some of our boys released from prison,' said Ratcliff, before adding, despondently, 'We've had a run of bad luck on that score. Anyway, it'll be back-channel stuff.'

Kit sat back in the seat and exhaled slowly. This was an impossible situation for him. However, he knew what he would have to do. The thought that his bailing out of a chess match would result in British agents staying in a Russian jail was abhorrent to him. Ratcliff sensed how Kit was thinking and patted him gently on the back.

'I'm truly sorry Kit. If there was another way, we'd do it. Unfortunately, we're fresh out of alternatives.'

44

Kit looked at Ratcliff, he could see how uncomfortable Ratcliff felt about putting him in this position. A bird splash-landed on the lake and both men looked at it. The surface of the lake had a thin crust of ice forming. The sight of it made Kit shiver, or was it the decision facing him? He wasn't sure, but he knew that couldn't refuse. Finally, Kit nodded to Ratcliff.

Almost as an afterthought, Ratcliff added, 'Who knows, old chap; you might even win.'

7

Edinburgh: 2nd January 1920

Fiona Lawrence was a mathematics prodigy. At twelve years old she had already reached a level not only far in advance of her fellow school children it would have sent a few university lecturers rushing to their textbooks to bone up on philosophical Boolean algebra.

For relaxation, she played chess. In fact, she played a lot of chess; friendships for Fiona tended to be with adults rather than children. Kids of her own age found her advanced intellect and interest in things mathematical, distinctly odd. Only from time to time did Fiona miss the company of children her own age. However, a few minutes exposure to other giggling girls talking about the latest romantic novel they were reading swiftly disabused her of any notion that she was somehow missing out.

Fiona's ability at chess had long since outstripped her teachers at the chess club and other players in the area. This is why, as she sat in the John Knox Presbyterian Hall in the centre of Edinburgh, she felt an excitement that she'd, perhaps, never felt before. The chance to lock horns with a genuine equal.

This was another thing that separated Fiona from other children her age. She had an unabashed certainty of her own cerebral superiority. Fiona really believed she could beat a prospective potential world chess champion like Filip Serov.

When playing chess, the tiny warrior always wore battle red. She viewed the colour as an extension of the game. For her it was a sign of aggression and strength. In a room full of sombrely dressed Presbyterians, she would stand out. This was exactly what she wanted.

Just before eleven in the morning, there was a commotion in the hall as the Russian made his entrance. He was flanked by one rather large man and another smaller, mean-looking, man. Fiona could barely suppress a smile as she saw her opponent. He had no idea his day of reckoning had come.

*

The morning for Serov had begun with a bracing walk across Princes Street Gardens. The park occupied the valley running along Princes Street on one side and Castle Rock, the volcanic plug which led up to Edinburgh Castle, on the other. The sun was shining, although this was just a detail as it seemed to be generating precious little heat. Serov didn't care. He was enjoying the freedom and the relative warmth, at least in comparison to Mother Russia.

He found Edinburgh much to his liking. There was an openness to the city but also a seriousness, dignity even, which appealed to him more than he cared admit. He quickly banished such thoughts and continued to walk through the gardens with a mood that swayed between elation at his surroundings and sadness that his work would begin in earnest, taking him away from the tranquil solitude he was enjoying so much.

It was difficult for Serov to hide his lack of enthusiasm for the Presbyterian Hall as he climbed out of the car. The building was dark and austere like the other buildings he had seen, but there was also an oppressiveness. Serov felt this was in keeping with the role of religion for the working man. He didn't like this building or what it represented. However, he was here to win more than just a series of chess matches.

Smiling like a politician, he shook hands with a church minister named Upritchard and his very earnest although not unattractive daughter. To his surprise he found Upritchard to have none of the earnestness of the building or his daughter. In fact, he seemed positively honoured to have Serov visit them. This was followed by more introductions as he walked into the hall. He had forgotten each of their names within seconds.

As dark and oppressive as the exterior was, the interior more than matched it in its ability to crush the spirit. Serov hoped that he could make short work of the series of opponents seated at tables which formed a "U". He looked around the room. A quick count revealed around a dozen eager players waiting to commence battle. None of them seemed younger than fifty. All were smiling up at him expectantly. Then he caught sight of the twelve-year-old Fiona Lawrence. Wearing bright red, she stood out from the dark suited men like a witch among altar boys.

Their eyes met.

Fiona Lawrence smiled at Serov. There was no humour or cordiality, however. Serov immediately detected the smile of a predator. He knew this would be the match. More than this, he knew she knew this too. Almost imperceptibly she nodded to him thereby confirming his suspicions. He disliked her on first sight. He would make an example of her.

Before the matches began, Daniels called him over to pose for photographs with the church elders and the chess club president. Formalities out of the way, Serov was introduced briefly to his opponents. Fiona Lawrence was sitting on the last table. They shook hands. Her hand was very small. Following the introductions, the games began in earnest.

Serov walked from player to player making a series of quick-fire opening moves, he was always black. That is until he reached the table of Fiona Lawrence. She had switched the board around, allowing Serov to play the white pieces. Theoretically this gave Serov a slight advantage. He glared in anger at the pocket predator. Before she could react, he swiftly turned the board around so that she would have a better chance.

Fiona Lawrence raised one eyebrow and the smile left her face. Upritchard, who was trailing Serov around, much to the grandmaster's irritation, glanced at the rest of the room. Everyone was watching rapt at this battle of wills. To a man and woman, each was thinking the same thing.

Serov's 'for it' now.

Miss Lawrence was a source of great pride, if not much affection, at the chess club. Antagonising Fiona Lawrence, even if you were a grand master, was to take the chess equivalent of your life in your hands.

After a tense few moments Fiona Lawrence, to the intense relief of Upritchard and the disappointment of the room, opted to avoid a diplomatic incident. She reached down to move her first white piece. Her selection caused gasps.

Fiona moved a3. The pawn in front of the Castle moved two squares. This was in complete opposition to classic, safe opening moves using either the King or Queen pawns. It was named the Anderssen opening, after a former world champion who had devised it. The move was used very rarely for the simple reason that its fundamental weaknesses were exposed as the game progressed. This meant the chances of winning were much lower than more traditional openings. Against someone of Serov's skill it stood no chance, theoretically.

Serov's face darkened in anger. Such a move, against someone of his standing, was tantamount to an insult. The little witch was effectively forfeiting her chance of winning in favour of a highly complicated and messy pitched battle. He hated the menace, madness, and confusion of such games.

As Newton once observed, each action has an equal and opposite reaction. Seeing the anger cloud Serov's face made the child prodigy smile again in a manner which, to those witnessing it agreed, bordered on Satanic.

Serov moved his King's pawn two squares and marched back around to the first table in a very dark mood. For the next thirty minutes, driven by a controlled fury, Serov lapped around the room laying waste to the great and good of the chess club. All except Miss Lawrence.

He ignored her. Completely.

Instead, he focused on finishing off the other players. He did this with an alacrity that bordered on contempt. The period of inactivity incensed young Fiona, much to the delight of Serov, as he completely disregarded her lap after lap.

This new theatre in the mind war between grandmaster and schoolgirl had, by now, attracted the attention of many more people than just the chess club. Billy Peel was a late arrival to the venue. However, his highly tuned newsman's instinct for tension had detected 'an atmosphere' in the room. He set to work.

With eleven out of eleven victories under his belt, Serov was finally able to focus his full attention on the young opponent. As he finished his penultimate game, he turned from his vanquished opponent to see Fiona Lawrence was no longer at her table. She was, in fact, speaking to Fechin. This was alarming and dismaying in equal measure. It was alarming because he hadn't realised Fechin could speak English. It was a source of dismay because he had no idea what he was saying to her. From the genial smile on the young girl's face, he guessed that it was information she would use against him.

He was right.

As this horse had already bolted, he could only glare at Daniels to indicate his displeasure at Fechin's actions. The sharper-witted Daniels noticed what was angering Serov and called Fechin to join him immediately. The look on the face of Daniels was enough for Fechin. Realising that his conversation with Serov's opponent may have been ill-advised, he quickly parted from her and scampered over to Daniels with the air of a schoolboy about to face corporal punishment.

Serov and Miss Lawrence both approached either side of the chess table like two gunfighters. Each wore a scowl, neither blinked as they stared at one another on their way to the seats. The atmosphere was febrile.

All around the two warriors a rush ensued to view the battle. Dignity and Presbyterian solemnity were thrown to the wayside as pensioners clambered over tables to get a view of the titanic tussle about to ensue. Unusually for a Presbyterian Hall, never mind a chess club, one of the members was surreptitiously taking bets. The odds on an unexpected victory for the twelve-year-old home favourite against the world renounced Russian grandmaster were an ungenerous two to one against.

Notwithstanding this, there were several takers at this price, including three bob from the very Reverend Upritchard. He hedged this with another two bob on a draw, which was evens. His daughter looked at him with raised eyebrows. Upritchard immediately recognised disapproval in the firm set of her mouth. He sighed. So, like her mother.

Serov stared down at the board and then he looked at his opponent. With great deliberation he put his hand on the King-side Knight and moved it. Without looking away from her opponent's eyes, Fiona Lawrence put her hand on a pawn and made her next move. The battle had begun.

8

London: 2nd January 1920

Kit was in a sombre mood which his meeting with Ratcliff had only made worse. He related to his friends' details from his meeting with Ratcliff. It was clear he was torn between refusing and a sense of duty towards his old commander. Both Esther and Bright urged Kit to play.

'I'm not sure a chess match falls under either duty or national interest,' concluded Kit doubtfully. He sat back in the chair gripping the arms tightly.

'Maybe so, Kit' said Bright, 'But if what he says is true then maybe if you play then it'll help get some of our boys released. Ratcliff doesn't sound a bad sort. He's not putting a gun to your head, is he?'

This was the key issue for him.

'No, he's not. This makes it all the worse, oddly. I don't owe him any debt and it's not as if we were close. He's a good sort, but I suspect I'd think differently if I'd crossed him.'

'Why do you say that Kit?' asked Esther out of curiosity.

'He was a very intense sort of chap. Almost fanatical in his dislike of the Bolsheviks. He genuinely fears the influence they could wield in England.'

'How extraordinary,' said Bright.

'I agree but then again, he's privy to more information than I. He spent a lot of time over there. He was out there long before me. In fact, he probably knows Russia more than anyone I've met. If he's in a funk about what they could do then I suspect, there's probably some basis for it and politicians will listen to him. He's very well connected.'

'All the more reason why you should play, Kit,' pointed out Esther.

Kit smiled in gratitude at Esther before adding with faux despondency, 'Oh yes, being publicly humiliated by a Russian grandmaster will really help my mood.'

It sounded though as if a decision had been made. On the bright side, reflected Kit, it would be something to tell Mary about in his daily letter. In truth, there had not been much to say. He missed her horribly but tried to avoid thinking badly of her schoolfriend who was getting married.

Miller was despatched to send a telegram in response to the challenge. He drove the short distance to the Telegraph office. There was a long queue as he arrived. Thankfully, the young woman at the counter was very much to Miller's liking and the time passed much too quickly. Miller smiled at the young woman when it was his turn, but she was much too business-like to notice. Can't win them all, thought Miller and read out the messages. The first telegram was to Georgy Bergmann confirming his acceptance of the challenge. The second telegram to Ratcliff was to let him know his decision. Miller noted that after recording the messages the young woman had glanced at him surreptitiously. He pretended not to notice. Instead, he replicated her business-like air and desire to expedite the commission.

*

Kit sat in the apartment with Sam snoring gently on his knee. Normally self-possessed, he felt anxiety grip his stomach at the thought of what lay ahead. It had been years since he had played chess seriously. Before the War, he had been a fine player. Unquestionably one of the strongest in the country. His title had probably made him one of the most prominent players although Kit modestly acknowledged that he was far from being the best. After returning from the War, he had taken the game up again but made no attempt to play seriously against top players.

Now he felt like an athlete, just back from injury, being asked to compete against an Olympic champion. He didn't give two bob for his chances. It was some comfort to know victory would only be a welcome by-product of the match rather than the sole object.

*

Later that day, Kit's Rolls Royce sped up Regent Street towards Oxford Street. The rain which had been threatening all morning finally arrived. It created a steady, hypnotic beat on the car window transporting Kit's mind to a limbo, free from worry about the match or Mary. His reverie was broken by an oath from Miller as the rain made visibility more difficult. Kit watched shoppers scurrying along the pavements wielding umbrellas like lances at a medieval joust.

'You should make time to practice, sir,' said Miller as they drove back to Kit's flat.

'I doubt it'll make much difference. He's too good, Harry.'

'Not like you to be so pessimistic, sir.'

'I was lucky against him first time. I think he took me for granted. Oddly, he's more of a snob than I'll ever be. I've never, I hope, treated anyone like they were inferior. Feel free to correct me if I'm wrong here Harry,' smiled Kit.

'Not with me, anyway, sir. Of course, I can't talk for other folk, mind,' laughed Miller.

This made Kit laugh also.

'Fair enough Harry. He's a strange cove, though. I never took to him. He just had this air of superiority about him. Contempt even. He thought he was better than me, not just at chess, which, I hasten to add, he certainly was. But there was an air of intellectual or, even, moral superiority because he believed in an inherently superior system of government or ethics than I. Unfathomable really. Anyway, he made some schoolboy errors in our first match because he wanted to humiliate me. I managed to win that one. Just about anyway. He destroyed me in the second match, but maybe I was a bit jaded in that one.'

'Why was that sir?'

'Well, it was before I met Mary, if you take my meaning, Harry,' laughed Kit.

Miller grinned replying, 'Say no more, sir, say no more. Did she put you off your game?'

'I was but a shadow of myself I can tell you,' said Kit, grinning at a memory of an encounter long ago.

*

Roger Ratcliff sat in his rooms near Kensington. There was a knock at his door, turning to Cornell, who was standing by the window he could see his friend was not making a move for the door. Finally, with just a hint of sourness, he said, 'Don't worry yourself old chap, I'll go.'

The apartment did not so much suggest bachelor as shout it from the rooftops. Ratcliff's cleaner had long since given up trying to impose order. This had been his base for almost thirty years. Much of that time, by necessity, had been spent abroad on postings in India and then Russia. Scattered throughout the room was the legacy of his travels. All around were books, objets d'art and various instruments of science picked up from the countries he had lived in.

Opening the door, he was greeted by a messenger who handed him a telegram. It was from Kit. He quickly read the short note and turned around to Cornell, 'Kit's in.'

Cornell looked at Ratcliff for an explanation. Ratcliff held up the telegram and then read it out, 'Sir, will play match with Serov. Will contact Bergmann today to confirm.'

Cornell nodded but remained silent. His face was impassive bar one eyebrow that was raised just enough to suggest scepticism. This was a feature that Ratcliff had often observed in his friend and colleague. He studied his friend as he gazed out of the window.

They had first met in India; Ratcliff had been Cornell's commanding officer. Unlike many officers serving in the Raj, both were linguists. During their posting in the Northwest frontier, each learned Urdu to work more closely with the extensive network of local agents who supported the army in the region.

The onset of the Great War had brought both back to serve in France. At an early stage during the War, Mansfield Cumming, or "C" as he was to be known, had spoken to them of the newly established Secret Intelligence Service. Both spoke Russian fluently and were obvious candidates to join the fledgling service following their experience of dealing with agents in Kashmir.

The three had met in a small restaurant in Soho. Ratcliff was an Oxford-educated major in the army. In late 1916, Cumming was sufficiently worried about the situation in Russia to ask them to join other British Intelligence officers in Petrograd.

Their role was not to join the recently established, Russian Bureau. This was led by Samuel Hoare. Instead, they were to go deep undercover and liaise with Oswald Rayner in a clandestine, inner circle, called the "Far-Reaching System". This group operated independently, and without the knowledge of Hoare's team. Their role was to keep Russia in the War.

This went beyond the usual remit of influencing key members of the government and keeping London supplied with a stream of intelligence on the situation in Russia. They were empowered to use whatever methods they deemed effective. The box of tricks they brought to bear in the cause of interfering in the Russian state included bribery, theft and, on occasion, murder.

The Far-Reaching System developed a string of alliances with sympathetic members of the Russian aristocracy. Both recognised a common problem. The slow erosion of the Tsar's power, a consequence of his mismanagement of the War. It had led to a growing movement for change. The Russian supporters of Rayner's team were prepared to accept extraordinary levels of interference in Russian politics in order to continue their involvement in the War and protect a social order that was under threat.

Ratcliff was one of the first people in the network of British agents to take seriously the rise of Lenin's Bolsheviks. Although only one of several groups rising in Petrograd at the time, they were making a much greater impact, and Ratcliff had seen Lenin make a speech, in person. The image had never left him.

Ratcliff had been at the station on that chilly morning of April 16th, 1917, when Lenin had set foot onto Russian soil for the first time in ten years following his exile. He had climbed onto the bonnet of an armoured car and made an address that was, by turns, passionate and chilling.

The magnetism of the man was undeniable. Ratcliff knew, as he watched him control the emotions of the crowd with utter mastery, that he was dealing with a formidable adversary who threatened more than just the Russian government. There was an insolence, a contempt for the crowd but also a charisma that repelled Ratcliff. Lenin's closing words, and the fervour they provoked in the crowd, were indelibly printed on his memory.

'Long live the worldwide Socialist revolution!'

Worldwide.

Worldwide. Hearing Lenin speak was to grasp the threat posed to the rest of the world. As Ratcliff looked around him, he recognised other British agents, including his friend, Arthur Ransome, although he sometimes wondered where his loyalties lay. He knew them all, but they didn't see him and nor would they. All were Hoare's men. The Far-Reaching System would always operate independently.

He wondered if they understood what they were seeing. Would they be able to communicate the power of this man's words? How could you describe the impact he was having on the crowd that had come to greet him? It was clear to Ratcliff that he couldn't leave things to chance. He and the other members of the Far-Reaching System were now at war.

The images of the last few years flashed through the mind of Ratcliff as he sat in his rooms in London. Ultimately, they had failed to keep Russia in the War and the old social order had collapsed into chaos and communism.

The demented reality of Russia was a country led at the top by highly intelligent fanatics. However, at local level, semi-illiterate thugs ruled by fear. The middle classes and the aristocracy were quickly being annihilated or had taken flight.

Amid the chaos, Ratcliff had taken the opportunity to forge a strong network of agents, all opposed to the new regime. He had also assumed a new identity as a Latvian-Russian, like many other British agents, to explain the difference in their accent. He went deep undercover to avoid being caught by the secret police. This had saved him. Soon after the Bolsheviks took power, the network of agents fell apart. The memory of the betrayal was a pain burning deep with him.

He looked up at Cornell. His friend was rubbing the back of his head again. He needs a doctor, thought Ratcliff, but he was tired of telling him.

'Do you think much of our time back there?' asked Ratcliff.

'Where? Russia or India? Neither, if you must know. Damned mess it all turned out,' snorted Cornell.

This disappointed Ratcliff, but he didn't respond. It was difficult to deny things had not turned out as they had wanted. They had failed to overthrow the Bolsheviks. Now the Civil War was all but lost, the Far-Reaching System network betrayed then shattered and their high-profile Russian supporters against the Bolsheviks, like Yusupov and Kerensky, were either planning to escape or had already done so. Visionaries such as Churchill, who understood the threat posed by the creation of Comintern, a body set up by the

Bolsheviks to enable the overthrow of western democracy, were ignored.

Ratcliff could see Cornell looking at him. 'You don't think he can win then?' asked Ratcliff.

Cornell's smile was mocking. He snorted contemptuously.

'Against Serov? He'll be humbled,' was Cornell's curt assessment of Kit's chances. The eyebrow was not at full extension. He wasn't joking.

Ratcliff shrugged and laughed but not altogether convincingly. Cornell was possibly the most cynical man he had ever met. This cynicism had grown over the years since Russia.

'It won't be easy, I agree, but I would never underestimate Kit. When the chips are down, he's a fighter. A true fighter never knows when he's beaten, Colin. He'll make a match of it, just watch.'

'You can watch,' Cornell put a pipe to his lips and began to puff away thoughtfully.

Ratcliff smiled. 'You really don't like him, do you? I almost think you want Serov to win.'

Cornell shot Ratcliff his sceptical look again but said nothing in reply. Ratcliff shook his head and laughed.

'I, for one, am relieved.'

He walked over to his drinks trolley and poured himself a small whisky.

'A bit early for this, I know, but I think this news merits a little celebration. Care to join me for a quick nip?'

'I think you're right.'

'About what?' asked Ratcliff.

'It's too early,' came the disdainful reply.

61

This amused Ratcliff and he laughed. Clutching his tumbler, he returned to his seat, feeling oddly comforted, despite the painful memories of the last few years.

9

Edinburgh: 2nd[d] January 1920

Serov's match with Fiona Lawrence had sadly descended into exactly the type of bloodbath he preferred to avoid. His preference in this kind of forum was for his opponent to overcome their initial excitement and go to the slaughter like a good lamb. This required them to play the game with just enough knowledge of classic opening moves in the early stages of the game before facing annihilation in the middle game, courtesy of Serov's superior intellectual weaponry.

His schoolgirl opponent was having none of this. Suicidal sacrifices followed audacious flights of fancy resulting in a chess board which bore no relation to anything Serov had seen before, never mind prepared. Worse, the game was taking far too long. There was no chance of his losing, but equally, his Satanic opponent was taking great delight in spending inordinate amounts of time contemplating her obvious moves whilst making the more insane moves within seconds of his, forcing him to spend more time than he had to respond.

Frantically, he glanced up at Daniels. The big man looked like thunder and kept reminding Serov of something he didn't need reminding of. They would soon be keeping several senior members of the Scottish Trade Unions Congress waiting.

The match with this she-devil was over ninety minutes old. No conclusion was in sight. Serov ran his head through his hair unable to disguise his anxiety. At this moment he felt a sudden stab of pain in his shin. She'd kicked him on the shin under the table.

He glanced up at the twelve-year-old face of evil. She was gazing at him with an angelic smile. Looking around him wildly, he realised two things. Firstly, no one had seen the little sprite assault him, their attention was too focused on the game. Secondly, he was in a fight to the death. Resisting his initial instinct to ram the heel of his palm into her face, he quickly moved his Queen to check her King.

This was when he felt the second, and greater stab of pain. Not physical pain. Instead, it was the blow to his gut at the realisation he was about to lose his most powerful piece. The audible gasps from the audience did not help Serov's mood and he could not bring himself to look at Daniels. Out of the corner of his eye he had caught the big man throwing his head back in anger and then step back away from the game.

Fechin was looking on in fascination.

Fechin.

What had the little cretin talked about with the malevolent imp before him? He glared up at the moron. At this moment, Fechin realised something very important, something which would probably be raised by Serov to Daniels and, worse, Bergmann. Furiously he began to rifle his mind for an alternative narrative to spin to his colleagues. Because with absolute certainty he now knew Fiona Lawrence's, seemingly innocent but highly specific, questions around their schedule and timings were being used to influence the outcome of the match.

Billy Peel was not a chess expert. Its role in the class struggle was somewhat opaque. However, even he could see that the little girl was not just putting up a fight; there was a real possibility of an upset. The look on Serov's face was by turns, angry, frenzied, and panic-stricken. Peel was unsure how he felt about this from the point of view of world revolution, but as a newsman, he was now finding his sympathies shifting in an unexpected direction.

Turning to Reverend Upritchard, he asked in a stage whisper, 'Are you a chess player yourself?'

Without removing his eyes from the bloodshed a few feet in front of him, Upritchard replied, 'I dabble occasionally, but Miss Lawrence and Mr Serov are playing a game from the heavens.'

Serov was also thinking that Fiona Lawrence's play had a biblical dimension. However, he would certainly have quibbled about the provenance being heaven. The odious little sorceress had about as much in common with an angel as Fechin.

Fechin.

He resolved, when the match ended, to strangle the imbecilic dwarf. To his left, he saw Daniels making a gesture with his hand across his neck. He hoped this meant that he planned on cutting his opponents throat, but he guessed it meant he should sue for peace.

Catching the eye of the young Medusa, he raised his eyebrows and held out his hand to agree a draw. Honours would be even. Both could walk away from the bloodbath to lick their wounds and fight another day. Preferably not with each other, thought Serov or, better still, with axes.

Unknown to Serov, Fiona Lawrence had seen the interaction between the two big Russians. With a shake of her head, she indicated the match would continue. Once again, the audience gasped. She was going for the kill.

'Jesus H. Christ,' said the Reverend Upritchard to Peel, 'Poor Serov'.

Somewhat surprised by the minister's turn of phrase, the mystified Peel asked, 'Why? What just happened?'

'Serov just offered our Fiona a draw.'

'And?'

'She said no. She thinks she can win.'

Peel looked at the board. Pieces were, quite literally, scattered like confetti across the board. He couldn't make head nor tail of it. In this regard, he had more in common with Serov than he hitherto would have imagined. Turning to Upritchard he whispered, 'Why?'

'Christ only knows,' answered the man of God, honestly.

Peel wasn't so sure if this was a call upon their maker to help the good Reverend understand better what was going on or an admission that the workings of twelve-year-old prodigy's mind were beyond his ken. He was even less sure that repeatedly using the son of God in this context wouldn't be frowned upon by the brethren, had they heard.

Serov saw his opponent refuse his kind offer with something approaching apoplexy. The look of horror on his face was noted first, with some satisfaction, by Fiona Lawrence and soon after by, a less happy, Daniels. This caused him to stride out of the hall to give vent, in Russian, to a string of oaths that were clearly audible inside and certainly required no translation.

However, as confident as she appeared on the outside, Fiona Lawrence recognised that victory was unlikely. Although a Queen up, she had little or no support by way of other key pieces. For the next ten minutes she contemplated her next move aware of the virtual disintegration of her opponent's composure. Moving her one remaining pawn she looked at Serov.

By now Serov was prepared to beg for a draw. He raised his eyebrows again, more in hope than expectation. This time, by dint of a small change in her facial expression, she gave the impression that she was prepared to accept the draw.

Resisting the impulse to leap out of his chair and hug her, Serov immediately held out his hand. With a final twist of the knife, Fiona made him wait three beats longer than the spirit of the game normally dictated, before accepting the draw.

A cheer went up, none more so than from Daniels who was relieved that the damn game was over albeit a full hour after it should have ended. With barely a goodbye to the great and the good of the chess club, Serov was hurried out the door by the burly Daniels, his diminutive assistant and off they went to their long overdue appointment followed by Peel.

Meanwhile, Fiona Lawrence, for perhaps the first time in maybe seven years, was subject to an overflow of affection so intense she could barely contain her emotions. The tears flowed like a river. And that was just the very Reverend Upritchard. After a minimal protest, Fiona was hoisted up on the shoulders of the cheering club members. Quietly, almost unnoticed, she wiped a tear from the corner of her eye.

10

The clouds above seemed heavier and darker as they left the Presbyterian Hall. Serov looked up and wondered what had happened to the blue sky. Or, perhaps, it was just his mood. He was only half aware of a second diminutive individual following them into the parked car.

Fechin climbed into the front of the car. Daniels, Peel and Serov sat in the back. It was only then that Serov realised they had an additional passenger. He glared at Peel and then looked at Daniels. After a few moments, Daniels explained to Serov, in excellent English, 'Comrade Bergmann requested that Comrade Peel join us. He is a reporter for the Daily Herald. I've read his work. He's a supporter of the struggle.'

This calmed Serov momentarily and he reached out to shake the hand of their new companion. In equally good English, he said to the newsman, 'Pleased to meet you Comrade Peel.'

'Comrade Serov,' said Peel by way of acknowledgement, impressed by the linguistic abilities of his Russian companions.

As Serov said nothing else and was clearly in a foul mood, Peel also remained quiet. There was, undeniably, an atmosphere in the car. Serov was fighting an overwhelming impulse to wring Fechin's neck. As he was driving, he reluctantly accepted it would not be a good idea. Instead, he fantasised about dragging him by the hair into the back of the car and punching him. Finally, unable to contain himself anymore, he said in Russian to Daniels, 'Would you kindly ask that idiot colleague of yours what he said to the witch?'

Fechin had spent the last hour thinking of an answer to this. He interrupted Daniels before the big Russian could reply and said in Russian, 'She was asking if we spoke English. Then when she realised, we could, she wanted to know more about Russia.'

Serov looked contemptuously to the front and said derisively, 'What? Like the weather? Or what kind of puppies we keep?'

Fechin, unable to detect the sarcasm in Serov's voice, could hardly believe his luck. He nodded his head excitedly, 'Yes, exactly.'

Daniels and Serov exchanged looks.

'Are you sure you didn't talk about what our plans were for the day?' asked Daniels, trying to keep his voice neutral.

'No, do I look stupid?' said Fechin scornfully.

To be fair, he did. This was due to a scar that ran from his mouth and curled upward giving him a leer that was could be interpreted, from a distance, as the look of someone untroubled by deep thought. The scar was a result of an unfortunate accident with a bomb from a few years earlier, in his anarchist days, when he was, almost single-handedly, trying to overthrow the Tsar. It led to his flight from Russia.

Daniels decided to wait until they met up with Bergmann before telling him of the suspicion, which both he and Serov shared, that Fechin's indiscreet babbling to the not-so-innocent youngster had contributed to Serov's failure to win. The tactics of Fiona Lawrence gave every impression of someone who knew Serov needed to win, and quickly, to get away. The only possible source was Fechin. Fiona had used this intelligence to devastating effect against Serov which cost him victory.

Fechin remained silent. He sensed the mood wasn't so much antagonistic as downright homicidal. Once more, Daniels questioned Bergmann's wisdom in using Fechin. The lean and loquacious Muscovite presented a stark contrast with the immense and intense Daniels.

Had Daniels stopped and really thought of it, however, he would have seen the simplicity of Bergmann's reasoning staring him in the face. Aside from his hatred of all things imperial and his fluency in English, Fechin was genuinely psychotic. The big Ukrainian was beginning to get a glimmer of this by now.

Bergmann had first unearthed Fechin in early 1917. This was just after the Bolsheviks had really begun to grow in influence. Fechin had given Bergmann a highly selective account of his struggle against the bourgeoisie. Bergmann's investigations revealed a very different picture. Fechin was not only on the run from the forces of law and order, but also from several of the anarchist groups operating in Petrograd at the time, including the Bolsheviks. The true story went something like this.

Born Valentin Korovin into a middle-class family in Moscow, Korovin, whilst no academic, had managed to earn a place at Moscow University. He read languages, majoring in English and German. The latter was an attempt to align himself more closely with the work of his heroes, Marx, and Engels, and to read their glorious prose in the original. His conversion to Marxism was the defining moment in his life. He resolved during his years at university to become a soldier-scholar. Temperamentally, and intellectually, he was more suited to the former than the latter. In an unusual, and almost certainly never repeated, moment of insight, he came to realise this himself. His next problem was how to direct this passion towards the class struggle. Salvation was at hand.

A drunken conversation one Friday night brought Korovin's first introduction to anarchists. In this case it was a group known as the Mercenaries for Marx. This small group consisted of one former army officer and his two sons, one of whom Korovin had befriended at university.

He took up active service one year later after graduating with a degree. Surprising his new colleagues, he requested military training and was given it by people probably even less qualified than he.

Finding an outlet for Korovin's military zeal proved difficult. His incompetence with a gun became apparent when he winged one of his instructors on the rifle range. In any circumstances this incident would have been frowned upon. However, in this instance, the instructor was the group leader's son. Thankfully, it was only a flesh wound and Korovin was able to claim, albeit unconvincingly, faulty equipment rather than human error.

However, Korovin's tendency to injure his own men in friendly fire could not be hidden long and resulted in his expulsion from the group. Working in Moscow with several new recruits, a plan was hatched for a bombing campaign to create as much pre-Christmas mayhem as possible. Train stations were identified as providing the perfect marriage between quantity of people, low security, and maximum disruption. It meant that a problem at one station could create an impact at others out of all proportion to the original input from the anarchists. Even better was the potential of adding

71

hoax bombs in other stations to the mix. This would amplify the confusion and mayhem.

Christmas of 1915 saw things go badly wrong for Korovin. Three days before Christmas, the ever-eager Korovin volunteered to carry the "real" package into the city centre while three colleagues took hoax bombs to three transport hubs.

Korovin duly contacted the station to let them know there was a bomb. The evacuation of Moscow Central took place and the bomb was duly uncovered. Diffusing it was unnecessary, Korovin had left a hoax bomb in the station by mistake. Across Moskva river, the real bomb took out the car containing Korovin's collaborators and a small section of the Borodinsky Bridge.

Korovin did not wait around in Moscow to learn of his fate from the high command. He took flight and spent a year lying low in Tbilisi. This incident had provided Korovin with a cold dose of reality. Previously he had believed that he would be willing to fight and die to liberate the workers from their chains. The prospect of being killed by fellow anarchists did not figure high in his plans and swiftly disabused him of any notions towards martyrdom. This left him with a dilemma: how best to continue the struggle? The answer became clear and from an unusual source.

Ireland.

Odessa was throbbing with quasi-communist groups jockeying for position as instigators of the dictatorship of the proletariat. Some were led by former members of the middle classes keen to bring a sound intellectual energy to the febrile atmosphere of the town. Korovin, now renamed Genady Grabar, arrived there just after Easter 1916. A keen follower of the fight for freedom by Ireland's patriots against the forces of imperialism, Grabar was particularly inspired by the Irish republican, Patrick Pearse.

Pearse was an Irish teacher, barrister, poet, writer, nationalist, and political activist. His activism extended beyond pamphlets and newspaper editorials. By 1916 he was actively involved in the planning and leading of the Easter Rising. Grabar was more entranced by Pearse's warrior-poet legend than his early demise at the hands of a British firing squad. Inspired by Pearse's approach, if not his execution, Grabar appropriated some of the methods used by the deceased IRA man. The idea grew in his mind, nurtured by reading cheap fiction, of a lone agent, an avenging angel. His vision was one of a mysterious figure, fighting with, but independent of, all strands of communism. He would take anarchism to its logical conclusion through the agency of an unseen, unknown angel of death. He named the avenging angel, "The Sword of Light", in honour of Patrick Pearse.

"The Sword of Light" had been the Gaelic League newspaper founded by Pearse. In possession now of a name and a strategy, "The Sword of Light" sought to implement his brand of terror on an unsuspecting bourgeoisie.

Sadly, Grabar's career as a lone wolf anarchist was brought to a spectacular end by a combination of flawed thinking and, quite literally, poor execution. The idea was for several men, dressed as postmen, to deliver packages containing a bomb with just a long enough fuse to allow for its reception by the target and the escape of his comrade worker, or tramp, in this case. The plan was simple in conception, deadly of consequence. It required a precision in planning matched with technical genius in bomb making. Grabar had neither. It

73

resulted in him becoming, by turns both a laughingstock among the various anarchist groups as well as, once again, a man on the run.

One summer morning in early August 1917, six tramps, dressed as postman, set off at thirty-minute intervals from different parts of Odessa carrying a bomb to an address of a nearby member of the business class. Grabar was so sure of success he had posted anonymous letters to the big Odessa newspapers as well as the local leaders of the groups he sought to align with in the fight to free Russia from the yoke of the aristocracy.

An early inkling of potential problems with his bombs had nearly ended in disaster for Grabar himself. He had avoided serious injury but was left with an unattractive, leering scar near his mouth. Sadly, the lesson remained unlearned, particularly for the unfortunate individuals who had been duped into helping.

By midday it was apparent to Grabar that his plan had gone horribly wrong. Three of his bombs had indeed gone off. Unfortunately, they had exploded in the hands of the hobos carrying them to their target. The other three had failed to go off because, starved of oxygen inside the package, a detail that a more expert bomb maker would surely have considered, the flame had simply died. Just like "The Sword of Light" as it turned out.

By early evening, "The Sword of Light" was no longer a mysterious unseen slayer. Evening newspapers all over Petrograd proclaimed the name of the vigilante vagabond slayer as one Gennady Grabar. Police had received an anonymous tip off from a lady called Olga on the identity of the killer. As Grabar was to explain to Bergmann afterwards, her treachery had been motivated by a misunderstanding over the remuneration she felt entitled to following a romantic interlude.

A combination of the October Revolution and meeting Georgy Bergmann was to prove the salvation for the, now, renamed Vassily Fechin. Following the Revolution, Russia was in chaos. To bring control to the anarchy unleashed by the fall of the government required strong leadership backed up by even stronger enforcement of the leader's wishes. Fechin, now an inhabitant of Petrograd, joined the one organisation likely to overlook the need for employer references in favour of a genuinely unhinged outlook on life.

The Cheka.

The All-Russian Extraordinary Commission and commonly known as Cheka, was the first of a succession of Soviet secret police organizations. Established in December 1917, Fechin was welcomed with open arms and the slate was wiped clean over his past misdemeanours. As an organisation, Cheka was normally suspicious of using people with anything approaching an education. However, an exception was made in the case of Fechin. This was not just because of his disinhibition towards extreme violence but also because he was fluent in two strategically important languages: English and German.

Bergmann had also been part of the early intake. Despite not being Russian, his fluency in English, which surpassed even Fechin's, meant he was accepted quickly by the new organisation. Soon a combination of his obvious leadership skills and linguistic ability resulted in him being given senior responsibilities in counterespionage. By mid-1919, at his own suggestion, he was reassigned to carry on the revolution in

Britain. Fechin followed him and they linked up with another English-speaking Cheka agent, Leon Daniels, who had been posted to Britain some months earlier following his demobilisation from the army.

Yes, Fechin was very much Bergmann's boy, reflected Daniels. The last year working with him had only confirmed Daniels in his view of Fechin as both dangerous and stupid in equal measure. As much as he may have wished it, Daniels doubted Bergmann would get rid of Fechin. It was too late now. The operation was about to begin. At the very least he wanted to remind Bergmann of the big risks posed by having a card-carrying imbecile like Fechin given any kind of responsibility. Events were to prove the hefty Cheka agent right.

11

Later that day, Kit received a telegram from Bergmann inviting him to make the first move by reply. He and Bright were sitting in Kit's apartment following breakfast, relaxing reading over the newspapers in companionable silence. Bright listened as Kit read out the telegram.

'Is having the first move good? I'm not much of a chess player, sadly,' admitted Bright.

Kit considered his response for a moment then replied, 'I can't quote any statistics, but conventional wisdom suggests white has a slight advantage. A bit like playing rugger on your home ground.'

'Good, so you're sure to win then,' said Bright with a grin.

Kit laughed, 'If only it were so easy.'

They both sat in front of Kit's chess board. Looking at it for a moment Kit then moved his King's pawn two places forward. Bright studied the board for a moment, then knocked over his black King to indicate resignation.

'You win. That was devilishly clever, old boy,' smiled Bright.

Kit laughed as did Miller, who was looking on.

'You had him there, sir,' said Miller, 'I could see mate in twenty moves.'

77

'You must show me your game plan, Harry, twenty-three for me,' smiled Kit.

'You really are out of practice, Kit,' responded Bright.

Kit turned to Miller and said, 'Sorry about this Harry but there's going to be a bit of too-ing and fro-ing over the next few days. Would you mind going to the telegram office. The message is d4. Stop.'

In fact, Miller was delighted with this piece of news.

'I think I can remember that sir,' before adding hopefully, 'I can wait for a reply if you like.'

Kit thought for a moment, then replied, 'Probably not. We don't know how close they are to an office. It may be a while before they get the message. We'll judge this as the game progresses.'

Settling back in his armchair, Kit picked up a Daily Herald which Ratcliff had sent to him with an article circled written by Billy Peel. Kit read through the short article and then looked up at Bright and showed him the newspaper.

'Do you read the Herald very often?'

Bright laughed, 'Not really my sort of thing. Didn't have you down for a socialist.'

Kit grinned, 'I'm not completely unsympathetic to these issues, you know. It may seem hypocritical given this,' he gestured around the room, 'I accept inequality exists, but it doesn't mean I like it. If I can do anything to give people a chance to improve their lot I will. Anyway, there's an interesting article on my opponent in yesterday's paper.'

Kit threw the paper over to Bright. After a few moments Bright looked up.

'Sounds like an interesting fellow. Doesn't mince his words about Britain and the Civil War in Russia. Are we really fighting a proxy war in Russia?'

'I don't doubt we're making mischief.'

Bright continued to read the interview, 'Doesn't strike me as the happiest of chaps. Seems angry about everything.'

'Intense, I would say, more than angry. I don't think I ever saw so much as a smile when I played him.' Kit was silent for a few moments as something appeared to cross his mind. 'I must find out more about this chap, Peel. He mentions our match. I wonder if he intends covering it for the Daily Herald. I can just imagine the tenor of the reporting he'll give our match.'

'I'll say. Reading this it sounds like he gets his salary from Lenin himself.'

Kit nodded in agreement.

'Yes, it looks like he's going to be siding with our Russian friend. To be fair to Peel, he doesn't have a go at me personally. His gripe is with the class system and my title more than anything. He's using it to counterpoint Serov's more humble origins. It's interesting that he picked up on how the Russians will see this as an important propaganda tool. This is something my old commander thought also.'

'Why?'

'I'm not sure yet. Just a feeling. If the rest of the article hadn't been so full of rhetoric about class struggle, I might have taken it as a veiled warning,' replied Kit.

'But you were aware of this,' pointed out Bright.

'True. But Peel wasn't to know that. Anyway, maybe it's my imagination. Right, are you ready? Harry can drop you off at the hotel'

'Oh? Where will you be?' inquired Bright, a little surprised.

'I'll be along soon,' said Kit reaching for his overcoat. 'I want to see Spunky. See what he says about all of this.' He pointed towards the newspaper article.

*

Spunky Stevens sat with his feet up on the desk puffing contentedly on his pipe. He gazed outside his window which overlooked Holland Park. He liked the new offices for the view, but much preferred his old office in Whitehall. Pressure to reduce costs had meant relocating the Special Intelligence Services offices the previous month.

As disappointed as he was to be away from the centre of things, his office on the second floor allowed Spunky to indulge himself, in quieter moments, by looking at the array of young ladies going for a walk in the park. On more than one occasion he had scurried out of his office to make their acquaintance. A knock at the door interrupted the thoughts of Spunky. The door opened, and he found himself looking up at Kit.

'Hard at it I see, old chap,' said Kit with a smile.

Spunky chortled as he rose to his feet, 'Meditation dear boy. I've taken to it since meeting that Indian chap, Ganga Singh, last year in Paris.'

Kit wandered over to the window and looked out at the many young ladies walking in the park. Spunky could see where his gaze was directed and smirked.

'I'm sure you've been reflecting deeply on the human condition. The physical condition, that is. How do you like the new offices?' asked Kit.

One particularly attractive lady walked into view. Both men remained silent in appreciation for a few moments before Kit added, 'Silly question really.'

They sat down and Spunky relit his pipe. He glanced at Kit and asked, 'So what brings you to the other side of the tracks old chap?'

'Have you heard about this match I'm to play with Serov?'

'Indeed Kit, rum fellow that. The boys at the club are considering running a book on it.'

'Really, any takers for the home favourite?'

'Poor choice of word old bean. It would be fair to say that the word "favourite" and Aston are not being spoken off in the same sentence.'

'I don't blame them,' admitted Kit. 'I'm a bit rusty.'

'And he's a bit better, I gather. Future world champion they say.'

'Has the old boy said anything about it?' Kit was referring to Mansfield Cumming, head of the Secret Intelligence Service.

'Not to me anyway, but you know what he's like. Keeps his cards close to his chest.'

'I remember. He had me trying to get the Romanov family to come to Britain whilst neglecting to mention he knew the Bolsheviks were going to start a revolution.'

'Yes, sorry about that,' said Spunky with sincerity.

'You knew also?' Kit laughed in surprise.

'Yes, I'd had wind of something. Anyway, this match, you know it could put us in a better position to free some of our boys from Russian prisons?' asked Spunky, keen to move away from the subject of the Romanov's.

'Roger said as much. Did you see the article by Billy Peel, in the Daily Herald, by the way?'

'Yes, quite a tribute to your opponent, I thought. Looks like your imminent defeat could herald the beginning of the revolution. Although I'm unclear why a dock worker in Rosyth would be encouraged to take up arms against His Majesty's Armed Forces based on a chess match.'

'I struggled with that also but no matter. Chap seems convinced on this. Good luck to him.'

Kit fixed his eyes on his old school friend and said, 'I was interested in knowing a bit more about Peel. I've a feeling he's going to go to town on this match. I'd like to know what to expect.'

Spunky remained silent for a few moments, seemingly lost in thought. After a few more puffs on the pipe he said, 'If you're asking me if he is in the pay of the Kremlin, I can honestly say, probably not. From what I've heard, he's his own man, albeit hard line socialist.'

This seemed to satisfy Kit. The two friends chatted for another few minutes before Kit took his leave.

'Pass my regards to the old man, Spunky,' said Kit nodding towards the stairs outside Spunk's office. They shook hands and Kit walked down the stairs. Miller was waiting outside in the car. Holding the passenger door open for Kit he asked, 'Flat?'

'Yes please,' replied Kit.

'Why don't you pop down to the Telegraph office it's on our way. I'd like to send Mary a telegram.

Kit quickly scribbled a note and handed it to Harry after he had pulled up outside the office. Miller leapt out of the car and went over to the Telegraph office. He noticed the same young woman behind the counter. Walking straight over to her, he showed the message he wished to send. She looked up and, although momentary, it was clear she recognised him. Looking at the message, Miller could see, almost imperceptibly, her eyebrows raise, before she resumed her usual professional demeanour.

Her hair was cut fashionably short and seemed more auburn than he had remembered. He guessed her to be in her early twenties. No sign of a ring on her finger. He wondered how her face would look when she smiled. Miller paid for the telegram, nodded to her without smiling and left.

The smile appeared on his face as he left the office and stayed there all the way to the car. Kit noted the smile but said nothing. He glanced in the direction of the office and caught sight of an attractive young woman at the counter. It was just momentary and then she disappeared.

12

Oldham: 3rd January 1920

Georgy Bergmann accompanied Serov away from Ramsbottom Cotton Mill in Oldham. The day had been surreal. It had started in central Manchester at a hotel with a series of chess matches against county standard players and finished with the Russian chess grandmaster giving a fiery speech, in faultless English, to a meeting of even more fiery Trade Unionist and mill workers.

It was an emotional speech that spoke of a man who had raised himself up from an orphanage to become a world-renowned chess player and champion, if not of chess, then of the oppressed. This had brought a satisfying cheer. In fact, had the audience been the local mill owners, they might have been just as inspired by Serov's rise-from-humble-origins-to-prominence story as the local workers, reflected Bergmann cynically.

Dressed in the unambiguously radical rhetoric of socialism, however, the unthinking audience were swept along by the narrative and cheered the Russian to the rafters. Bergmann looked on in quiet amusement at the onlooker reaction to the, essentially, anti-communist narrative of an individual's triumph.

At the end of the meeting, Bergmann brought Serov over to a tall, fair-haired man. His striking blue eyes compelled Serov's attention. He had a small moustache which made his face seem older and more serious. From his bearing it was clear to Serov he was a former army man. There was something more about him, an aura of authority. Serov guessed this must be Mr Kopel. He wondered, idly, if it was Kopel who was really in charge, such was the careless sense of power emanating from him.

'May I present Mr Ezeras Kopel,' said Bergmann grinning broadly up at the younger man. Serov could see immediately how Bergmann was in thrall to the younger man. It confirmed him in his impression of their relative ranking.

'Please to meet you, Comrade Serov,' smiled Kopel. Serov also found himself succumbing to the charisma of Kopel. The smile was warm, and the voice had a timbre which made his accented Russian all the more attractive.

'Please call me Filip. I detest formality, Mr Kopel.'

'As do I,' replied Kopel.

Kopel's praise of his speech also revealed a mind that Serov felt was almost equal to his own. While Serov was completely comfortable in the knowledge of his own intellectual superiority, he was self-aware enough to know he was not the most companionable of people. In Kopel, he recognised someone who combined a deep reservoir of intelligence with an easy grace in company. Had he not already taken such a liking to the Latvian he would have defaulted to his usual dislike of any intellectual rival.

Kopel followed Bergmann, Serov, and Daniels to the car. Bergmann and Daniels sat in silence as Serov and Kopel discussed the work of new Marxist thinkers such as Lukács in

Hungary. Fechin, sitting in the front, listened transfixed to their discussion as he drove them back to their hotel in Manchester.

Bergmann, too, was impressed by the chess grandmaster. Kopel's idea to bring Serov over was proving inspired. He was every bit as impressive a speaker as he was a competitor at the chess board. The twelve matches from this morning had resulted in twelve comfortable wins. The local press had picked up on Serov's tour thanks to the sterling platform created by Billy Peel in the Daily Herald. Best of all, the match with Kit Aston was in progress with press interest growing steadily.

The trip to the mill and meeting the workers had given Serov much to think about albeit for entirely different reasons. Since his trip to Edinburgh, a nagging feeling was emerging from within him that the conditions necessary for the overthrow of the bourgeoisie were sadly lacking in what he had seen so far of Britain. When he had the opportunity, he would discuss this with Kopel. Perhaps his time in Britain could help Serov understand better the progress, or indeed need for, class struggle.

His presumptions coming over from Russia on the conditions of the workers and their mood were strangely at odds with what he was witnessing for himself. Cases of hardship, cruelty and neglect were not as visible as Russia. The Trade Unionists were a passionate bunch, but Serov could find precious little evidence to see what they were angry about.

Compared to Russia, where poverty was acute, and the conditions for workers were brutal, the British seemed to be relatively well off. Even the healthy physical appearance of the men he met was in marked contrast to the sallow faced, under nourished, subsistence peasants in his home country.

The conditions of production were, of course, as Marx described. The workers were enslaved by the machine and the over-looker. However, unlike the Trade Unionists, the workers he'd met had been disappointingly lacking in the grievance he had expected and, in many cases, positively cheerful. Based on the two cities he had visited; it was difficult to discern what fetters needed to be cast off the workers. All in all, it was all very disheartening.

When they arrived back at their hotel, Bergmann picked up messages from reception. They included the latest move from Kit in the match. Clutching the telegram, he showed it to Serov and Kopel.

'If you've time we can respond to Aston soon.'

Serov looked at the telegram and snorted derisively before responding immediately, 'Bishop takes pawn. I'll show you upstairs in the room if you like.'

'I'd love to see more of what you have planned for Aston,' smiled Kopel.

Then he and Bergmann led Serov away. As they headed towards the stairs, Kopel turned and glanced at Daniels who nodded in response. Daniels and Fechin headed off in another direction. Neither spoke as they exited the hotel.

*

Herbert Yapp had enjoyed his day very much. The opportunity to shake the hand of a man who had shaken the hand of Lenin was one of the highlights of his life. He had been moved by the story of Serov. The story of his rise from the orphanage to become, perhaps, the greatest chess player in the world was inspirational. Utterly oblivious to the contradiction in terms, it demonstrated to Yapp how the proletariat could be an unstoppable force when it could produce individuals like Serov.

Meeting his companions had also been an interesting experience. Bergmann was clearly a man not to be trifled with. Yapp would have loved to understand more about his part in the glorious revolution. He wondered who the other man Serov had spoken to was. He could not remember seeing such clear blue eyes before. His manner suggested a diplomat, but Yapp was not aware of Russia having many such people in the country.

Of Daniels and Fechin, he was less certain. He sensed a danger with them. From first sight he guessed shrewdly that they were Russian agents. The idea of Russia having agents in his country gave Yapp mixed feelings. On the one hand he welcomed any movement which would result in the overthrow of the capitalist bloodsuckers. On the other, as a matter of principle, he didn't like having foreigners in his country. They undermined wages. This was abhorrent to him and was to be resisted. Yapp didn't stop to consider what British workers were being denied a job by the presence of two Cheka agents.

Yapp followed his usual route home from the working man's club where he had spent a stimulating evening with his comrades discussing the day's events. Stimulating in the sense that not all his comrades had reached the same level of enlightenment that he had achieved. The arguments had raged long into the evening. It never ceased to amaze Yapp, over a pint or four, how blithely unaware his fellow workers were of the degree to which they were subjugated. This would change as their political education grew. Recognising the need for a classless society based on complete equality would come when they were exposed to more outstanding individuals like Serov.

Yapp wasn't sure if it was the effect of the fifth pint or the whisky chaser that accounted for the vision he saw approaching in the dark street. Looking behind him he saw that the street was empty. It was just him and this looming apparition. This was a problem as he was feeling distinctly uncomfortable at the sight of the man. It wasn't so much his size, although he was a large man, nor was it the funny looking Bishop's mitre that he was wearing on his head. Granted this was unusual in Oldham, even on a Sunday morning. No, of more concern, was the unintelligible chant he was repeating, which sounded vaguely Russian, accompanied as it was by the twirling of a long, heavy-looking, metal rod, windmill style, in his hand. Then he heard footsteps behind him.

When the gap reached twenty yards, Yapp made the decision to cross to the other side of the street. The impairment to his faculties brought on by the evening's activities meant this decision was several seconds too late. Just as he was about to cross the road, he felt his foot get tapped from behind resulting in him pitching forward. This was the last thing Herbert Yapp saw, as the metal rod came crashing down.

*

Inspector Maurice McEwan looked down at the dead body of Herbert Yapp. It was well after midnight. He was cold. If he could have been anywhere but here, he would be. However, as murders went, this was an unusual one. McEwan could see the man was clearly lifeless. The doctor hadn't arrived yet, but the cause of death wasn't going to be difficult to identify - a blow to the head caused by the object lying, helpfully, beside the dead body.

McEwan took off his hat and scratched what remained of his hair. He quickly put the hat back on again for fear of catching a chill. Where was the damn doctor, he wondered? He clapped his hands causing a young policeman to look up and inquire if the Inspector needed anything.

'A roaring fire, whisky and a good book,' replied McEwan sourly. A puzzled look crept over the young constable's face and McEwan shook his head to indicate nothing was needed.

McEwan bent down and took a closer look at the probable murder weapon. It was at least five to six feet long and made from metal. In fact, after ten years as an Inspector in the Oldham police force, this was the first time he had seen anyone killed by a Bishop's crosier.

Although not a devout man, the Inspector recognised the rod must be religious in provenance. He assumed it must be Christian, although the design was somewhat bizarre. Religious symbols fringed the bottom of the rod. At the head of the Castle were a pair of sculptured serpents with their heads curled back to face each other, with a small cross between them. They were stained red, presumably by the victim's blood.

Attached to the serpents was a piece of fabric. There was probably blood on this fabric, but at this moment McEwan couldn't tell as it was also coloured red. There were some gold letters but the alphabet unfamiliar. At a guess, McEwan would have adjudged the cloth tied to the crosier to be a Russian flag.

13

London: 3rd January 1920

Miller dropped off Esther at her hotel and then drove the two men back to Kit's flat. Another telegram was on the floor. Kit picked it up and read it aloud. Laughing morosely, he turned to Bright and said, 'He's just taken my pawn with his Bishop. He must fancy his chances to do that so early in the game.'

'Why do you say that?'

Kit walked over to the board. Looking at it for a moment, he made Serov's move. They had now made four moves each.

'At this stage I prefer to use the Knight or one of my pawns to mop up the advance guard. The Bishop isn't really part of your infantry unless you intend going all-out attack. Your Knight can jump in, execute his mission, then escape.'

'That's good news isn't it. If he takes you for granted he may make some mistakes.'

Kit smiled, 'I like your optimism. I daresay he feels he can beat me in whatever fashion he chooses. The thing of it is, he probably can. Serov doesn't just want to beat me; it seems he wants to club me to death while he's doing it.'

For the first time in the evening both found it possible to laugh as some men, destined for the gallows, might in the face of certain death.

*

The next morning found Spunky Stevens polishing his monocle to get a good view of the young ladies passing him and Kit on the park bench. Ensuring his eyewear was clean was imperative as Spunky had lost his other eye courtesy of German shrapnel early in the War. Invalided out of the army, he was quickly snapped up by spymaster, Mansfield Cumming. He became a vital part of Britain's intelligence network thanks to his expansive network of former Oxbridge contacts. His genius for organization soon made him indispensable in the organisation.

Kit looked at his old friend who was overtly surveying the territory. Spunky had long made it policy not to hide his thoughts, or indeed, intentions when it came to the opposite sex. Spunky believed in complete transparency. To the surprise of his friends, a combination of boyish charm and staggering honesty resulted in his enjoying a wide variety and high frequency of female company.

'Tip of the iceberg, of course,' explained Spunky to his friends. 'You don't get to see the dozen gals that turn me down.'

Kit looked at Spunky. This made Spunky smile and he turned to Kit and said, 'You must understand the terrain. From all this planning and strategy, execution must follow old boy.' His gaze followed a young lady accompanied by her mother, or governess, strolling through the park.

Sam was sitting on Spunky's lap enjoying a spot of dog watching. Spunky gazed down at the little terrier. 'I have a feeling that Sam is doing exactly what I'm doing. Do you ever give him the chance to meet young ladies?'

Kit laughed at this but did not answer and instead watched as his friend kept casting his eyes outside the office window.

'Sorry, old chap. A bit carried away there, but my word, Kit. I'm beginning to see the benefits of this move every day,' said Spunky yet another young lady caught his one good eye. 'Anyway, Billy Peel. An Ulsterman, been over here for yonks. Did his bit during the War. As you will have gathered, he's a bit of a hard line socialist. Been arrested a few times. Usual thing. Trade Union marches and the like. Haven't read many of his articles personally, but I gather he makes Marx look like a gin-swilling colonel at your local Conservative party.'

'Sounds like a character. Do you know why he's so hard line?'

'Not had enough time old boy,' admitted Spunky.

'I understand. Thanks, I appreciate you finding out so much.'

Spunky looked at his old friend with a frown. Kit couldn't quite read this look.

'Look, why the interest in Peel anyway, Kit?' asked Spunky finally.

Kit raised his hands, 'Honestly, I don't know. Probably I'm in a funk about the upcoming Serov catastrophe. I'm facing humiliation. My suspicion is someone like Peel will look to rain down on me seven kinds of you-know-what. Some of the things in the article were odd but I can't explain why.'

Spunky looked at him with a half-smile, 'I sense Kit the bloodhound is on the trail of something nefarious. Is there a fifth column in our midst?'

This made Kit roar with laughter. After a few minutes he looked at Spunky, 'Thanks, I don't feel I've been good company of late.'

'Perfectly understandable old boy,' replied Spunky sympathetically. 'You've fallen pretty hard for her, haven't you?'

Kit nodded in reply but said nothing more. What could he say? The aching hollowness inside him was its own answer. Spunky saw the look of pain on Kit's face and looked away, embarrassed to intrude on such anguish.

*

Later that afternoon, Kit picked up an early edition of the Evening Standard from a seller outside his apartment. The lad selling the paper was barely in his teens. Kit gave him a tip and took away the paper. His attention had been drawn by the headline. It read: Trade Union Official Murdered!

He showed the headline to Esther and Bright who sat with him in the car. He read the article out loud to his companions.

'Police are baffled by the bizarre battery of,' Kit looked up at his friends, 'I love the alliteration.' Continuing with the article, '...a man in Oldham. Trade Union official, Herbert Yapp was on his way home from a meeting in a local working men's club, when it is believed an unknown assailant attacked him. Police have not confirmed the cause of death, but it is believed he was murdered by a single blow to the head. Police have appealed for any witnesses.'

'How shocking, this world seems full of ghastly murders' said Esther.

'Strange,' said Bright.

'Even stranger, Richard. Listen to this,' said Kit. 'Herbert Yapp had earlier attended a meeting along with other Trade Unionists in which Russian chess grandmaster Filip Serov. The visiting Russian had just given a rousing pro-communist speech...'

94

Kit glanced up at Esther and Bright, 'What do you make of that?'

'But surely, it's just a coincidence,' said Esther.

Kit looked inside the paper to see if there was anything more on the story.

'I'm not sure I believe in coincidences, Esther. I wish there were more on the story.'

'But what possible connection could Serov have to this? It's fantastic,' replied Bright, unable to hide his scepticism.

Kit smiled, 'My suspicious nature. Mary would agree with me though.'

Esther laughed, 'She would. You're two peas in a pod, in this regard.'

Rather than leave Esther back to her hotel, all three returned to Kit's flat. They were greeted with a telegram containing the next move in the chess match. After depositing their coats in the cloakroom, Kit went over to the chess board and made Serov's move before sitting down to ponder a response.

The match was in its early stages. The pattern thus far recalled several matches familiar to Kit. All had been won by white. Although Kit was in no doubt Serov had a variation up his sleeve, there seemed little reason to depart from the classic responses. Kit made his mind up quickly and asked Harry to send a telegram to his opponent.

'Yes sir. I don't suppose you want me to wait for a response.

Kit glanced up at Miller. Something in what he'd asked made him wonder. He decided not to pursue this and merely said, 'No thanks, Harry. No need to wait.'

Miller left the apartment, watched by Kit.

Esther sat down near Kit and began to sketch him as he stared at the board. Kit, without moving, glanced at her.

'Do I have to stay in this position?'

Esther laughed, 'Yes, just a couple of minutes, I'm getting tired of painting watercolours in the park. A figurative study might be just the trick.'

'You've never asked to paint me,' smiled Bright.

Esther responded by making a face at him, 'I have some ideas on that, Dr Bright. They'll have to wait until we're married.'

*

In a nearby office, someone else was reading the same article with interest. Billy Peel set the Evening Standard down and gazed reflectively out the window. Peel, like Kit, did not believe in coincidences. It seemed unlikely that Serov would be implicated in such a crime, not the least because Yapp would have been on the same side of the fence, politically. He made a mental note to find out more about Yapp, and if his class struggle credentials were as strong as everyone had been led to believe.

However, the two Cheka agents presented a different proposition. Both were probably killers; Peel had suspected this from the first moment he'd met them. Bergmann was also someone who could order such an act and, probably, be capable of its execution. The only question if one believed this train of thought, and Peel did, was why? What possible motive would the Cheka agents have for murdering someone who was a supporter of class struggle. This made no sense to Peel. His spider senses, which he trusted implicitly, were tingling. Whenever he sensed a story, it was the same reaction. Grabbing his coat, he went over to the office of the editor.

George Lansbury, editor of the Herald, saw Peel enter his office with something approximating dread. That he did not like Peel was not an issue. He hated most of the journalists he worked with. They were a bunch of prima donnas in his view; always demanding to be centre of attention, always believing in a fantasy that they had an adoring public. This fantasy was, sadly, fed by the occasional supportive letters from the public. Peel was the worst in this regard.

The problem for Lansbury was that Peel was good. There were better writers on the newspaper, but few were smarter than the Ulsterman. Even fewer matched Peel's sense for a story and nobody had a way of sensationalising it quite the way he could.

This created a conflict for Lansbury. Like Peel, he genuinely strove for the truth. He passionately believed in the need for a newspaper to hold governments, judiciaries, and legislatures to account. In Britain, this meant the Establishment. Like Peel, Lansbury believed the Establishment sprang from the same small pond. Unlike Peel, Lansbury abhorred hyperbole and detested over-dramatizing stories. Doing this only diminished, rather than enhanced, the message. However, the newspaper owners loved Peel and Lansbury's hands were tied when it came to the diminutive Ulsterman.

'George,' said Peel entering without knocking.

'Come in,' said Lansbury, unable to hide the sourness in his voice.

Peel immediately detected the tone but, as usual, ignored it. 'I need to go to Oldham.'

'A little early for your summer holiday, Billy,' replied Lansbury sardonically.

97

'Very funny. I'm not sure the sun has ever shone in Oldham. Hidden behind the smoke from the mills no doubt.'

'No doubt. Perhaps you can shine the light of truth on this mill town then. May I ask why you want to go Oldham?'

'I want to look into the murder of the Trade Union official,' explained Peel.

Lansbury sat up, a little surprised. 'I thought you'd left crime behind.'

'The victim, Herbert Yapp, met Filip Serov, earlier that day.'

'Good God, you're not suggesting that there's a connection, are you? Wait a moment, Billy, you're not going to accuse Serov...?'

Lansbury had always been highly sympathetic to the Russian government. The prospect of Peel stirring up trouble with Serov was something he was keen to avoid. He dreaded to think what scandal Peel could dredge up on Serov if he put his mind to it. His rapid reverie was thankfully interrupted by Peel before it had fully landed on what might be happening in a typical Russian orphanage.

'No of course not,' answered Peel, 'but I want to find out more about the case. The police haven't released much about the murder beyond the usual appeal for witnesses.'

The connection with Serov was new news for Lansbury. Reluctantly he had to admit, as ever, Peel's instincts were correct in the need to follow up on what had happened. On the positive side it would take Peel away from a few days and hopefully give Lansbury one less child to worry about in the nursery. For a moment he could not stop himself fantasizing about having guard dogs patrol the perimeter of his office. The image of them snapping at the newspapermen brave enough to come to him for more space or a bigger headline gave him a warm glow.

With a wave of his hand, he agreed to allow Peel the expenses for the trip up to Oldham. It was only when Peel had left the office that Lansbury's mood sank again, as he realised how any perceived special treatment for Peel would only increase the demands from the rest of the adolescents in the newsroom. He rubbed both his eyes with the heel of his palms.

14

Oldham: 4th January 1920

Kopel read over the typewritten note. He looked at Fechin and smiled benignly. On several levels, it was a surprise. Given English was only his second language, Kopel was impressed with the absence of errors. Perhaps this was a function, he thought ruefully, of the low expectations he had of the little Muscovite.

More surprising was his flourish at the end. He had named the group, "The Sword of Light". It was very evocative, and Kopel had immediately congratulated Fechin on this. Not that he cared, but he was conscious of the need to encourage Fechin from time to time.

'Well done, Fechin. I think it captures the tone and the message very well. The misdirection about Yapp is very good. The police will waste a lot of time on this one. I like the "Sword of Light", very good.'

This seemed to make Fechin embarrassed but pleased all the same. He was desperate to please Kopel, sensing neither Daniels nor Serov liked him much. The provenance of the group's name was clearly unfamiliar to Kopel. It would be a nice surprise for him when he realised how Fechin had added another layer of misdirection on his own initiative. It was badly needed. The fiasco in Edinburgh was still fresh. He needed to regain some esteem from his colleagues, particularly Kopel, who had doubtless been made aware by Bergmann or Daniels.

Daniels, inevitably, seemed less impressed by both the name and the idea of the note. Kopel was quick to observe his reaction. As much as Kopel respected Daniels, he certainly wasn't a big picture man. There was a lack of panache in his comrade. Perhaps this was just as well. He took orders, he executed them, literally. What more did he need really? One last review of the note, it read:

Welcome to the Revolution. Herbert Yapp was executed yesterday. He was a traitor to the cause of class struggle.

The Sword of Light

Kopel put the note into an envelope and addressed it to Billy Peel, care of the Daily Herald. This would make a nice scoop for Peel. He'd maybe ask Bergmann to follow up separately with Peel on the progress of the chess match. It was critical that the profile of the encounter was maintained.

Over breakfast, Kopel, Bergmann and Serov discussed the progress of the game. Although Serov was glad that Bergmann had returned, meeting Kopel was a turning point in his level of enthusiasm for this trip. As much as he liked and even respected Daniels, the big Russian was not the most communicative. On the other hand, Fechin was much too talkative. None of it interested Serov. More importantly, he neither trusted nor liked the man. He guessed Fechin sensed this also and, increasingly, they avoided each other's company. Kopel's company was proving not only to be enjoyable but stimulating. Aside from his obvious intelligence and despite

101

his relative youth, there was a natural gravitas. Furthermore, he was exceptionally good company. He had a fund of fascinating stories about the Revolution. They encompassed the events leading up to its onset through to the aftermath.

Contrary to what had been reported by the party, the Revolution had been a bloodless affair. The revolutionaries had not stormed the Winter Palace; rather, they had been welcomed inside, like tourists on a guided tour. Serov had laughed when he heard Kopel mock the official line about these events, which Bergmann also confirmed, but afterwards he felt a little hollow. It was as if something, somewhere, was wrong. The idea that the revolutionary government would lie was an unwelcome dose of reality.

'The next few moves will be predictable,' confided Serov. 'We're still in the opening exchanges. I doubt Aston has the skill to innovate around the classic moves in this model. He won't want to risk it because white has won this way before.'

'I'm assuming that you can innovate, as you say, and ensure black triumphs this time,' smiled Kopel.

'Of course. I have several variations in the middle game that lead to white resigning.'

This seemed to trouble Kopel who asked, 'But not too soon, we need to keep the game going long enough to attract public interest and have you play Aston face to face.'

'Don't worry, I will keep him alive as long as you need me to.'

This made Kopel smile.

'Excellent, we don't want to kill Aston off too soon.'

*

Inspector McEwan sat at his desk in Oldham police station. After a day on the case, he had no witnesses. Instead, he had a chief constable shouting at him and the local press queued outside demanding to know more about the murder. He had nothing. Worse, he thought, I have something: the murder weapon.

The crosier had been stolen from a Russian Orthodox church in Manchester four months previously during a visit from a Russian Bishop. McEwan remembered the case although he had not been involved personally. Half-hearted efforts by the Manchester police led to an investigation which had, unsurprisingly, resulted in no arrests and no sign of the object in question. It had clearly not been a priority and the case file probably buried in a drawer marked 'inconvenient'.

Now McEwan had a dilemma. A big dilemma. Should he reveal more about the murder weapon and its origin? By doing so he could put immigrants in the region at risk of either revenge attacks or abuse. He didn't dare think about the wider ramifications for Whitehall in London. Not revealing more of what they knew might limit the investigation and deny potential access to new information from informants. It would also highlight how little they did know. This was equally unpalatable.

And then another idea occurred to him. One that could not be traced back to him, and would anger the police commissioner which, in McEwan's book, was merited after the carpeting he had endured earlier. McEwan sat back in his chair and smiled to himself. A few moments later he rose from his chair and walked out of the office. At the administration desk he found what he was looking for: the duty roster. Checking the list, he picked two names out before glancing around the office. The two men were sitting near one another not doing very much, as usual, thought McEwan sourly. They would be off duty soon and, no doubt, make straight for the pub.

They would do perfectly.

Catching the eye of one of the men he indicated by use of his index finger that he wanted to see both in office, pronto. Both men jumped up and followed Inspector McEwan into his office. Inviting them to sit down, he leant forward confidentially, 'So what do you make of this Yapp murder then? Have you ever heard of anyone being bashed over the head like this before?'

Neither Detective Constable Sargent nor MacDonald had, but for the next ten soul-annihilating minutes, McEwan endured their theories on the murder. At the end of this purgatory, both men, by dint of the increasingly succinct answers to McEwan's questions, hinted that they were now ready to knock off work. As much of a penance as it was to be in their company, McEwan took some enjoyment in stretching things out a little longer before releasing them to their evening in the pub.

*

Billy Peel sat in the Bell and Whistle a pub located near Oldham's police station. On a number of levels, Peel loved pubs. Although a moderate drinker himself, he found them a rich source of material for news. Pubs meant alcohol. Alcohol meant drinking. This, inevitably, led to a deterioration in people's common sense, even in those cases where some was present. Peel mercilessly exploited this, and it happened often, thankfully. Sometimes he obtained information through luck; being the nearby recipient of overheard conversations, sometimes he acted directly to obtain it, however he preferred to avoid this as a rule.

It was often expensive, potentially unethical and, worst of all, unlikely to be refunded by that prurient oaf, George Lansbury. He regretted this thought immediately. George's heart was in the right place. They had fought many battles together on marches, supporting strikers but sometimes he could be just too pious for Peel's taste.

Earlier that day, Peel had strolled into Oldham police station. It took only a few minutes to understand there was as much chance of receiving information from the Oldham constabulary as the Pope leading morning prayers at the local mosque. Rather than waste time sitting with his press brothers, he picked up what information he could in casual conversation including, importantly, key gaps in reporters' knowledge. Which were many.

All Peel needed was to find a policeman stupid enough to accept drinks from a stranger and open up about interesting cases in the station. Patience was key. Sometimes Peel could sit a whole evening in a pub and glean nothing. On other occasions, the ones he lived for as a newsman, he would hit the mother lode.

Just as he was considering which type of night it would be, he saw two men enter the pub. Peel's sure-fire instincts told him three things: they were police, they liked to drink and, to be confirmed, they looked like they had the collective intelligence of a gerbil.

The key was never to rush in. Bide your time lest they become suspicious. It took an hour which was significantly less than Peel thought would be needed. Both policemen were on their sixth pint of ale. This struck Peel as both excessive and an unhealthily fast way of drinking. He found little to admire in men who considered themselves hardened drinkers.

105

Character and courage were defined in ways such men would never understand.

Stepping up to the bar, he made sure he was beside the two targets. Then he waited to be served. And waited. Peel's modus operandi was beautifully simple. He used his lack of height to great effect. He could become almost invisible when he chose to. After a few minutes standing at the bar and being ignored by the blameless barmen, Detective Constable Sargent noticed the lack of service.

'They don't seem to be seeing you pal.'

'I know. Are they always so slow?' asked Peel ruefully.

A public servant to his toes, Sargent waved at the barman to attract his attention, 'Oi, Paddy, over here. Customer waiting.'

The barman, who was Irish, but not a Patrick, strolled over with a fixed grin. He recognised the two men as coppers, otherwise they would have been dealt with more summarily.

Peel ordered his pint then, kindly, offered to buy his new friends a drink. As it would have been rude to turn down such hospitality, the two policemen accepted with alacrity. Introductions were soon made.

'I'm Billy, gentlemen,' said Peel as he held out his hand. "I'm selling some encyclopaedias and,' Peel paused for a moment as inspiration struck, 'Bibles, in the area.'

'Is that so. We're in the job.'

'Police.'

'Very good Billy,' winked MacDonald. "I'm Detective Constable MacDonald.'

"And I'm Detective Constable Sargent.'

106

Peel looked at Sargent for a moment just to check if they were taking the rise out of him. Neither seemed to be making a joke so Peel ploughed on regardless.

'Your health gentlemen. You do an important job protecting our community and ridding our streets of the criminal element.'

The three men clinked glasses. 'It's nice to be appreciated Hilary, isn't it?' said Sargent.

Hilary? Once again Peel wasn't sure if this was a joke, but he knew that some poor men had been given this name, no doubt causing years of bullying at school.

'I couldn't do what you do, gentlemen. All those criminals, all those murderers,' prompted Peel, eyes raised up in the universal invitation to tell him more.

And they did.

Before long they were recounting their role in cracking cases, international crime rings, anarchist cells. To hear them tell it, Peel concluded, these two men had single-handedly wiped crime out in the northwest. He congratulated them on their extraordinary powers of deduction before prompting them further on the ineffectiveness of their colleagues. This was always fertile ground and within minutes it bore fruit.

'We've one case that's has the plain clothes stumped.'

'Really?' urged Peel. Said with just the right degree of intonation and combined with the raising of an eyebrow, it could prompt all manner of responses.

'Heard about the Trade Union man that was mugged?'

'No, what happened?' asked Peel moving closer. It had long since been his experience that when he did this his interviewees did so also, revealing much more in the process.

107

'A local Union bigwig was bashed; on his bonnet,' explained Sargent, pointing to his head to ensure the point was understood. Pitt groaned inside. This could be a long evening.

'No, really? And no one knows who did it?' inquired Peel.

'Not a clue, trust me. No witnesses. But the killer left a murder weapon behind.'

Peel nearly leapt of his chair at this. He confined himself to a silent hallelujah and said nothing. Instead, he widened his eyes theatrically and nodded encouragement for the drunken policeman to continue. The invitation was taken up with something approaching relish.

'It was some sort of religious stick.'

'Religious stick?' said Peel looking at Sargent unable to believe how stupid the man was. 'What type of religious...stick?'

Sargent shrugged. 'No idea. You know. A stick.'

Peel didn't know and felt an overwhelming desire to scream. Resisting this impulse, he turned to look at MacDonald. The worthy constable shrugged also. Peel looked down at his pint and seriously considered smacking both men with it. Religious stick? What kind of morons were these people, he wondered? Still, it was better than nothing. If he broke the story, then it might force the police to release further details. He could work with this. Even Lansbury would be hard pushed to deny the trip had not been worthwhile. As he thought about the murder weapon and the lack of any witnesses, all his instincts were telling him the same thing.

This was only the beginning.

15

London: 5th January 1920

It was a brilliant January day. The sun's rays slanted through Kit's window glinting off the pieces on the chess board. The room felt warmer although it was icily fresh outside. It seemed the room's mood was dictated by the extent of light outside. Kit let the light fall on his face, and it warmed him. He left the window and sat down by the chess board and studied it for a moment. He glanced up at Bright and Esther who had moved to the window.

'What have you planned today?'

'We were thinking of looking for an apartment in town,' replied Esther smiling up at Bright. Her fiancé took hold of her hand as she said this.

'I'm not sure I could stand to live up at Cavendish Hall,' added Bright.

Kit laughed and looked at the couple. Esther, as ever, seemed like an ethereal presence. Her hair and white silk dress were framed by the dappled light coursing through the window. Richard was a very lucky man, thought Kit.

'I don't blame you. Is Emily at Cavendish Hall full time now?"

'If she isn't already, I imagine she soon will be,' laughed Esther. Bending down, she picked Sam up, who made clear his delight by nuzzling her neck.

Bright laughed, 'My rival.'

'No contest,' said Esther making a face to Bright.

'I think he wants you to adopt him,' smiled Kit.

The little dog barked in approval causing Esther to laugh.

'He certainly is a tonic,' said Esther.

Kit returned his attention to the chess board. After a few moments he made another move. Reaching over to the board, he took his Knight and made the peculiar "L" shaped movement of this piece. It landed on the square of a black Knight. He lifted Serov's piece and put it alongside a few other pawns at the side of the board. Bright looked over, with interest. Eyebrows raised he said with a smile, 'Shall I start singing Land of Hope and Glory yet?'

Kit laughed and replied, 'Best leave it a bit longer Richard. You may want to bone up on The Internationale just in case, though. I fancy it may be needed.'

'Freedom is just privilege extended unless enjoyed by one and all,' recited Bright with a smile.

This made Kit glance up sharply at Bright. Even Esther seemed surprised, 'I'm impressed. It's nice to know my future husband is erudite.'

'And a radical, apparently,' laughed Kit.

'I was a bit more radical as a student. I've calmed down a bit now,' admitted Bright.

'I should hope so,' said Esther, grinning. 'You're about to marry into the aristocracy. Well, minor aristocracy if truth be told. I hope that's not a problem.'

'I shall bear the disappointment as best I can, my dear,' responded Bright looking at the most beautiful girl he'd ever met. He didn't look particularly disappointed, noted Kit with a smile.

'Anyway, our Lordship,' pointed out Esther, eyes narrowing in a way that made Kit's heart burn for Mary, 'You seem familiar with this song also.'

'True,' acknowledged Kit. 'My oldest friend taught me the words in Russian and English. Came in useful, I can tell you. I might be able to tell you one day.'

Returning to the board Kit said, 'So Serov will probably take my Knight now. I'll take his pawn then he'll take mine. We'll be all square, so to speak, but things will start to get messy from this point. Well, from my point of view anyway. Serov will only see order and inevitability.'

Esther glanced up at Bright who merely rolled his eyes. They both hoped Kit would become more positive about his chances.

*

The overnight train from Manchester arrived in London just before dawn. The station lamps were still glowing brightly in the gloom. Peel could sense a city beginning to wake. Outside the station, market stalls were opening. One young boy was unloading a cart of fruit and vegetables as his father made ready the stall. Peel walked over to them and picked a couple of apples from the pile.

'Morning son. Too early to buy these?' he asked.

'Never too early sir,' beamed the boy.

Peel flipped a shilling into the boy's hands and walked on. He waved his hands to the boy and then the father who were calling out to him for his change. He heard the boy shout thanks.

Rather than head back to his flat in Bayswater, Peel made straight for the offices of the Daily Herald. The place was already humming with activity. Ignoring everything around him, Peel set to work. Still frustrated by the lack of precision from his dimwit informants, Peel struggled to write a suitably compelling headline. He settled on the following: Trade Unionist Murdered by Crucifix – Police Baffled

He suspected Lansbury would dilute this. To be fair to Lansbury he'd had enough trouble over the years with the law. But no matter; the basic story was robust and would create a stir. The more he shook the tree the more likely fruit would fall. It was now clear to Peel that no connection could be made with Serov's visit. Notwithstanding his usual suspicion around coincidences, for once this seemed genuinely pure chance.

For the moment.

As he was finishing the report a young man came by his desk and dropped several letters. Peel stopped typing and glanced at the letters. They could wait. He resumed typing. Removing the sheet from the typewriter, he proofread the report several times. It would create a stir, no question. Rising from his desk, he made his way to the office marked "Editor".

George Lansbury read over Peel's report from his trip to Oldham. Twice. As much as he hated to admit it, Peel had delivered the goods. This was a scoop, and no mistake. The Daily Herald would break the story about the murder weapon, forcing the police to reveal more details. Of course, there was only one problem, and he broached it immediately with Peel.

'Good work, Billy. I just hope no law was broken in getting this,' said Lansbury eyeing Peel closely.

This made Peel smile, but he decided not to indulge Lansbury on this and moved the subject on to more important matters.

'Will it make the final edition?'

Lansbury glanced at the clock on the wall, it was nearly eight in the morning.

'If you run down now.'

'Front page?' pushed Peel. Inevitably.

Lansbury looked again at Peel. Of course, it was front page. Peel knew it. He knew it. At that moment Lansbury was reminded of why he found Peel so irritating. Then again, was ambition combined with talent innately wrong? Possibly when it came with Peel's special brand of arrogance. The feeling that Peel would walk over anyone to get to a story was palpable. Lansbury was not like this. But, then again, wasn't this what made a great newsman: commitment to the story?

With a moment bordering on epiphany, Lansbury realised this was what drove Peel. Was it possible, disguised beneath his "pit bull" persona, he was genuinely not the self-serving individual he had always believed him to be? He looked Peel in the eye. What he saw was not ambition. For ambition is merely an extension of ego and the ego is rarely objective. It feeds off denial and builds on lies. Peel wanted the truth. Unvarnished, undiluted, and untainted. He would follow wherever it took him, at whatever cost. Finally, Lansbury nodded. Peel left the office headed downstairs to speak to the printers.

*

113

It was early afternoon before Inspector McEwan's phone began ringing. He had expected something around then. Picking it up he was greeted by shouting at the other end. He moved the earpiece further away as the sound of the thunder reverberated down the line, uncontrolled in its fury. After what seemed like several minutes, the storm abated.

'Chief Constable. Always good to hear from you,' lied McEwan, 'I'm sorry, but can you tell me what exactly the problem is? I didn't quite catch what you were telling me if I'm being honest.'

McEwan held the earpiece away from his ear again as the chief gave vent to his thoughts on McEwan's powers of deduction, management of the case and, most importantly, control of the flow of information.

'Am I to understand, there has been a leak of information on the Yapp murder?' inquired McEwan innocently.

Several swear words followed; an impressive array of nouns, adjectives and even one verb, preceded confirmation of this fact. The rest of the conversation was just as one sided but with the result that McEwan was ordered to release full details of the murder weapon to the press and to investigate the leak. This would uncover nothing, both knew this, but it was necessary to keep up or recover the appearance of good governance.

When the call finished, McEwan took his feet off the desk where he'd perched them to enjoy more comfortably the disembowelling from the chief constable. Now, it was his turn to roar at the boys. It made no sense to pick on just the culprits. After all, he'd set them up to do this. From time to time, it was never the wrong answer to hand out a good carpeting. Kept them all on their toes and acted as a reminder of the need for confidentiality. In many respects, it was mission accomplished.

A few hours later, McEwan read the article. There was some dismay at the level of detail. He was sure both Sargent and MacDonald had seen the murder weapon. The only conclusion that could be drawn was that neither had any idea what it was. Worse, neither had inquired what it was. An even more scary thought struck McEwan, perhaps they had been told the name of the object and had simply forgotten. McEwan shook his head with dismay. His job was never going to be easy if he had to work with muttonheads like these.

*

If Serov had found the Northwest unattractive but prosperous, his view of Birmingham was, if anything, even less enthusiastic. The excitement of visiting the cities and meeting workers and Unions was beginning to pale. Edinburgh had seemed more open, the air cleaner and the temperature to his liking: cold bordering on freezing. The further south he went, the more he began to miss seeing the sky rather than the grey blanket that seemed to hang permanently, like a pall, over the Northwest and Midlands.

One good development was the absence of Fechin. He had been dispatched by Kopel on some unknown task. Sadly, Bergmann was no longer in their company. However, Kopel was more than compensation for the absence of Bergmann. Daniels continued to accompany them, but he was less of an issue. Having Fechin around was like having a migraine. A nagging, relentless headache. Although Fechin rarely spoke to Serov, the rat-like features and sneer, albeit unintentional, made his presence unpleasant.

115

The good humour of Kopel allowed Serov to relax. In fact, Serov recognised he was falling under the Latvian's spell. The easiness of his manner in no way detracted from the impression of a high-level intellect. Unusually, at least in Serov's experience, he sensed a man who was a sportsman also by the nonchalant physical grace he possessed.

The other impressive aspect of Kopel was his ability to listen. Serov found himself talking about his early life in a way he had never done before. Certainly not like the speeches he made back home to the workers, or here in Britain. They were well-drilled marches through the events that had shaped his convictions. Instead, he spoke on a more personal, emotional level as if to a confessor.

The three men travelled together in easy company. The day's first visit was to play in the usual series of games at a chess club. This was followed by a trip to a Workers Club where Serov met the usual parade of uninspiring, albeit, committed radicals, who shared his vision of a country where the workers ruled, and private property no longer existed. Except, the more he encountered the future rulers of this socialist utopia the less sure the Russian was of this vision.

The chess matches, since his bloody battle with Fiona Lawrence, had been mostly walkovers. No one had challenged him in the way the young girl from Scotland had. He no longer felt frustrated by the result. With more time to reflect, he realised that she had played a weak hand with something approaching genius.

It almost made him smile as he recollected her various ruses to upset him. She had executed her plan brilliantly. But it had provided him with an unexpected insight for his future attempts at taking on the great players of the day: Lasker and

116

the young Cuban, Capablanca, who was making a stir on the other side of the world. Chess was not a board game; it was not even a mind game. It was war by other means.

Before Fiona Lawrence, he had thought his weapons were the pieces on the board. Now, he knew otherwise. They were but one theatre in a wider conflict of the mind. He laughed to himself at the thought of a mathematician like Lasker dealing with the machinations of a twelve-year-old prodigy who was not above using physical violence. At the hotel, Kopel brought Serov back to reality from his reflections by showing him the latest telegram from Kit.

'Do you want to see the board?'

Serov grinned and tapped his forehead. Borrowing a pen, he scribbled his response. Kopel looked at Serov for an explanation.

'I might have mentioned the other night; we exchange Knights and one pawn. From this point, the game can go in several directions. Aston will almost certainly be able to see how two, maybe three routes give white a material advantage. I know at least two other directions which have never been captured in chess textbooks. Either way, we are moving into unknown territory.'

'And Aston won't have prepared for this?' smiled Kopel.

'Highly unlikely in my view unless he's better than I thought,' replied Serov with the certainty of a man who knew Aston would not have thought of these end games.

'You don't think he is,' said Kopel reading his mind.

Serov paused for a moment before answering.

'He's good. I'm better.'

This seemed to satisfy Kopel, and the conversation moved on to other topics. Serov noted that Kopel did not offer much information on the whereabouts of the other two men but he was enjoying their conversation too much to ask.

16

The Daily Herald newsroom broke into a round of applause when Peel entered. Even Lansbury, standing by the entrance of his office with a half-smile, was applauding. Peel gave him a brief nod and sat at his desk after his embarrassed wave signalled an end to the acclaim.

He began to sift through his mail cluttering his desk. After a few moments he sensed someone standing beside him. Looking up he saw Lansbury. Peel nodded again and said, 'Hope this hasn't upset you too much George.'

Lansbury laughed, 'You'd be surprised, Billy. Good work.' A clap on the shoulder and Lansbury was gone as quickly as he had arrived. Peel returned to sifting through his post.

Ten minutes later Peel rapped on Lansbury's door. The editor shook his head indicating he was in a meeting with some of the printers. Peel walked in anyway. Lansbury did not try to disguise his irritation.

'Billy, I appreciate all you've done this last day or two, but can't this wait?'

Peel didn't bother answering, instead he handed Lansbury the note signed by "The Sword of Light".

Lansbury read the note, his face falling with each word. Finally, he looked at the rest of the attendees.

'Gentlemen, we need to hold the front page for another thirty minutes.'

This was greeted by groans of dismay by everyone. The editorial had already been agreed and printing was already in progress.

'You'll have to trust me. Can we reconvene in twenty minutes or so? I need to talk to Billy about this,' said Lansbury holding up the paper in his hand.

The other men left the room leaving Peel alone with Lansbury. Peel sat down and looked at the troubled face of his editor. It was not difficult to guess why he was worried.

'Where did you get this?' asked Lansbury.

Peel handed the envelope to Lansbury. It had been addressed to Peel with a Manchester postmark dated from two days ago.

'I only saw it this morning,' explained Peel.

'What makes you think it isn't a hoax?' asked Lansbury. The letter was dynamite but equally, if it turned out to be a hoax, it would have serious consequences for the Daily Herald beyond just humiliation. Sending the police off on a wild goose chase would create future problems for the paper. There had been enough problems with the police in the past. Lansbury had worked hard to rebuild relations. He relied more on good relations with the police than he was prepared to admit. More practically, a better relationship helped to gain access to stories. Wasting police time was a cardinal sin for newspaper. Especially so after all he and the newspaper had been through in the past. Lansbury had to be certain.

'I don't have a secondary source on this George. Just this. We won't have time to dig up anything on this group now. You have to decide if we go with it or not.'

'I'm aware of what I have to do,' said Lansbury sarcastically.

'There's one thing that might make it credible,' said Peel ignoring the dismissive tone of Lansbury.

'Go on.'

'There may be an Irish republican angle to this.'

'What? Why?' exclaimed Lansbury in astonishment.

'The name.'

Lansbury looked mystified, so Peel continued to explain. 'The Sword of Light is part of Irish folklore. It was brought to Ireland by some king, can't remember who, don't really care, but no matter. It was the embodiment of justice. Specifically, it was meant to punish Ireland's enemies.'

'Bit of a jump to say it's Irish republican, though,' said Lansbury, still doubtful but conscious, trustful even, of Peel's sure-fire instincts.

'You remember Patrick Pearse?' asked Peel.

'Yes, we were stupid enough to make that man a martyr by executing him in 1916. I suspect we haven't heard the end of it either.'

'He ran a newspaper before he led the Uprising. Want to guess what it was called?'

Lansbury exhaled loudly. For a minute he was silent as he weighed up his options. Finally, he asked Peel, 'But why Herbert Yapp? I don't understand the connection.'

'When I was in Oldham, I did some digging into potential motives for killing Yapp. As I see it, he was highly vocal against the arrival of Irish immigrants into the area. He said they were taking jobs from English people. A man of the people, unless, of course, those people were foreign,' said Peel. Lansbury noted the tone of contempt in the voice of the Ulsterman.

'You've ten minutes. Bring me a front-page story.'

121

Peel was already out of the office before Lansbury had finished the sentence.

The Daily Herald hit the newsstands later that morning with the following headline: Irish Republican Connection to Yapp Murder

The story included the printed letter received by Peel in full. However, it wisely omitted any mention of "The Sword of Light". By the time copies of the newspaper were being snapped up by the public, the letter and the addressee were both in an office at Scotland Yard.

*

Chief Inspector James Jellicoe of Scotland Yard looked at Peel. Their paths had crossed on several occasions. Neither appeared to derive much pleasure from the renewal of their acquaintance. Neither tried to hide the fact.

'Why was this sent to you?'

'I don't know.'

'You're investigating the Yapp murder for the Herald,' stated Jellicoe sullenly. He had a strong feeling about the letter. He suspected it was genuine. This was aggravating because it also signified the potential for further murders and more publicity. None of this would reflect well on the police unless a miracle resulted in the quick resolution of the case. Jellicoe was not a man who either relied on, or believed in, miracles, although his colleagues noted he often called upon the supreme unction of the Lord in times of stress. They had rarely seen it granted. Maybe something in the Chief Inspector's angry tone.

'Yes, but this was sent before I broke the story about the murder weapon. Look at the postmark'

The Chief did so, his heart sinking a little.

122

'Why Irish republican?'

Peel explained.

Jellicoe looked at the newspaper article again. Grudgingly he had to admit it was well handled by Peel. Importantly, by not mentioning the name of the group, he had seen off any possibility that the police would have to spend much time filtering hoax copycat letters.

'Thanks for not mentioning the name of the group,' conceded Jellicoe, 'That'll help us.'

Peel said nothing. Instead, he looked at Jellicoe. The Chief Inspector was not given much to humour or, indeed, any kind of warmth. His face was always mournful. This impression was exacerbated by the rather hangdog moustache and beard that made him resemble King George V. The Daily Herald had many dealings with Jellicoe over the years. His nickname in the press room was "his Highness". Even George Lansbury, the most correct of men had, on occasion, used the epithet.

'You've seen the news release by the Oldham police on the murder weapon?' asked Jellicoe.

'I did. A bishop's crosier. My informant didn't mention this. He described it as a stick.'

'A stick?' said Jellicoe incredulously.

'Not the brightest light in the house,' responded Peel, his eyebrows raised.

'Clearly,' said Jellicoe shaking his head, his heart sinking at the thought of men found their way into the police.

The interview was thankfully short, as far as Peel was concerned. Even if Jellicoe took himself and life seriously, in Peel's judgement, he was no fool. Jellicoe would've quickly ascertained the potential gravity of the situation; he would also know that Peel was entitled to use whatever came his way for

123

the purposes of breaking a news story. But oddly, Peel had earned the trust of the Jellicoe, at least for now, thanks to his handling of the letter.

From Jellicoe's point of view, he needed to have Peel on his side. His instinct told him there would-be other letters, other murders. If, as seemed likely, future correspondence was forthcoming, it would be directed to Peel. Going forward, Jellicoe determined to maintain a good relationship with the diminutive Ulsterman to ensure some control of the news story. He was certain there was more to come and none of it would be good.

Following the meeting with Peel, Jellicoe placed a phone call to Inspector McEwan in Oldham. The jurisdiction of the investigation was Oldham, but it made sense to warn McEwan that there was a possibility this might change. More murders, if the Irish connection was true, might not necessarily be restricted to Oldham. In fact, it was highly unlikely they would. Jellicoe's heart sank as he considered the possibilities.

The idea of a campaign of murder on the mainland by an Irish group was unthinkable. He was aware of how nasty things were becoming in Ireland. The violence perpetrated by the British police force nicknamed the "Black and Tans", owing to the colour of their uniform, was gradually becoming well known in Britain and a source of controversy. It seemed to Jellicoe entirely plausible for Irish republicans to have set up a terror group to exact revenge for the attacks taking place on civilians in Ireland.

Jellicoe introduced himself to McEwan and told him of the purpose of the call. McEwan had not yet seen the Daily Herald article and was taken by surprise by the news.

'Irish, you say? Why do we think this?'

Jellicoe took McEwan through the logic, which seemed plausible on one level but did not explain other inconsistencies.

'We didn't mention in our release,' explained McEwan, 'but the crosier in question is not Roman Catholic. If it had been, it would've fitted the narrative perfectly.'

It was Jellicoe's turn to be surprised. 'What type of crosier was it?'

'Russian Orthodox.'

Alarms began to ring in his mind. This is getting out of hand, thought Jellicoe. Were the Bolsheviks working with Irish republicans or was the Socialist League re-emerging from the shadows? Was it an attack on Britain, against class inequality or was it a religious minority lashing out against an oppressor? He shook his head, desperately wondering how he could shift this case away from his desk and onto to someone else's.

'Russian? Good lord. I'm not sure what to make of this. Look, Inspector, this may not be the last of these murders. We must take this group seriously. But clearly, based on this new evidence, we can't discount the possibility of Russian involvement. I think I may need to refer this elsewhere if you take my meaning.'

'I think I understand you sir,' said 'McEwan, who was silently cheering the news that overall responsibility for the case was going off his desk.

'You've had no breaks in the case aside from this new information?' asked Jellicoe, more in hope than expectation.

'None, sir. However, we'll shift our focus away towards the Irish angle and see where it takes us.'

'Good idea, McEwan. Let's keep in touch.'

The end of the phone call saw Jellicoe rise from his desk and look out of his window. This left him with a two-pipe problem, he thought amusedly to himself. Should he wait for the next killing to take place, for there would surely be a next killing, or would it be better to risk some slight embarrassment by bringing in the Special Intelligence Service now?

Outside his window he could see the street full of people walking on the pavement, some cars were on the roads. The people seemed like ants scurrying to and fro. For a moment, a frightening image entered his mind of the impact a bomb, from an anarchist, would have on the street below. The immediate carnage followed by the fear, the terror for people in cities. Jellicoe had often wondered why anarchists had not used such weapons. It would've been all so easy. It was not like they were trying to win the hearts and minds of people. They just wanted to kill.

His thoughts returned to the murder in Oldham. What was the reason for killing Herbert Yapp? With a heart that felt like a lead weight in his chest, he realised more murders would need to take place before he could answer this question. As it turned out, Jellicoe didn't have too long to wait

17

Sir Montagu Forbes-Trefusis had been knighted at the age of twenty-seven. This was a record for the Forbes-Trefusis family. The previous record holder was his grandfather, Spires Forbes-Trefusis. Nobody then nor now could, if pinned down, quite give a reason why he had earned this honour at such a young age other than possession of an impressively upper-class name. Envious colleagues at the Foreign Office, where Forbes-Trefusis worked, agreed that the honours list of 1889 had not been a vintage crop.

Whatever question marks existed on the Forbes-Trefusis line's hereditary right to be knighted, there could be no question over the work ethic of the current family patriarch. Like his forefathers before him, he rounded off an outstanding career at Eton, followed by Oxford Balliol, with an immediate entry into the Foreign Office. He had risen through the ranks by dint of connections, intelligence, hard work and yet more connections to become a deputy under-secretary in national security. This was a position occupied by many previous Forbes-Trefusis men.

He took to his role with an enthusiasm bordering on fanaticism. Doubt was not a word that existed in his vocabulary. Britain was a force for good in the world. What was good for Britain was good for the world. The advancement of British interests was a proxy for the advancement of mankind. It just needed clear-sighted men, like him, to advise and guide policy that ensured Britain was at the forefront of international diplomacy, not an order taker from those nations, many as they were, who looked on with envy at the empire.

Over the period in which Forbes-Trefusis worked in the Foreign Office, he had been vocal in advocating a foreign policy that did not so much border as inhabit the idea that attack is the best form of defence. From the Far East to Africa, he was instrumental in asserting Britain's desire for peace through the agency of a strong military.

Notwithstanding his purview of the need for a muscular Britain, Forbes-Trefusis had a wide circle of friends including the Bloomsbury set. He enjoyed close friendships with Duncan Grant and John Maynard-Keynes. Although both men disagreed with him on policy, the combination of hawk and dove provided mutual comfort from time to time.

On those occasions when asked if he had any regrets or, more specifically, any failures, Forbes-Trefusis was surprisingly candid on the subject, albeit within the confines of his private club in St James's.

Russia.

The failure of Britain to prevent the October Revolution, rankled. For many years he had pointed out the risks that lay with Britain's indecision on whether to view Russia as a future enemy or potential ally. The craven attitude of the politicians over Tsar Nicholas's more extreme repressive measures resulted in a lost opportunity to build on the common interests that resulted from having heads of state, Nicholas, and George V, who were cousins. Had this been done early enough

Forbes-Trefusis believed Britain could have avoided entanglement in the Great War and averted the overthrow of the Romanov family.

The Great War had changed Forbes-Trefusis, however. The loss of one son at Passchendaele had caused an almost Damascene conversion. For the first time he began to question if policy ends could be achieved by military means alone. He opposed military intervention in post-revolutionary Russia. This brought him into conflict with former allies, such as Churchill, putting him into the orbit of more diplomatically minded Foreign Office officials, doubtless relieved to have the vigorously argumentative Forbes-Trefusis batting for them.

The Forbes-Trefusis epiphany had not made him a pacifist overnight, but he did become a voice within the National Security office arguing for accommodation with the Bolsheviks rather than the overthrow favoured by Churchill. They remained good friends as they were aligned on most other topics of the day such as Ireland. Forbes-Trefusis could never forgive the Irish for having started an uprising whilst many of their countrymen were dying in France, and later, his own son. About Russia, Churchill and he agreed to differ; they rarely discussed the subject face to face.

As Forbes-Trefusis skipped down the steps of the Foreign Office, for what would be the last time, he looked up at the sky. Against the chaos and confusion of commuters on the street, it seemed so calm with the ever-consistent grey clouds drifting lazily towards, well, wherever clouds go.

Pulling up the collar of his coat against an icy wind, he stepped forward briskly into the waiting car at the bottom of the steps. The big driver was new, which was not new. He was used to this. The drivers seemed to change more frequently these days. He missed, Asif, his driver of many years greatly. Now, he rarely bothered to learn the names of the new drivers, such was the turnover.

'Whites,' said Forbes-Trefusis, before opening his leather satchel and taking out some papers. After a few minutes, Forbes-Trefusis became aware that the car was travelling in the wrong direction.

'Where do you think you're going?' barked Forbes-Trefusis irritably.

The big driver responded in a foreign accent, 'The road was blocked.'

Forbes-Trefusis looked sceptically at the driver. Unfortunately, as he had not been paying attention he could not really argue. This changed when the car stopped suddenly, and a small man leapt in unexpectedly. At this point Forbes-Trefusis realised that he would not be going to his club any time soon.

*

'I never thought I'd be reading the Daily Herald every day,' said Kit, glancing over to Esther and Bright. 'This chap Peel seems to be covering my match and the Yapp murder.'

Bright laughed, 'Do you think there's a connection?'

Kit laughed but did not reply. He was wondering about this also. On the surface there was nothing obvious to connect the two but, it was a coincidence, and this always acted like a stone in his shoe.

'The Times is covering your match now, I see, and I noticed yesterday the Telegraph also,' said Esther looking up from the newspaper, adding teasingly, 'You're becoming quite famous. Well, even more famous.'

'I'll bet that's Bergmann sending details through of the moves,' responded Kit with a grin. 'I think that's what they want, publicity. Let it build slowly and then a high profile, public execution.'

Esther and Bright glanced at one another; both raised their eyes to the heavens. This time Kit noticed the eye rolling.

'You may laugh,' said Kit with a grin, 'I'm the one in the firing line here.'

'Who is this Bergmann anyway?' asked Bright.

'I've never met him funnily enough. I've spoken with him on the telephone once and the other times it's been via telegram or letter. My guess is he's part of a Russian drive to re-establish diplomatic links or even an embassy. Possibly, he's Cheka, who knows?'

'Never thought to investigate him?' continued Bright.

Kit put his paper down and looked reflective. 'I suppose I'm just doing what my old commander asked me to. My heart's not in it. To be honest, I really don't care about the blessed match. It's a distraction. I'm at the point now where I'd be happy if Serov wins. I say "if", I mean when.'

Kit returned to his paper and scanned various headlines. Nothing captured his attention. He glanced down at the Court Circular. The King and the Queen would be visiting the Teddington and Hampton Wick Memorial Hospital, near where Kit was playing Serov at Hampton Court, the same afternoon as his match. He mentioned this to Esther and Bright. Of the three of them, only Esther had any recent brush with the Royal family, but this had been before the War with her grandfather. The memory of it brought a tearful smile to her face. She felt, once more, an emptiness in the pit of her stomach.

A knock at the door broke the sombre mood. Miller went to answer, reappearing moments later with a telegram. This was the latest move from Serov. Kit reviewed the telegram and made the move for Serov. It did not involve taking a piece, but it made Kit look at the board for a short period before speaking.

'Interesting.'

''Why?' asked Esther looking at the board also but without any idea of what she should be seeing. She looked back at Kit expectantly.

'By moving this pawn into a position where it will be sacrificed, he wants to open up the left side of the board. This is an invitation for me to develop this line here,' said Kit indicating a vertical line of squares on the board, 'And it will put me a pawn to the good.'

'That's good, surely,' pointed out Bright.

'Yes and no. Yes, because it's always good to have an advantage, however slight. But it introduces a new variation to the game which I haven't seen before. He's probably tested out its evolution. I haven't.'

'So, you're damned if you do and damned if you don't take the pawn,' said Bright beginning to understand where Kit was heading.

'Correct.'

Kit shook his head in consternation. Getting up from his seat he went to a set of drawers and took out a small rectangular tea box. Inside was another chess set. Setting it down alongside the main board he arranged the pieces to mirror the latest stage of play in the game with Serov.

'It looks like a child's play set,' said Esther. The smile on Kit as he looked back at her confirmed her intuition. 'Must be dreadfully old then.'

Both men laughed at this. Then Esther and Bright watched in fascination as Kit moved the pieces around the board at lightning speed, experimenting with different permutations. Kit looked up and smiled at the rapt couple.

'The thing is Serov can probably do this in his head. He'll certainly have had time over the last few years to work out the strongest moves. I've a matter of a few days. I wish I'd someone who could help me a bit on this,' Kit looked up at his two friends suddenly, 'Sorry, I wasn't meaning to cause offence'

Bright laughed, 'None taken. I'm sure we both wish we could help more. When are you playing this blighter anyway?'

'Less than a week now,' said Kit before adding ruefully, 'If I last that long.'

'Don't worry old chap,' said Bright with a grin, 'I'm sure he'll toy with you long enough to deliver the knockout blow in as public a setting as possible.'

'Richard!' exclaimed Esther, turning to Bright in shock.

Then she turned to Kit, who was lying back in the sofa laughing heartily before asking, 'I have a question, and it is a serious one: do men ever grow up?'

'No,' said Bright.

'Miss,' added the other, suitably reprimanded, schoolboy.

This finally brought a reluctant smile from Esther, but she accompanied it with a shake of the head to indicate her unwillingness to relinquish disapproval quite yet.

Kit returned his attention to the two boards. 'Damned if I do, damned if I don't all right. I'll pass on the opportunity to take his pawn now.'

'Good man,' encouraged Bright, 'He who runs away etcetera. Delay the inevitable, that's the ticket.' This caused more mirth for the two men and another reprimand from Esther.

'These are worrying signs of regression, children,' observed Esther sternly, 'I've marked your card as a bad influence, Kit.'

'You could be expelled,' warned Bright, desperately trying to avoid smiling.

Miller reappeared once more wheeling a trolley with tea and pastries. This brought an end to the ribbing. As he served the tea, Kit asked him to deliver the latest move to the telegram office. Miller looked at the board and then at the message.

'He has him on the run Harry,' said Bright, smiling.

'I'll dig out the bunting, sir,' replied Miller.

Miller went to grab his coat and went out to the corridor. As he opened the front door, he found a man standing there about to knock. The man took off his hat. His hair was dark, flecked with grey. He was slightly taller than Harry, but it was his eyes that drew his attention. They were a piercing blue. Deep frown lines rose vertically between his eyes. The deadly serious face spoke of a troubled life.

'Is Lord Christopher Aston in?' asked the man in heavily accented English.

'Yes sir, who shall I say is calling?'

'Alexander Kerensky.'

Miller gave a start. He knew all about Kit's connection to this man which explained his solemn appearance. It was the first time Miller had met a Prime Minister before, albeit a former one. As he returned to the group inside, he, once again, reflected on how much his life had changed since the day he crawled out into No Man's Land and rescued Kit.

Kit and his friends looked up in surprise as Miller reappeared followed by Kerensky.

'Alexander Kerensky, sir,' announced Miller.

Kit rose from the seat and went over to Kerensky, arm outstretched.

'Alexander, what a wonderful surprise. Can I introduce you to my good friends, Esther Cavendish and Doctor Richard Bright?'

Kerensky went over to Esther and gallantly kissed her hand before shaking hands warmly with Bright.

'Thank you, Prime Minister,' said Esther looking up into the eyes of the exiled Russian. They were hypnotic both for their colour but also because of the sense of deep sadness that lay behind them. This was a man who had led the Russian nation following its near collapse, due to the incompetence of the Tsar. He'd tried to keep Russia in the War. Eventually the people turned on him also.

Following the Revolution, he had been unable to resurrect support against Lenin. As the Bolsheviks imposed a ruthless grip throughout the country, violently eradicating any opposition, he had to flee the country.

Kit invited Kerensky to sit down and served him some tea.

'How did you and Kit meet Mr Kerensky?' asked Bright.

Kerensky glanced at Kit who merely laughed in response and shrugged his shoulders. This made Kerensky smile also and return his gaze to Bright and his beautiful fiancée.

'I shall take that as a yes.'

135

Part 2: Middle Game

18

Petrograd, Russia: 25th October 1917 (November 7th, 1917) -Early morning

Kit burst into the room without knocking. Two men looked up at him in surprise. This was partly due to his unusually dishevelled state but also because of the look of alarm on his face. The room was sparsely furnished. A table and five chairs and a bottle of vodka with some empty glasses. It felt like there had been no heating in the room for months. Outside sounds of men shouting filled the cold night air.

'It's over. Two of the bridges have gone. The other two,' Kit stopped and shook his head in incredulity.

'What of the other two?' asked Roger Ratcliff, confused.

'Troitsky Bridge and the Palace Bridge are being held; are you ready for this? They're being held by the Women's Death Battalion and some cadets.'

'Good lord,' exclaimed Colin Cornell, 'What's Kerensky thinking?'

'Not sure he has many options left, Colin. The Cossacks have abandoned him. What's left of the army is at the Winter Palace. Some of them have erected barricades, the rest are waiting for their moment to desert. It's hopeless. More than that, it's finished.'

'We need to make sure Kerensky gets away,' said Ratcliff.

'Yes, that's why I rushed back,' replied Kit. He looked around the room. 'Where's Olly?'

Ratcliff looked at Cornell then back to Kit, 'He went out to look for Kristina, would you believe? The revolution starts, and our lover boy abandons ship. Young fool. Can't say I blame him though.'

Turning to Cornell, Ratcliff asked, 'Can you and Kit go to the Palace. See if you can get Kerensky to see sense? He has to escape.'

Cornell nodded but Kit looked sceptical.

'What's wrong Kit?' asked Cornell.

Kit sat down at the table before saying, 'They'll be looking for him. Checkpoints are already being set up around the city. We need cover.'

'What do you suggest?' asked Ratcliff.

'The American Embassy. If I can get a car from them, we can use that to get Kerensky away. Even the mobs will think twice about stopping a diplomatic car.'

Ratcliff looked at Cornell, 'What do you think?'

Cornell replied, 'Worth a try, I'm out of ideas. So, I'll go to Kerensky and meet you in the west side of the courtyard. I know Lieutenant Vinner well. He'll make Kerensky see sense.'

'I'll come with you, Kit,' said Ratcliff. I can use my influence with Secretary Whitehorse. He'll help, I'm sure. We don't have time to use official channels; Ambassador Francis would never allow it.'

*

Two cars cut their way through the commotion and the chaos. Each vehicle proudly flew small Stars and Stripe flags on the bonnet. The red seas parted for them as they motored through the palace gates into the courtyard of the Winter Palace.

The first thing Kit sensed as he drove through the gates was not so much the confusion as the calm. Instead of seeing mobs attacking the buildings, or soldiers defending the Palace, there was an eerie tranquillity. There seemed to be no sense of what was happening outside the gates. The absence of violence was a relief, but it also suggested something more worrying. The Provisional Government had not just fallen, it was gone for good. Russia was now in the hands of the mob.

Ratcliff followed Kit towards the rendezvous point. Ahead he could see Cornell talking calmly with two sailors. He recognized them as Alexander Kerensky and Lieutenant Vinner. Clearly, they were in disguise. Ratcliff was unsure how successful this would be, but alternative options were non-existent at this moment. There was a third man with them, but Ratcliff could not identify him.

Kerensky and Vinner climbed into Kit's car. Cornell went to Ratcliff, accompanied by the other man.

'Kit,' said Kerensky as he entered the car. 'Thank you for this. You know Vinner?'

Kit nodded to the lieutenant and replied in Russian, 'Yes, we've met, before, Prime Minister.' They sped off immediately followed by Ratcliff.

'We need to find our troops and rally them.'

'Prime Minister, with respect, the Bolsheviks have taken the bridges, the railway stations, the state bank and the telephone exchange. We need to escape from the city. Rallying troops will need to wait until you're safe. You'll have to assemble anti-Bolshevik forces outside Petrograd before the Bolsheviks gain control elsewhere.

Quietly, almost to himself Kerensky said, 'How is this possible? How can a rag tag bunch of hoodlums just take over the country?'

Kit answered, 'You don't need to be large numbers, sir. You can paralyse a city just by occupying key points like a telephone exchange, a railway, bridges then you're in charge.'

Once outside the Palace gates, Kit pressed hard on the Renault's accelerator. All around the street groups of people were wandering, many of them disconsolate soldiers unsure whether to fight, flee or fasten onto the revolutionaries. Ratcliff and Cornell followed close behind.

'You know we hail from the same town,' said Kerensky quietly.

Eyes on the road, Kit asked, 'Who Prime Minister?'

'Lenin. We're both from Simbirsk. My father taught him would you believe,' responded Kerensky, unable to hide the bitterness in his voice. 'My father taught him.' His voice trailed away.

Kit turned to Kerensky and then returned his gaze to the road. No more was said as the two cars hurtled away from the Winter Palace.

141

19

Birmingham, England: 6th January 1920

In a Birmingham hotel, it would be fair to say that Kopel and Fechin were sharing a less tender moment. Both Fechin and Daniels trembled in the presence of Kopel's anger. This was the worst they'd seen him, and they had seen some monumental rages in the past half year. Most of the time he combined a powerful sense of leadership with charm. However, occasionally the storm would break. It was well and truly raging now. He was brandishing the Daily Herald. Fechin looked at the front page of the Daily Herald, with the headline about Irish involvement with the Yapp murder and quivered.

'Look boss, I agree in hindsight that it wasn't the smartest thing to have done.'

This masterpiece of understatement stopped Kopel dead in his tracks. He glared at Fechin in astonishment.

'Not the smartest thing?' he whispered. 'Vassily, it was unquestionably the dumbest thing you've ever done in your pathetic life. And now you say you've sent the second letter off without my seeing it?'

Fechin couldn't speak, he nodded like a scolded child about to be punished severely.

'What did you write Vassily?' It was a whisper.

Fechin's heart sank even further. He hated it when Kopel whispered. He hated it when he called him by his first name or glared at him with those blue eyes. If Kopel was displeased with his initial efforts at misdirecting the police towards Ireland, the new letter would cause a volcanic reaction.

Reluctantly, fearfully Fechin spoke.

'I wrote, 'The revolution continues. Sir Montagu Forbes-Trefusis was an oppressor of the working man. He was executed last night. Our day will come. Then I used," The Sword of Light" signature.'

This seemed to cause an abatement of the storm. The content of the note could easily be interpreted as a part of the class struggle. A third note, following the next execution could clarify things, maybe redirect attention back to Russia, which was Kopel's ultimate objective.

'That's exactly what you wrote, Vassily. Nothing else? Remember, the newspaper will publish it exactly as written.' The eyes did not stare at Fechin so much as rip open his defences and reveal the contents of his soul.

And that was the problem. Fechin had written exactly this, except for one crucial difference. A difference so critical, it would likely cause the next explosion. He felt himself, physically shrinking as he said, 'Not quite, boss.'

'Not quite?' said Kopel. The voice was quiet again.

This did not augur well. Fechin's innards quaked at what would follow.

'The part where I said, "Our day will come",'

'Yes, Vassily?'

Fechin paused as he saw Daniels lean forward.

'I wrote that as, "Tiocfaigh ar la", it means...'

'I know what it bloody means,' roared Kopel, 'I'm still trying to understand why you wrote it in Irish you cretin. Do you know Vassily, before I met you, I actually believed there was a cause to fight for. Now I'm not so sure. I mean what's the point of class struggle? Tell me Vassily, and I ask you this in all seriousness: are the rest of the workers as stupid as you?'

Kopel was pointing to the hotel bedroom wall. It said something of Fechin's complete discomposure that he looked at the wall, which, for the purposes of Kopel's rant, represented all downtrodden humanity. Kopel ignored the surreal sight of Fechin looking at where he was pointing and continued his dismantling of Fechin's self-esteem.

'Because here's my problem. If class struggle really is the right thing to do then we have one enormous, insurmountable challenge. We'll never triumph if the foot soldiers carrying out the plans are a bunch of blockheads like you.'

Fechin visibly flinched in the face of the vicious onslaught from Kopel. He risked a glance towards Daniels, sitting to his right. Contempt was etched all over the face of the big Russian. He wished him somewhere else, somewhere he could not witness, and no doubt remind him in the future, of this humiliation. But it wasn't over yet.

'First you kill your fellow anarchists in Moscow. Oh yes, Vassily, don't think I didn't know about that. Then you blow up those poor tramps. Think of it, all those lives laid waste because of your incompetence. All the very people we should be supporting, killed by a five-foot imbecile. Tell me Vassily, do you know why I let you write the notes?' This question was asked quietly, his face was inches away from Fechin's.

Daniels leaned forward; he didn't know either. Fechin shook his head.

144

'It sure as hell wasn't so that you could use your bloody initiative!' roared Kopel.

This was going from bad to worse for Fechin, although Daniels was enjoying the show immensely. He was almost feeling sorry for his colleague. Taking the rest of his remaining dignity in his hands Fechin decided to offer some form of mea culpa with a hint of grievance.

'Perhaps boss,' whimpered Fechin, 'if you'd let us in on your plans, this sort of thing might not happen, I wouldn't have done something so stupid.'

'Yes, you would have, Vassily, because you're a moron. Just as it's the nature of a scorpion to sting, it's your nature to be stupid. And no Vassily, I will not let you in on my plans, not now, not ever. You will not improvise on them. You will do as I say. That applies to both of you.' With that said, Kopel stormed out of the room in search of Serov.

'Oh, that's great you idiot,' said Daniels irritably, 'now he's mad at me.'

'To hell with you,' said a thoroughly miserable Vassily Fechin.

*

Chief Inspector Jellicoe could smell the fish market before he saw it. It was early morning, the sun wasn't shining, the atmosphere felt damp on his skin. Billingsgate Fish Market should have been a confusion of activity, buyers and sellers engaged in the strange dance of negotiating, bargaining, buying, and selling. Instead, it was a different kind of chaos as angry traders demanded to be let into the market to set up their stalls and make their living.

Eyes straight ahead, Jellicoe ignored their protests. He ordered the constables to maintain control of the crowd and marched ahead towards the Italian-style arcade facing the Thames. The constables improvised on this order with something approaching relish as they took out their truncheons. Jellicoe could hear the boos and whistles as the stall holders reacted to the police. He shook his head and walked directly towards the one police officer he recognised.

Inspector Philip Treacy greeted Jellicoe at the door of the arcade. One look at Treacy's face told him a particularly grim scene awaited him. His intuition was to prove more accurate than he could ever have imagined. He asked his colleague anyway.

'Well, Treacy, what do we have?'

The serious expression on Treacy's face turned to one of surprise.

'Has no one told you?'

'Wouldn't be asking if they had. I was only informed of the dead body,' responded Jellicoe, not without some irritation. It was very early for him.

If Treacy picked up on this, he didn't respond. Instead, he replied sombrely, 'Perhaps you should look yourself, sir. This way.' He nodded towards the entrance.

The two men walked through the arched doorway into the large open space lit by a roof of louvered glass. Despite the superb ventilation, the place reeked of the sour smell of salt and rotting flesh. For once it wasn't the dead body causing the problem. Jellicoe wondered idly how anyone could spend minutes in such an atmosphere never mind work there day in day out.

The space was enormous and empty save for unopened stalls around the sides. But only one thing was attracting

Jellicoe's attention. It was a sight Jellicoe that, in over twenty years of police work, had never encountered before.

'Oh' said Jellicoe.

'Oh, indeed sir,' replied Treacy, not without a hint of smugness. How would anyone describe this sight to the Chief Inspector without being made to feel an idiot?

Jellicoe walked over to the dead body. After a moment or two he moved slowly around it. It didn't matter from what angle he looked; the sight was no less astonishing. Finally, realizing he needed to say something, if only to maintain a veneer of professionalism, control even, he asked, 'Any identification of the man yet?'

'Yes sir, one of my men is of the belief that it's Sir Montagu Forbes-Trefusis.'

Jellicoe was none the wiser.

'Who is he?'

'A civil servant, sir. Works in the Foreign Office, I understand,' replied Treacy.

'I see,' said Jellicoe, who plainly didn't see. It was difficult to relate what was before him to anything other than the wildest imagining of a writer of a penny blood.

Another, older, man came over to join them. Treacy took one look at the man's whiskers and made him to be a doctor. For reasons he could not explain, Jellicoe always associated the possession of whiskers with the medical profession.

'This is Dr French,' explained Jellicoe. The two men shook hands briefly. Both men turned to look down at the former civil servant. Out of the corner of his eye, Jellicoe could see French shaking his head. This was probably the first time he'd seen such a murder before also.

147

'I daresay the cause of death is the stomach wound,' said Jellicoe to the doctor. The doctor noted the sardonic tone. A half-smile creased his lips.

'Yes, there's quite a lot of blood, so the poor devil probably died immediately as result of the...' French left the sentence unfinished and looked at Jellicoe expectantly.

'Medieval jousting lance?' offered Jellicoe.

'Quite.' nodded French. 'The lance.'

20

Mid-morning at the offices of the Daily Herald, invariably saw a calm, business-like atmosphere unless new news was breaking which required further editions of the morning paper. The journalists who remained saw Lansbury and Peel locked away in the editor's office. Curiosity was mounting on what was being discussed. The working assumption was another communication from the Irish republican group in contact with Peel. They were accurate in at least one respect.

Lansbury and Peel looked at the latest handwritten letter from "The Sword of Light". It was too late for the morning edition. The discussion centred, not if it was genuine, but whether to run a special afternoon edition of the paper.

'You were right about the Irish angle, Billy.'

Peel wasn't so sure. He looked again at the note. As a protestant, he had little knowledge of the Irish language beyond recognizing it when he heard it spoken or saw it written. Lansbury could see scepticism on his face.

'It must be Irish republican in origin, right?' asked Lansbury. Even he was familiar with how Gaelic looked, and the phrase was familiar to him.

'Yes, it would seem so. Still, I'd like to check this with a Gaelic speaker, all the same,' replied Peel, eyes on the letter.

'What makes you doubt it? Inquired Lansbury.

'Just to be certain on the spelling and use of the fada.'

'Fada?' asked Lansbury.

Peel pointed to the accent over the letter "a". Lansbury nodded but was still determined to press ahead with a single sheet afternoon edition of the Herald.

'By the time we get this out, the murder will have been announced anyway. If not, I'll contact Scotland Yard. In the meantime, write up the story and only then, check this...'

'Fada,' added Peel.

'Fada,' repeated Lansbury.

*

Later that evening, Roger Ratcliff looked at the Daily Herald story on the murder of Forbes-Trefusis. After finishing the story, he held the paper up for Colin Cornell, who was over by the window as usual. Cornell looked at the headline but only gave the story a cursory glance. He seemed more interested in Ratcliff's reaction. Ratcliff looked like thunder.

'You knew him?' asked Cornell.

'Of him,' replied Ratcliff grimly. 'Strange cove. Once upon a time he was a big supporter of a more assertive British approach to international diplomacy. Lost his bottle somewhat during the War.'

'How do you mean?' asked Cornell.

'On our side, for example, he backed the creation of the Special Intelligence Service for a start. He was aware of the deep cover work we did in Russia to prop things up a bit. But after the Bolsheviks came to power, he changed. He lost his son in France. From then on, he argued against military engagement in Russia. Before he'd have backed Winston to the hilt.'

Ratcliff looked at Cornell. He was worried about him. His normal pallor seemed even worse. His hand rubbed the back of his head, like he was experiencing a monumental hangover or perhaps it was a migraine. He seemed to be suffering frequent headaches.

'Been out on the sauce, old chap?' smiled Ratcliff, trying to lift the mood, his own principally.

'Chance would be a fine thing,' replied Cornell, walking over to get a better view of the newspaper.

'Have you been to see the doctor, like I told you? You look ghastly. You seem to have lots of headaches these days,' continued Ratcliff with obvious concern for his old friend.

Cornell glanced down at Ratcliff but said nothing in response. He doesn't look well, thought Ratcliff.

*

Miller brought up the afternoon edition of the Daily Herald to Kit, Esther and Bright. All were sitting in Kit's living room looking at the two chess boards and chatting. The face-to-face match with Serov was five days away and all the newspapers were featuring the latest moves from the game.

Kit turned around to Miller as he entered the room. He noticed Miller was carrying an afternoon newspaper, which Kit normally didn't read. Returning his gaze to his two friends, he continued an explanation started before Miller's return.

'So, Serov will find out I've taken his Bishop. His Queen will no doubt exact suitable revenge,' said Kit, indicating the move on the second chess board.

Miller waited until Kit had finished before handing him the newspaper, 'You should see the latest news sir.'

Kit glanced down at the headline, 'Good lord,' said Kit spinning the newspaper around so that Esther and Bright could read also. It read: Another Murder by Irish Republicans.

151

'Who on earth are this group anyway, Kit?' asked Bright.

'Honestly, I have no idea,' admitted Kit, equally mystified. 'I've not had much to do with Ireland over the years.'

'Did you know this chap Forbes-Trefusis? Cracking name by the way, Sir Montagu Forbes-Trefusis,' read out Bright, 'Never any chance he was going to be a dockworker.'

Kit ignored the gallows humour and said, 'I've met him, but didn't really know him very well. I heard he was a bit of a fanatic at the start of the War. If I remember correctly, he lost a boy in France, poor chap. Not been the same since. None of us are, I suppose,' added Kit absently.

Bright studied Kit but didn't ask what he meant. He didn't need to. As a doctor during the War, he'd seen too much of the damage wrought on bodies and minds exposed to the conflict. Nobody who had been in France, and lucky enough to return, came back the same person. There had been moments when he thought he'd lose his mind also such was the stress of trying to repair the awful injuries. Esther rested her chin on Bright's shoulder and read the story.

'There seems be nothing but bad news in the papers these days. Always some murder or another. I would've thought people had had their fill of it.'

Kit directed his attention away from the chess board for a moment and gazed at Esther. Her comments had been general, but it made him recall the recent murder of the Trade Union official and his conversation with Spunky. The fact that Peel was reporting on both the chess match and the murders was a connection that had put Kit's senses on alert.

He couldn't explain why this should be so, but he knew something felt peculiar. The Irish republican involvement might be something Spunky could shed light on. Impatient, as ever, to know, he rose from his seat to go to the phone. He dialled a number. A minute later he was through.

'Hello, yes, this is Lord Kit Aston. Can you get me Spunky please?'

In the background he heard Bright snort. He sneaked a quick glance and saw Esther looking at him askance. As he was holding on with no one else on the line, he pretended to talk with someone.

'What do you mean he can't come now?'

In the background Bright was now coughing with laughter. Esther seemed very concerned. She leaned over to Bright, 'Let me get you a drink darling, are you alright?'

'Fine, really,' said Bright frowning at Kit whose smile was beaming.

Spunky finally took the call.

'Hello Spunky, it's Kit. I was calling to find out more about these murders by Irish republicans. What's going on? There hasn't been much about the murders themselves in the papers and even less about why they think there's an Irish connection.'

After a few moments when Spunky was speaking, Kit added, 'I see, yes, I'd love to know more. Thanks, Spunky and apologies for interrupting your evening. Is she anyone I know, by the way?'

As he said this he glanced at his friends and winked. This caused Esther and Bright to laugh. Both could hear a voice reply but the sound was indistinct. It was enough to make Kit laugh.

Finally, Kit said, 'Oh, I see, it's your book club, is it? What are you reading? Fanny Hill?'

*

153

'I haven't a clue why these letters are being sent to me, Chief Inspector,' said Peel, once again in Chief Inspector Jellicoe's office.

Jellicoe didn't immediately respond to Peel. Instead, he studied him closely. Silence was an interrogation tool he often used as it usually opened up a suspect more effectively than direct questioning. Unfortunately for Jellicoe, Peel either knew what he was doing or employed similar techniques himself. Silence hung in the air like cigarette smoke, a lingering, unwelcome presence. Jellicoe suspected Peel's protestations of innocence were true, and yet he knew there had to be a reason why "The Sword of Light" was using Peel as their contact. It was clear Peel did not know why, but there would come a time when he would.

The question remained who or what was "The Sword of Light"? A deranged individual, an Irish republican group operating in Britain, or something else? Aside from the letter there were no leads save for the odd choice of murder method.

Peel understood Jellicoe's dilemma. The Chief Inspector's suspicion arose as much from his lack of leads as anything untoward he may have done. He felt a degree of sympathy for Jellicoe. There was probably a lot of pressure on him now to make progress in the case and it wasn't being helped by the publicity he had created. It said something for Jellicoe that he had not reproached him for gaining such a scoop.

After a long silence, Peel said, 'I won't publish this, but so as I'm clear, you're saying you have no other leads aside from the letters and the murder weapon. Correct?'

'Correct,' acknowledged Jellicoe.

'I've spoken with a lot of people who are on the fringes of Irish nationalism. No one's heard of this group. Worse, they've no idea who might have created it.'

Jellicoe looked at the Ulsterman and thought for a moment.

'This is not for publication. We've been pushing hard on informants in the Irish community, here and Dublin. It's the same response: this group is new. No one knows who's involved. They seem to have appeared magically out of thin air. Either that or people are afraid to speak.'

'And there's no link between Yapp and Forbes-Trefusis?' asked Peel

'No link that we can find.'

'I can't publish the medieval lance?'

'No.'

Peel smiled and began to rise. 'Sorry. One more thing. Presumably, the crosier was stolen. Did it come from a Roman Catholic church?'

Jellicoe looked surprised by the question and then laughed, 'I don't think my answer will shed much light on that. It was stolen from a Russian Orthodox church, would you believe? A Russian flag was tied around it. I suppose that's why we're a bit confused.'

Peel still didn't believe in coincidences.

21

Cheltenham: 7th January 1920

Cheltenham was a pleasant change from Birmingham. In fact, reflected Serov, just about anywhere would've made a pleasant change. It had been an agreeable drive down with Kopel. They had passed through some beautiful green countryside which Kopel had called the Cotswolds. If Serov didn't know better, he would have sworn that Kopel was an anglophile such was his knowledge of the history and culture of the land on which he was spying.

Although he would never have admitted this to Kopel, Serov had enjoyed reading the novels of Jane Austen. While he detested the inequality of the world depicted by Austen, he enjoyed them as entertainments. They contributed enormously to his study of the English language. As he walked past the Regency buildings, his memory of the books he devoured growing up came alive. It felt like he was in her world.

The sun was shining now, and the air felt clean as he walked through the historic centre of Cheltenham. Once again, he was struck by the absence of true poverty and depravation he was used to back home. Perhaps he could speak to Kopel of this. The Latvian Russian had been stationed in England for a few years now. He seemed able to reconcile an interest in the country with a desire to see it move along the lines prescribed by Marx. There was bound to be an alternative narrative for a country which, ostensibly, had no great need to change.

He passed a newspaper seller. Beside him, on a billboard was a big headline: Another Murder. In this regard, Serov noted, England was no safer than Russia. He continued his stroll back to the hotel thankful to have an afternoon off from visiting Trade Union officials and party members. This was another topic to broach with Kopel. He was tiring of the treadmill of matches in the morning followed by factory visits followed by meetings. Daniels and Fechin seemed to have more free time than him.

Although he felt completely confident in his ability to beat Aston, it wasn't something to leave to chance. Preparation time would be welcome. As he thought about this he paused and looked around him. The street was noisier than the big cities in Russia. There were more cars on the roads and more people in the streets. It was warmer, obviously that helped. But the people also seemed more alive. All around there were street sellers and buskers making music.

They had an energy he did not recognise in his home country. As much as he would love to have put this down to the quiet desperation of the proletariat trying to survive, the evidence was of something else, and it bore little relation to what he was hearing at the meetings. In fact, no relation at all.

Kopel, Daniels and Fechin sat together in Pittville Park in the heart of Cheltenham. Facing them was the Pittville Pump Room with its colonnade of Ionic columns. On the lawn facing the pump room were families enjoying an unusually sunny January, late in the afternoon.

'It's a beautiful building, isn't it?' remarked Kopel.

Daniels and Fechin each had no opinion on the subject. Rather than risk silence, Daniels offered a truthful if not effusive response, 'Yes'.

Kopel glanced at Daniels and smiled. Daniels shrugged. Kopel decided against further small talk and returned to business. The walk in the park had been a last-minute idea to bring the team together again. The dressing down he'd given to Fechin was still festering. Kopel realised the need to build bridges again. As useless as he was, Fechin still had an important role to play.

'I'll join you tonight,' said Kopel, 'I want to make sure everything goes to plan.' Daniels noted how Kopel looked at Fechin as he said this. The unfortunate Fechin had spent most of the day sulking following the rather public demolition at the hands of Kopel. To help rebuild the small Muscovite's dented confidence, Kopel entrusted him with a small task.

'Off you go Vassily, we'll see you back at the hotel,' added Kopel with a smile and a good humour he certainly wasn't feeling toward Fechin. He would have a word with Bergmann about his choice of personnel when the opportunity arose. The thought of Bergmann stopped him for a moment. He wondered if he'd ever have that conversation. If things went as he planned...

Fechin welcomed the chance to be away from the others. The reaction of Kopel to his error over the letter struck him as disproportionate. The mistake clearly lay with Kopel for not being more open about his plans. The anger and humiliation he'd felt earlier was, however, slowly dissipating. What remained was an open wound. It was always him. The hangover of humiliation has a physical dimension. Fatigue seeped into his bones like water in a cloth. A part of him wanted to get back to the hotel and shut himself away in a room. Instead, he had more work to do tonight. The thought of what lay ahead perked him up.

Another source of energy was his hatred of Daniels. It had grown in direct relation to the level of degradation he had undergone. If there was a way he could get even with the big thug, he would. As he drove through the early evening traffic, he considered all his options. There weren't many, he realised.

Arriving at his destination he stepped out of the car at Shipley's Garage. Greeting him was the eponymous garage owner, Ernest Shipley. Like Fechin, Mr Shipley was made to smaller dimensions which were in inverse proportion to the extent of his meanness. A good day for him was one in which he could put one over on an unsuspecting member of the public. Visitors to Cheltenham were always entertaining targets. Occasionally, heaven provided rich bounty in the form of a foreign visitor. Today it seemed as if the creator was smiling on him. One look at Fechin suggested someone from outside Britain. He guessed Slavic.

Unfortunately for Shipley, his essentially ill-natured personality was all too visible to anyone that met him. For this reason, Shipley's business was not in robust health. However, for an owner with no dependents, nor likely to breed any, it was enough.

'Good evening,' said Shipley with a smile that revealed a set of teeth which were, if anything, in worse condition than their owner. Even Fechin found himself recoiling.

159

'Good evening,' replied Fechin not bothering to smile. There was no reason to. He and the man before him were hardly likely to be exchanging Christmas cards this year.

Shipley's smile became even wider when he heard the accent. He had guessed correctly. It took a considerable effort to stop himself rubbing his hands together. With something approaching glee he asked, 'How can I help you sir?'

Fechin pointed to the car, 'I need to fill up my petrol can. I also need a second petrol can. Have you one I could buy?'

'So, my friend, you have one in the car to fill and one you want to buy, is that correct?'

Shipley's appeal to friendship was always likely to fall on deaf ears with the disgruntled Fechin who merely contented himself with a nod of the head. For the next few minutes Shipley made himself busy filling the empty can for Fechin. Then he brought out another metal can.

Fechin took one look at the can in Shipley's hand. It had seen better days. Thirty years ago, it would have seemed an old can. A recent attempt at painting it could not hide the patches of rust. Shipley opened it so that Fechin could see and, more importantly, smell the contents. Although the cost seemed higher than other places he had visited, Fechin did not care as it was Kopel's money. He made sure to get a receipt, however, just in case Kopel demanded proof of how the money had been spent.

Shipley waved goodbye to Fechin, grinning widely. The little Russian ignored him, happy to be away from the garage owner. The drive back to the park was mercifully quick as the smell of the gasoline began to permeate the inside of the vehicle. Catching sight of his companions standing outside the

160

park, Fechin pulled over to let them in. Both Kopel and Daniels recoiled as they climbed into the car.

'What on earth is that smell?' demanded Kopel.

'The owner spilled some of the petrol,' said Fechin uncertain if this was true or not. However, it seemed plausible, and this was enough. With everyone aboard, the three men set off towards Gloucester.

*

Gloucester Cathedral was originally founded as an abbey by the Normans. Following the dissolution of the monasteries, Henry VIII re-founded the abbey as a cathedral. The dissolution had proved a boon to the royal coffers. To ensure the loyalty of major aristocratic families, Henry VIII created numerous offices for Bishops, in the aftermath of his break with Rome, using money appropriated from the Catholic Church to provide pastoral direction for his flock. The beneficiaries of these rewards tended to be royal bureaucrats rather than men with genuine vocations. One such office was the Bishop of Gloucester.

The current incumbent was John Gordon. This was a man, much like his predecessors, whose calling lay in understanding political and administrative exigencies rather than any great interest in the spiritual well-being of the diocese. Gordon was not altogether apathetic towards his episcopal responsibilities. It was a job, albeit a job which gave him a very high quality of life without requiring much by way of exertion in return.

Gordon liked to visit the cathedral, on his own, from time to time. He would sit in the nave at the same pew near the back. He used this time, not to pray, but to meditate. Over recent years he had become very interested in Buddhism. This epiphany had occurred after reading Sir Edwin Arnold's

161

poem on the life of Buddha, The Light of Asia. A private amusement for him was to quote from this poem in sermons to his Christian flock.

The cathedral was dark save for the glow of candles. The only sounds were echoing footsteps of the remaining visitors shuffling along the aisles drinking in their surrounds and the peace and presence of the divine. Gordon didn't need to close his eyes. What remained of the light and the muffled sounds resonating around him wove a hypnotic spell. Sometimes he would fall asleep for several minutes such was his immersion in the moment. On this occasion, his nap was more a consequence of the chloroform rag held to his mouth than psychophysical relaxation of his senses. It was sleep from which he would never awake.

Acting as lookout, Kopel motioned to Daniels and Fechin to pick up the limp body of the cleric. They followed Kopel through a side entrance to the cathedral, where the car was parked. Less than a minute later they were driving off at great speed.

'He looks dead,' said Fechin looking down at the unconscious Gordon, beside him in the back of the car, 'How much did you give him?'.

'Enough to knock out a male rhino,' responded Daniels who was driving.

'The smell in this car would've knocked him out,' noted Kopel sourly, glancing at Fechin. In truth it was overpowering. Even with all the windows open, little could counteract the soporific effect of the fumes.

They made a short drive to a farm near Cheltenham racecourse. Previous scouting by Daniels had established the presence of some outbuildings which lay empty and unused.

Daniels drove straight into one such building. Fechin leapt out of the car, propelled by a need for fresh air, and shut the large gates of the barn. Returning to the car he helped Daniels drag the prone prelate into the middle where there was a supporting pillar. Gordon was tied to this as if he were at a stake.

Fechin gazed down at the comatose cleric.

'Shall we try to wake him?'

'Good luck,' replied Daniels, not bothering to look at Fechin.

'No leave him,' said Kopel with finality. 'Vassily, bring the petrol.'

Fechin walked over to the car and opened the back. He took out the rusty can and carried it over to the stake.

Kopel nodded at Fechin, who proceeded to empty the contents of the rusty can liberally over the soon-to-be-former Bishop. The men stepped back from the stake. Intent on showing his trust in Fechin, Kopel handed him a box of matches. He nodded over to Bishop John Gordon. Fechin lit a match and threw it towards the body.

All at once the Bishop burst into flames. Kopel, Daniels and Fechin stood still, staring at the flames, the crackling sounds, and spirals of smoke.

Then, they looked on rapt, as the fire began to spread. Slowly, it moved away from Gordon, advancing inexorably along a thin trail of gasoline towards the car. Stunned, afraid and unable to obey the instincts of their mind, they watched the flame reach the car. The only noise was the sizzling celebrant until the car popped into flames. A small explosion followed.

Both Kopel and Daniels turned simultaneously to their diminutive companion. Fechin glanced up at both men. He couldn't tear his eyes away from the hatred and anger in Kopel.

The voice of Kopel was deadly quiet, 'Vassily, what the hell have you done?'

*

Serov rose early next morning for one final walk around the centre before his party returned to London. He had enjoyed the evening to himself but, he admitted, it would be good to have company again. He didn't see the other three men at breakfast. However, when he returned from his stroll, he spied Kopel and Daniels in the dining room of the hotel.

He walked over to them and greeted all with a smile. His early morning stroll had put him in fine fettle, even for Fechin. It had been a habit of his, even in the deepest of Russian winters, to take a morning walk. Invariably problems melted away, ideas presented themselves and solutions to chess problem were resolved when he did so.

'A beautiful morning outside, the weather in this country is really quite wonderful.'

Both men looked glum but Kopel, at least, made some effort to respond warmly. But there was no mistaking the shadow behind his blue eyes.

'Yes, it looks fine outside. You've been for your usual walk, Filip?' asked Kopel.

'Indeed, up to the park and then back. Very pleasant. Where is our friend Fechin?'

Kopel glanced at Daniels and replied, 'Vassily will not be with us for the rest of the trip. He's been asked to undertake

164

another mission. I'm not at liberty, of course, to explain more.'

'I understand. So, we are just we three then?'

'Correct Filip,' answered Kopel. 'We shall take the train down to London presently.'

This puzzled Serov for a moment, and then he realized Fechin must have taken the car. He nodded and left the two men to return to his room and pack his bags for departure. After he had left, Kopel looked at Daniels.

'It was for the best,' shrugged Kopel.

'I'm surprised you waited so long.'

*

Margaret Hill was also reflecting on what a nice day it was as she strolled through the farm. Three children and two husbands had done nothing to dampen her energy or her love for the farm she had been brought up on. It was hers now and always would be. Every day she would make a tour of the farm, the fields, the horses, the people. All would receive a cheery hello, a friendly chat, and a laugh. This January morning was no different; except in one regard.

She was surprised to see the gate opened in the larger of the two buildings. Breaking into a trot, she became aware of the smell as she neared the entrance. It smelled like there had been a fire. It was mixed with another smell that she could not quite identify.

The scene greeting her was one she would never forget. Not a squeamish lady by nature, she found the sight of a charred body tied to the stake as shocking as anything she had seen during her stint as a nurse during the War. It was partially obscured by the burnt-out car. With more courage than she would have believed of herself she stepped forward towards the car.

It was then she screamed.

Moments later she was running back to the farmhouse.

22

London: 7th January 1920

Lansbury and Peel looked at the latest letter from "The Sword of Light". It had arrived in the early afternoon post. There was now no doubt about the existence of the group or the possibility of a hoax because neither the Daily Herald nor the police had released the name of the group. This one had several differences, which Peel had noted immediately, and Lansbury had also remarked on. It seemed to have more in common with the first note than the second and yet the handwriting had changed.

Welcome to the Revolution! Bishop John Gordon of Gloucester was executed this evening. Religion is the opium of the masses. Sometimes history needs a push.

The Sword of Light

Lansbury eyes peel closely, 'You first. Why is this different?'

Peel's answer was clear and clearly chimed with Lansbury.

'Ignoring the handwriting for a moment, the first and third letters are Marxist in tone. The problem I had with pointing to an anarchist group was the name. It had to be an Irish republican reference even if the tone suggested Marxist.'

'And now?'

'I don't know,' replied Peel. He looked genuinely puzzled. 'Quoting Marx and Lenin in the same letter is either an attempt to misdirect us deliberately or they want us to make a connection to Russia.'

In fact, Peel was not just puzzled, he was genuinely disturbed. The connection with the visit of Serov was still fresh in his mind. He had no doubt that both Daniels and Fechin would be more than capable of murder. Bergmann seemed different but clearly it was possible he was a Cheka agent also. In fact, thinking about it, although Bergmann was clearly much older than the other two men, he sensed beneath the jovial nature a reservoir of power which could easily turn dark in a moment. It was premature to link the two stories in the paper, but it was something to delve into further.

'What do you recommend we do then, Billy?' pressed Lansbury.

'We have to go with the Russian angle now,' asserted Peel.

'Why?' Lansbury felt uncomfortable with this. He had long been an advocate of opening a dialogue with the new communist rulers. The prospect that they were implicated in murders in Britain, quite apart from their sickening nature, would make him look foolish, given his highly public sympathies. The Herald had long been critical of Britain acting covertly in the Russian Civil War in support of the Whites. However, this could not justify any criminal acts on British soil, in the eyes of the public. There would be an anti-Russian outcry.

Peel related what he had heard from Jellicoe. Both agreed it was not possible to mention the weapon used to kill Yapp but the link to Russia was now very strong. Like the threat from a republican group, the prospect of Russian involvement in mainland Britain was incendiary. Unlike the Irish story, any proven link between the three murders would be interpreted as a direct attack by a foreign government on this country. This would cause an escalation in tension between the two countries, perhaps worse.

As Peel thought through the ramifications of the story, he was clear on a few things. The Daily Herald had to go to print on the Russian angle. There was no evidence yet to make a connection with the chess match. But Peel felt a tingling sensation which he knew would only get worse unless he arrived at the truth. Thinking again about Fechin and Daniels, he felt certain they were capable of the murders.

There was only one thing he could do, now. Soon after finishing the story for the afternoon edition of the paper, he phoned Jellicoe to inform him of the latest development. The story about the murdered Bishop had only reached him a few hours previously. Unsurprisingly, Jellicoe greeted the update from Peel with dismay. In fact, when he put the phone down after finishing with Peel, he vented prodigiously, about the Irish and the Bolsheviks in turn, causing several nearby policemen to exit the corridor to avoid getting caught in the crossfire.

When Peel finished his call with Jellicoe he sat back in his chair and thought for a few minutes. If you believed in coincidences, then you were either lazy or you shouldn't be a newsman. Peel had learned this from his first mentor in newspapers. It was a mantra for him which had driven his success in journalism. There was always a way to connect events which, at first glance, seemed unrelated. Peel wanted to find the link. He also knew what he needed to do next.

Picking up the phone, he made a second call. When his call was answered, he said, 'It's the Orange Man.'

He immediately hung up. A few minutes later the phone rang. He listened for a minute then wrote something in his notebook. Standing up, he grabbed the coat from the back of his chair, swung it over his back and made his way out of the office. Several colleagues watched him leave; all wondered what was coming next.

*

Cars swayed and swashed along Wilton Terrace in London. The pavement was relatively quiet which suited Roger Ratcliff as he walked towards Belgrave Square. He felt tired and was looking forward to leaving the cold of Britain to travel to the South of France. He was no longer a young man; the time spent in the mud of France and the chill of Russia had taken a toll on his bones, his breathing, and his brio. A good friend, who was also his doctor, had already warned him against spending yet another winter in such a cold climate. This time he was going to take the advice.

Rounding the corner, he arrived in Belgrave Square. He turned to Colin Cornell. Ratcliff would have liked Cornell to join him, not just for the company, but also because he genuinely felt concern for his friend. Cornell was young enough to be his son and, although unspoken, he had come to view him in this way. Once more he caught Cornell rubbing the back of his head. Cornell noticed this and stopped immediately.

'What?' asked Cornell, irritably.

'If you won't listen to me, I won't say anything. There's hardly any point,' responded the older man irritably.

Cornell chose to ignore Ratcliff's meaning and asked instead, 'What will you say to Aston? He's hardly going to like it if you trot off to the Riviera when he's putting his reputation on the line for King and country, especially when you set him up to do it.'

Ratcliff looked at Cornell and shrugged resignedly. It was true, but there was nothing he could do. Kit was an adult; he would deal with what was coming. Yes, it was potentially an awkward conversation. However, he trusted that Kit was too much of a gentleman to make it an issue between them.

Ratcliff began to cross the road when all of a sudden there was a screech, and a car came to a stop. Unhurt but shaken, Ratcliff continued his way across the road briefly holding his hand up in acknowledgement to the driver.

'Idiot,' shouted the driver as he sped off.

Ratcliff turned to Cornell and grinned sheepishly, 'Should've looked where I was going.'

'He nearly accomplished what the Germans and Cheka failed to do you silly old fool,' said Cornell, not unkindly.

A minute later he was outside Kit's apartment building gazing up at the white exterior. Ratcliff shot Cornell a look. He raised his eyes questioningly.

'Are you coming up?' he asked finally.

'No, I'll see you later,' replied Cornell.

Ratcliff looked a little crestfallen. It was always the same. They had all been through so much together yet now the two former colleagues could not speak to one another. It was very sad. Maybe one day things would be different.

*

Jellicoe stood in front of a dozen plain clothes detectives at Scotland Yard. Flanking him were Inspector McEwan from Oldham, Inspector Treacy from London, and Inspector Dalton from Cheltenham. Along the wall were photographs of the murder victims and newspaper articles from the Daily Herald. The mood in the room was grim.

The Chief Inspector spent a few minutes introducing his colleagues from the other forces. Following this, McEwan, Treacy and Dalton all provided a brief synopsis of the investigations to date as well as a pen portrait of the known victims. The fourth victim was unknown but, as Dalton explained, he was suspected of being one of the killers who had either been killed by misadventure or had deliberately committed suicide.

When each of the policemen had completed their section, Jellicoe resumed his place centre stage.

'So, there you have it gentlemen,' he announced. 'Three, possibly four murders. Three victims. All unconnected save for the person responsible for their death and whatever twisted reasoning they had for committing such vile acts. It goes without saying that we must catch this madman or madmen soon. We are facing a grave threat that is possibly foreign in origin. This means we must be careful in how we investigate with foreign nationals living in this country because we do not want to create a climate of fear or, indeed, intolerance. Doing so could cause diplomatic tensions which would make matters worse. It's critical no one let's slip anything to do with this investigation, either to colleagues not involved or to the press. This will be treated with the utmost severity.' Jellicoe paused to let the import of this sink in.

'By the same token, we need to catch these people. You must follow up on every lead, and yes, this will mean speaking to members of the Irish and Russian communities who might include the killers in their midst, albeit unknowingly. We must find the killer. We must do it soon. Thank you, gentlemen.'

The policemen filed out from the conference room leaving the Jellicoe with the three other policemen. No one was prepared to speak. They all looked at Jellicoe expectantly.

'One thing I neglected to mention just now to the wider team, but I shall to you, relates to the national security aspect of these cases. Clearly, we have departments of state who, shall we say, are actively involved in promoting our national interest abroad. I won't dwell on who for obvious reasons. They are, I assure you, taking a close interest in these murders. I understand they're conducting their own investigations in the countries in question. If any information should come to light which can expedite our investigations, and which does not compromise the source of this information, I shall forward to you immediately.'

The three officers looked at Jellicoe. It would be fair to say they were all impressed by what they saw. In Jellicoe, they sensed a man who could head up an investigation as complicated as it was likely to be political. There was no question the level of scrutiny had risen. Each of the inspectors was relieved the chief inspector would be the public face of the investigation. The idea of dealing with the concerns of senior policemen, the press and politicians was anathema to the three men.

Jellicoe finished the impromptu meeting by saying, 'Good governance is critical in this investigation. We need to work with porous walls, share information regularly, maintain

173

frequent contact at all levels. Please, gentlemen, encourage cooperation as much as possible. Without it, we will fail. It's as simple as that. Understood?'

There were murmurs of agreement from each of the men. Wishing each other luck, and meaning it, the meeting finished. Soon Jellicoe was alone in the conference with his thoughts, and they were dark thoughts. The prospect of Russian involvement in these murders had introduced a new level of complexity not to say urgency also. This was the stuff of sleepless nights. The case desperately needed a break, something to give it direction, focus and momentum. His wish was soon to be granted.

*

Harry Miller answered the knock on the door. He opened it to a large man who seemed vaguely familiar. It took a moment for Miller to register who he was. Miller grinned and said, 'Hello sir, please come in.'

'Thank you. Is his lordship in?' asked Ratcliff.

'Yes sir, please come this way.'

Ratcliff had never been inside Kit's London home before. Walking along the corridor, he recognised a few paintings including one that looked suspiciously like a Canaletto. Another world he thought. A moment later, with some dismay, he wondered how much longer this world would last.

Miller opened the door and Ratcliff entered Kit's large living room. Kit was with two other people, a good-looking young man wearing a tweed suit that had seen better days and one of the most beautiful women that Ratcliff had ever seen.

'Major, what a pleasant surprise,' said Kit rising to greet his visitor.

'I'm so sorry Kit if I'd known you had company.'

174

'Nonsense sir. Let me introduce you to my friends. This vision before you is...' he paused for a moment before saying with a grin, 'Dr Richard Bright, and this is his fiancée Esther Cavendish. May I present Major Roger Ratcliff. He was my commanding officer for a period.' Kit did not add anything more and both Esther and Bright knew not to inquire further.

Ratcliff smiled and shook hands with both and smiled, 'As handsome as you are Dr Bright, I shall form my own judgement on who the vision is.'

Bright laughed, 'I shall try not to feel insulted sir.'

'Esther is Mary's sister,' explained Kit.

They all sat down and chatted for a few minutes before Bright and Esther, sensing Ratcliff wished to speak with Kit privately, made their apologies and left the two men alone.

'I'm dreadfully sorry Kit if I've interrupted something,' said Ratcliff dejectedly.

'Really sir, don't worry. But I sense you're not here on a social call.'

Miller brought in some tea and put it down on the table in front of the two men. Ratcliff took a sip before replying to Kit. Rather than answer the question directly, he looked down at the two chessboards sitting side by side.

'How's the game progressing?'

'Well, I'm a pawn to the good. We've both just lost our Bishops. I sent my move earlier today. I'm waiting for a response although my feeling is there won't be one.'

'What makes you say that?' said Ratcliff leaning forward.

'As you surmised when I saw you last week, he'll want a face-to-face meeting to apply the coup de grace. As it stands, I think we've reached an interesting point in the match. There's probably another fifteen or twenty moves to play. This will provide enough theatre for anyone foolish enough to come along and watch.'

'More of a rugger man myself,' laughed Ratcliff.

Kit laughed also before admitting, 'Won't be playing much of that anymore.'

'I know, sorry old man,' smiled Ratcliff ruefully, 'how's the old leg anyway?'

Kit chatted amusingly about his hatred of the prosthetic limb. The conversation turned to the Cavendish family, his two friends, and his hopes for a future with Mary. As he'd suspected, Kit greeted the news about Ratcliff's intention to spend several months in the South of France more as a cause for concern about Ratcliff's health than anything else. He seemed genuinely delighted that Ratcliff was taking the time off. The last few years had been an unending source of stress for the big man, a break was needed.

'I might have to escape London also and join you,' grinned Kit, 'When Serov humiliates me. I won't be able to show my face in good company. Sheldon's will kick me out in a thrice.'

'Oh well, you'll be fine with me in that case in Monte Carlo.'

They parted amicably with Kit leading Ratcliff to the door. After Ratcliff's departure, Kit sat down and looked at the chess board for a few moments. The thought that Serov may not play any additional moves had only occurred to Kit while he was speaking to Ratcliff.

This was often the case. A thought would strike him as he spoke which might not otherwise have occurred to him. It made him reflect for a few moments on the importance of talking to friends about things. This was not usually his way. His preference was to deal with all emotional matters alone; to

176

figure his own way through. He wondered if this was mistaken. Perhaps keeping things inside denied him access not only to the good council of friends but also those parts of his mind that could unlock solutions which might not otherwise occur through deliberation.

Kit sat alone in the flat, staring out at the night sky. The moon and the stars were obscured behind a dense, black shroud. Kit felt jealous of their ability to hide. He wished he could disappear also, sometimes. But where? And without her. Never.

A knock at the door intruded upon his melancholy. Expecting to see Bright, Kit went to the door himself. Instead, it was a young man delivering a telegram. After tipping him, Kit took the telegram inside and opened it.

He stared at the telegram. Miller arrived late to the corridor to see Kit staring in shock at the note.

'Is everything alright, sir?' asked Miller.

'No, Harry, it's just become worse.'

23

London: 8th January 1920

Harry Miller was holding the young woman from the Telegraph Office close. Only moments would pass before he was kissing her. He desperately wanted to draw this moment of anticipation out a little longer. At last, she was finally in his arms, looking in his eyes, lips apart. The sound of his heart beating was deafening. How could she not hear it? Blood coursed through his veins as the excitement grew. She was excited too; unable to breathe. Panting. Loudly. Her face moved closer to his. Her mouth opened. Then she began to lick his face.

Miller awoke with a start. Sam was on top of him. He wanted something.

'Thanks Sam,' said Miller, disgruntledly to the little dog. 'That was the best dream I've had in ages.'

Sam, front paws on Miller's chest looked down and tilted his head slightly. He nuzzled Miller. Sometimes these men didn't get the message first time.

'Let me guess. Food?' asked Miller.

Sam gave a yelp to confirm assent and leapt off the bed and scuttled into the kitchen, slipping, as usual, just outside the door in his haste. Miller rose more slowly, put on his slippers, and shuffled off in pursuit of the terrier. Half an hour later breakfast was prepared for Kit and Bright. He lightly rapped on the doors of both men.

Kit did not need any help in being dressed which was a relief. Miller found the idea bizarre that any fit and healthy adult would need such help. His only role in the morning was to get everyone awake and fed. After giving Kit a few minutes to wake he went into the room and opened the curtains.

'Thank you, Harry,' said a sleepy voice somewhere underneath a pillow.

Miller made his way towards Bright's room. He gave the door a brief rap then entered. Much to his surprise, Harry found Bright's room empty. The bed was as Miller had made it the previous morning. It was clear Bright had not slept in the room. Harry chuckled to himself.

'Lucky devil.'

At the breakfast table, Kit noted the absence of his friend.

'Where's Richard? Is he still in bed?'.

'Not sure sir. He didn't sleep in his room last night,' replied Miller, unable to suppress a smile.

Kit glanced at Harry with a raised eyebrow. He smiled also before saying, 'I don't think we should jump to any conclusions yet, Harry, if I read your smile correctly. And I think I do.'

Miller laughed, 'You should be a detective sir. Would you like the newspaper sir?' He placed the folded paper on the table beside Kit.

'No thanks, Harry, let's go to the hotel and pick-up Esther. Not to check obviously,' added Kit quickly. He, too, was smiling. He rose from the breakfast table and made his way into the living room. It looked like rain outside. Grey clouds moved with menacing purpose.

Kit stopped to look down at the two chessboards again. The latest move by Serov, delivered the previous evening, had been a surprise. It had caught him out. He had not anticipated a continuation of the game in advance of their face-to-face encounter, furthermore, the move had been audacious.

Miller looked at Kit staring at the board, 'Are we in trouble?'

'Deep trouble, Harry, deep trouble. I looked at this but didn't think he would be so brazen. He'll almost certainly take my Castle in two moves. Not sure how I can stop him. He's up to something. I wish I had more time to work out what that something is.'

'Shall I bring your revolver to the match?' smiled Harry.

'You may need to at this rate,' said Kit smiling grimly.

*

Kit walked into Esther's hotel. There was no sign of her. He walked over to the reception and asked them to ring her room. No answer. Kit was not sure whether to be worried or to smile. As he stood at the reception desk pondering his options when he saw Esther step out of the lift. As she glided over through reception looking around her, Kit was able to observe, with some amusement, the reaction of people to her as she passed them.

Men and women stopped and looked at her. Kit was not surprised. She was extraordinary. Her dark mauve dress was fashionably short stopping just beneath her knees. It emphasized her slender build and grace.

After a moment or two, she spotted Kit. She smiled and waved. A moment later the smile became a look of surprise and then a puzzled frown. It was a frown that reminded him so much of Mary, that Kit felt his heart crash through the wall of

180

his chest. Trying not to alarm her, Kit walked forward to greet her with a smile.

'Where's Richard?'

'I was hoping you could tell me,' replied Kit. 'He doesn't appear to have come home last night.'

'I don't understand. He left me around eleven. He didn't mention going to visit anyone,' said Esther, clearly perplexed and now a little worried.

They both went out to the car. Rain was beginning to fall gently. Outside the hotel a newspaper boy stood beside a street billboard. In large, black capital letters against a stark white background were written: Latest Murder.

*

The mood around Kopel and Daniels was distinctly better than in Kit's apartment. In fact, the absence of Fechin had added a degree of levity to the grim work they were conducting. Each were each reading an edition of the Daily Herald. Billy Peel had written the following:

As reported in yesterday's special afternoon edition of the Daily Herald, the double murder of Trade Unionist, Herbert Yapp and Civil Servant, Sir Montagu Forbes-Trefusis is now a treble murder. The Daily Herald was sent another letter from the same group claiming responsibility for the murder, in Gloucester, of Bishop John Gordon. Police are treating this letter as genuine.

We believe that far from being an Irish republican group active in this country the murders may be the responsibility of a foreign government: Russia.

We know, Britain's hostile attitude to workers extends beyond its own borders. Through its global imperialist

181

adventures, Britain has time and again sought to exploit the poor, the dispossessed and working men from Australia to India to Africa and beyond. Is Britain, at long last, facing its day of judgement?

Police remain baffled by how the three men are linked but seem now to be discounting Irish involvement. Both Yapp and Forbes-Trefusis might have been considered legitimate targets for Irish republicans. The latest letter and the murder of Bishop Gordon takes the investigation into new territory.

Daniels looked up from his paper at Kopel, 'How do you feel about this?'

'This is what I wanted. Peel is proving remarkably useful. I'm glad Bergmann chose him,' said Kopel, not looking up from the paper.

Daniels nodded but, in truth, was none the wiser. He liked Kopel but, unlike Bergmann, he feared him also. The problem was Kopel could be opaque. Like their former co-conspirator, Fechin, Daniels would have preferred more demonstrable trust from Kopel. Unlike Fechin, he accepted his role and did not question their plans or seek more information. He was always a soldier first and foremost. However, his curiosity about Bergmann overcame his usual reluctance to ask Kopel too many questions.

'What of comrade Bergmann?'

As he said this, he noticed Serov had just joined them at the table. Daniels scolded himself for being indiscreet and he hoped Kopel would not be angry. Kopel smiled up at Serov, who was usually the last to arrive for breakfast, and folded his newspaper.

'Filip, so good to see you. I trust you slept well.'

Serov looked around the breakfast room at the Waldorf Hotel. The surroundings were very much in the Art Deco style of the day. There was an open, airy feel to the décor that contrasted with the heavy, overworked interiors of hotels in his homeland. In place of heavy marble floors and railings, was parquet and thin metal rails, exuberantly shaped to delight the eye.

'Yes, thank you, I feel quite refreshed.'

'Well prepared also? Two days and you will be facing Aston.'

'Yes, I feel ready,' replied Serov before adding,' I'd like to visit the venue soon, if I may.'

'Good idea, Filip. We shall arrange this for later today. Is this convenient?'

A waitress came over to take Serov's order. She looked uncertainly at the big Russian, as she had overheard them speaking in a foreign language.

Serov smiled at her and replied, in accented English, 'Tea please.' Then added, 'Earl Grey.'

'I heard you talking about comrade Bergmann. Will he be attending the match also? It's been a while now since we've seen him.'

Kopel smiled towards both men and replied, 'I'm not sure now if it will be possible. Other matters have arisen requiring his attention.'

Daniels and Serov glanced at one another. Neither seemed entirely happy with the answer, but neither seemed inclined to probe further.

*

Kit and Esther sat in the living room of his apartment. Without Bright the atmosphere felt different. Both more relaxed and more tense, Kit couldn't decide which. They had spoken more to one another during the morning than they had at any point over Christmas, when they had first met.

At one point, Esther looked at Kit with a mischief he had not seen since those first days, 'Did I ever have a chance?'

Kit smiled, 'Well I certainly liked both of you. For what it matters, Esther, I don't think I've ever met someone so beautiful. I could see Richard was smitten immediately. I was quite jealous.'

'Of Richard and me?'

'Yes. And then I wasn't sure if it was you or Mary he liked.'

'I think this probably clarified matters for you regarding Mary and myself,' said Esther with a surprising degree of insight.

'Yes, I rather think it did,' admitted Kit smiling boyishly.

'What do you think has happened Kit?' said Esther, the frown returning to her face.

She looked as fragile as he had ever seen her. The loss of her grandfather, and now the disappearance of Richard were taking their toll. Dark circles had appeared beneath her eyes which were still red from the tears.

'I wish I knew Esther. He said nothing to me about meeting anyone. The only thing I'm completely certain of is how crazy he is about you. Whatever has happened, I don't believe this has changed or ever will change. The Cavendish girls have cast a spell on us.'

Esther looked at Kit and smiled gratefully. It wasn't much, but, for the moment, it was enough.

Outside the apartments, Harry Miller was sitting in the car rereading the newspaper article on the murders that were taking place when he saw Kit and Esther appear. He opened the door for them, and both climbed into the back of the car.

'That's terrible, isn't it?' said Esther as she sat down noticing the headlines on the newspaper.

'What is?' asked Kit, obliviously.

'The news. There was another murder. They burned him at a stake,' continued Esther with a shudder.

'How horrible. Is it connected with the other murders?' inquired Kit.

'Apparently so,' responded Esther.

They drove along in silence for a few minutes. Miller turned around when they halted at one point due to traffic, 'How is Miss Cavendish?'

Esther brightened up momentarily, 'I think the trip to Scotland has been good for her.'

'Not for me,' said Kit.

'Poor dear,' said Esther with not the remotest trace of sympathy. She noticed that Kit seemed a little distant and suddenly felt a wave of guilty. 'I'm sorry I didn't mean to sound mean.'

Kit looked far away in his thoughts and didn't respond immediately, then he looked at Esther and said, 'Sorry, I was distracted there. No. it's not that. There's something nagging at me.'

Kit looked out of the car window again, preoccupied. A frown was on his forehead. He was silent for a few moments, his attention clearly elsewhere. Miller peeked at Kit in the mirror. He recognised the look. It came when something was unclear. Something had disturbed him. There was a ripple on the water.

'I don't suppose they were able to identify the body?'

Miller answered, 'It was a Bishop sir. The Bishop of Gloucester, John Gordon. I have the paper here sir if you would like to see.'

'Bishop?' whispered Kit. Outside the car, the world seemed to stop and turn to gaze at him. The car continued moving, while all around him was silence and immobility. They passed a newspaper board, screaming its headline in bold, black capitals, "Bishop Burned Alive". Kit's mind was in tumult.

A Bishop.

A Knight.

A pawn.

The silence thickened the air. Esther looked at Kit, her face apprehensive. She could tell something was troubling Kit. Something that was not about Richard, or Mary.

'Is something wrong Kit?' asked Esther.

Kit nodded slowly, yes. Something was wrong. Something was very wrong indeed.

24

Esther accompanied Kit and Miller back to the apartment. They were greeted by a surprise. Sitting on the sofa was a rather dishevelled Bright. Dark rings under his eyes suggested he'd not enjoyed much sleep the previous night.

'Good Lord!' exclaimed Kit, shocked at the appearance of Bright, 'Where've you been?'

Esther said nothing but went straight over to him and received a hug.

'I'm sorry, the most extraordinary thing happened,' explained Bright. They all sat down, and Bright continued with his story.

'I'd just left Esther after supper, and was heading outside the hotel, when I was accosted by a man. I subsequently found out his name was Wilson. He's a porter at the hotel; his face was familiar. Anyway, this chap Wilson came over and told me about his son being taken very ill suddenly. The child was only two years old, and I could see Wilson was in quite a state. He'd obviously picked up on the fact that I was a doctor. Anyway, to cut a long story short, he asked if I could come and attend him. He'd not been able to find a doctor willing to come out so late. Of course, I said yes, and we took a taxi to his house in Islington. Terrible area, I must say. I'm glad I don't have to live there. They lived in a tiny two room flat, but very clean to be fair to them. As soon as I saw the child, I suspected it could be meningitis. Naturally, I was alarmed and immediately ordered Wilson to find a taxi; we needed to take the child to the nearest hospital. And that's pretty much where I spent the night.'

'The poor thing,' said Esther, 'How is he?'

'Hopefully, we diagnosed it in time. He should have a good chance. Meningitis is the devil. It can creep up on you very quickly. With care it can be managed; without it, well, I wouldn't have given the child a chance. I'm so sorry, I hope you weren't too worried darling.'

'We were both worried,' said Kit, 'But there was nothing else you could do. And jolly well done. You may have saved a child's life.'

Bright smiled at Kit's praise and his smile grew even broader as his fiancée gave a more eloquent demonstration of her admiration, one which required no words and caused Kit to look away in embarrassment.

After a minute, perhaps two, he asked, 'Have you two finished?' A noise coming from Esther suggested not. Another minute passed.

'Finished?'

'Yes,' said Esther triumphantly and walked off towards the kitchen.

Kit looked at Bright who, if anything, was even more dishevelled. On the plus side, he looked distinctly perkier. The conversation was interrupted by Miller who brought over a letter for Kit. He opened it and read the contents. A moment later he gave a gasp.

'What's wrong Kit?' said Esther returning from the kitchen with a glass of water for Bright.

'They have Olly,' said Kit, anxiety spreading across his face.

'Who is Olly? And they for that matter?' asked Bright, clearly mystified.

Kit looked vacantly at his two friends and then shook his head.

'Harry, who brought this letter?' asked Kit.

'A young lad hand delivered it,' responded Miller.

'Quickly, see if you can find him. He can't have gone very far.'

Standing up, Kit walked over to the window and drew back the curtain. For some reason he had a feeling the person who had given the letter to the boy might be below. The street was crowded, and it was difficult to make out faces through the droplets of rain on the window. One man did catch his attention, however. Standing across the road, dressed in a long dark coat was a very large man. He seemed to be the only one without an umbrella. The sighting was a brief one because the man suddenly turned and walked towards a taxi. He climbed in. Within seconds the car was gone. Kit's skin was tingling, however. He watched the taxi until it was out of sight, then turned to his friends.

'Olly is Lord Oliver Lake. Probably my oldest friend,' explained Kit.

'And they?'

Kit walked over and sat by the chess board. He looked down at the pieces and felt the anger rise slowly within him. Cold eyes burned through the chess board. He experienced an animosity towards the game, towards himself. His credulousness for participating in a game had resulted in three deaths and perhaps a fourth. The idea of being responsible for

189

the possible death of his oldest friend brought tears of frustration, then frenzy. With one sweep of his hand all the pieces on the chess boards went crashing to the floor.

Esther looked at Bright, startled by the reaction in Kit. Bright picked up the letter and showed it the Esther. The note was typed and dated 12th January 1920. It read:

Dear Mr Aston,

By now you may be reconsidering your participation in the chess match. Unfortunately, it will not be possible for you to leave prematurely. The match must continue to the end. Liberty is precious. At this moment, your friend, Lord Oliver Lake of Hertwood, would agree with this idea.

Kind Regards

S.o.L

Esther looked at Bright, 'Does this mean Olly has been kidnapped? But why?'

Bright looked at Kit. He'd never seen his friend like this before. His eyes were a frozen fury. He understood immediately the anger of his friend was suffused with guilt. Why Kit should be blaming himself, he could not comprehend, but clearly it was connected to the chess game.

'Kit, I don't know what's going on, but you shouldn't blame yourself for this. Whoever this "S.o.L" is, they're clearly mad.'

Kit looked up. Bright could almost see the flames burning in his eyes now. Kit covered his face with his hands. He rubbed his eyes with the heel of his palms and then put his hands down. In a moment, the flame died away. Turning to Miller, he said, 'Harry can you bring me over the phone?'

Miller did so. Kit dialled a number. A minute later he was speaking to someone.

'It's Kit. Look I must see you right now. I know who killed those three men. It's connected to the chess match with Serov.'

The call finished a few minutes later. Both Esther and Bright now understood more about the situation. They watched Kit rise and head out the door with Miller.

'Kit is there anything we can do?' asked Bright.

Kit stopped and thought for a moment.

'Yes, maybe there is. Can you go down to Sheldon's in St. James? It's Olly's private club. Say I sent you. Try and find out as much as you can, specifically if Olly's been around in the last few days.'

'Are you sure that's where he'll have been?'

Kit nodded his head. A shadow seemed to pass over Kit's face.

'Sadly, yes.'

25

It had been less than a week since Kit had last sat in Spunky's office. The story told by Kit and the new facts supplied by Spunky on the murders of Yapp and Forbes-Trefusis had created a clear connection with the chess match. Almost.

'I understand Bishop kills pawn and Knight kills Knight, but how do you arrive at Queen kills Bishop?' asked Spunky.

'What were you doing during history class?' asked Kit, smiling grimly. The two of them had been at school together.

'If you remember, I usually bunked off and spent a happy hour or two with the pub owner's daughter,' admitted Spunky proudly. He paused for a few happy moments as the recollection of those days crossed his mind like a fresh breeze on a summer's day.

'I don't think old Mathers knew I was reading history until I turned up to the examination,' finished Spunky.

Despite the tenseness of the situation, Kit laughed, 'I didn't know you were studying history until you turned up to the exam.'

Kit stood up and walked over to the window that overlooked Holland Park. Turning to Spunky he continued, 'Bishop John Hooper. Does he jog anything in those little grey cells of yours?'

'No, can't say he does,' responded Spunky happily.

'He was Bishop of Gloucester. Burned at the stake by Queen Mary for the heinous crime of being protestant.'

'Trifle harsh, don't you think? Wouldn't three Hail Mary's have done the trick?'

The two friends were interrupted at that moment by a knock at the door. An attractive young woman entered the office.

'Dawn, meet Lord Kit Aston,' said Spunky indicating his friend.

'Dawn,' said Kit shaking her hand.

'The Chief will see you now,' said Dawn.

'Has he finished with that other chap?' asked Spunky.

'No sir, he'll be joining you in the meeting,' replied Dawn.

They followed Dawn out of the office and up another set of stairs to the top floor of the house. As they climbed the steps, Kit glanced at Spunky with a smile. The latter returned the look and shook his head dejectedly.

'Sadly, I've never woken up at Dawn,' said Spunky in a stage whisper.

They arrived at a narrow corridor. Walking through the only door took them into an outer office which Kit took to be Dawn's. It was sparsely furnished. Just a table and chair with two large filing cabinets in the corner. There was another door which Dawn walked towards and knocked.

'Enter,' came a voice from inside.

Kit and Spunky both followed Dawn through two doors and walked inside a dark wood-panelled room. Old master paintings of naval battles adorned the walls.

'Stevens and Aston, sir,' said Dawn, who immediately left the room.

The office was dimly lit. Two men were there, either side of the large desk. With his back to the large dormer window sat the Chief, Mansfield Cumming. The daylight behind Cumming forced Kit to squint a little as his eyes grew accustomed to the light. He had met Cumming only once before, just after he had returned to Britain to recuperate. It was at his hospital, and he had accompanied Spunky. It was much later he heard from Spunky how the nature of Kit's injury had made "C" insistent on the meeting. Only Spunky was aware that "C" had also lost part of his leg following a road accident a few years previously.

At the time, Kit was not told who he was although he'd soon guessed. It was the man known only as "the Chief" or "C". It was a sign of the seriousness of the situation that he had agreed to meet him. Normally, "C" kept a hermit-like existence away from the operatives who, ultimately, carried out his orders.

From his time in the hospital, Kit remembered him to be nearer sixty than fifty, with silver hair and a very large, prominent chin. Another distinguishing characteristic was the monocle. Kit wasn't sure if this was due to a weaker eye or for theatrical effect. His eyes, Kit recalled, had a piercing but not unkind quality. Those eyes looked directly at Kit, but "C" remained silent. He gestured for Kit to sit down at the other empty seat, opposite the unnamed man.

There was silence for a few moments. Kit knew this was typical and he waited for "C" to initiate the conversation. Finally, "C" spoke.

'Good work, Kit and thank you for coming. This situation is unprecedented. Our response needs to be both urgent and carefully considered. I'm sure you'll appreciate how difficult this will be to manage. Kit, can you tell us what you know?'

Kit glanced at the other, as yet unnamed man, before looking again at "C", who simply nodded.

'Certainly, sir.'

Over the next five minutes, Kit related everything about his involvement in the match from the initial contact by Bergmann through to his discovery of the connection to the recent murders. To finish off he took out the letter he had received and handed it to "C".

"C" looked over the letter for a minute before handing to the other man.

'Well?' asked "C".

The other man said nothing and then returned the letter to "C".

'Are you aware of the significance of the signature, Kit?'

'No idea, sir. Can you shed any light on this?'

This brought a smile from the other man, who simply said, 'Funny you should use the word light'.

Kit looked at the other man again. He was smallish in stature with a hard glint in his grey metal eyes. The accent was Northern Irish. Out of the corner of his eyes, Kit could see a smile grow on the face of "C".

'Forgive me, I was forgetting my manners. Kit, may I introduce you to Billy Peel.' The smile broadened when he saw Kit's shocked reaction to this news.

'Mr Aston,' said Peel holding out his hand. There was no sign of friendliness in the Ulsterman.

'Mr Peel,' replied Kit coldly. He suspected whatever reason had brought Peel to the headquarters of Britain's Special Intelligence Service; it did not mean the newsman was any more in favour of the aristocracy unless he was an enormous hypocrite.

Peel seemed to read his mind, 'No Mr Aston, I still hate the class system in Britain. It just so happens that I hate the Bolsheviks more. Both systems oppress the working man. But I think this is a discussion for another time.'

Although not normally a man who required someone to use his formal title, Kit found himself developing an intense dislike of Peel and the deliberately provocative use of mister. In such situations, Kit followed his instinct, which was to smile benignly. He took the view that this was more likely to irritate than to ameliorate. In these situations, it was a minor victory of sorts.

'Indeed,' replied Kit non-committedly.

'If I may summarise gentlemen,' said "C" interrupting, 'The situation is this. We have Russian, or rogue Russian, agents operating in Britain. They are using the chess match as a signal to kill ranking British citizens for reasons unknown. You are unable to pull out of the chess match now, Kit, because it would almost certainly result in the murder of Olly Lake. However, if you continue the match then they shall achieve their object anyway given the superior skills of your opponent. Is this how you see the situation, Kit?'

'Yes sir.'

'I see. We know at least two members of the group, Georgy Bergmann and Leonid Daniels.'

'And Fechin?' added Peel.

'Ah yes. A nasty piece of work,' replied "C". 'But possibly no more.'

Peel looked at "C", clearly puzzled by this.

'We didn't release this publicly, but we believe he died by misadventure.' At this point "C" explained the unusual circumstances.

Peel nodded before replying, 'I wouldn't be so certain of it being an accident.'

This made "C" smile and then he continued, 'Bergmann we know nothing about. He is a mystery. Daniels, we do. It isn't good news. He is Cheka and a highly effective agent. He's fluent in English and German. He was a sergeant in the Russian army. He is clearly deadly. There may be other members in the gang of whom we are not aware. We have Mr Peel to thank for this intelligence, by the way Kit.'

Kit and Peel looked at one another. The feeling between them was no warmer.

'I'm glad that the two of you are getting along so well,' observed "C" sardonically. 'In fact, the two of you have at least one thing in common.'

'We've been used,' responded Kit grimly.

'Very much, Kit,' agreed "C". 'Both of you have been indispensable to this plan and, if I may say, you have played your respective roles most diligently.'

This stung Kit, but he resisted the urge to pin the blame on Roger Ratcliff. A quick glance at Peel reassured him that the newsman was feeling no more pleased by this than he was. At least he was not alone, thought Kit, rather ashamedly like a schoolboy facing detention.

'As to their intentions, we now arrive at the core of our problem,' continued "C". 'If they were to continue as they have started then I have to agree; their intention is nothing less than the assassination of the Royal family.'

Kit nodded unhappily. He had shared exactly this conclusion with Spunky just minutes before. Peel looked shocked by this news. Something Kit was quick to pick up.

'Are you a republican Mr Peel?'

Peel glared back at Kit. In truth, Peel had no answer. On the one hand, as a protestant from Northern Ireland, he had been brought up to oppose anything that would end Ulster's link with Britain. This meant opposition to Irish republicanism. However, as a staunch socialist, he was opposed to the class system and reserved a deep hatred for the Royal family. Admitting he was a republican was anathema, but correct, strictly speaking. In any other situation, Peel would have been amused by the dilemma. Sitting in front of a famous, and popular, manifestation of a system he despised, decided him against any admission one way or another.

'Very funny, Mr Aston.'

'If we could return to the matter, gentlemen,' admonished "C" softly, 'We appear to have limited time and options available to us. The kidnapping of Lake presents us with a challenge. I will not ask you, Kit, to stop the match. Is there anything you can do to prolong it?'

'I'm not sure, sir. Serov is in an exceptionally strong position.'

'But you are a piece to the good?' pointed out "C". This surprised Kit and he turned to the head of the Special Intelligence Service. "C" smiled and shrugged his shoulders. 'I've been following the match since the start. Truth to tell, I authorised it. Roger told us he had heard via back channels that the Bolsheviks were open to a deal. There would be a few conditions. This was but one. It was me who suggested using

Mr Peel. If it's any consolation to you then I am just as credulous as you.'

Kit nodded but the news appeared to give him no pleasure. He then answered Cumming's original point.

'It's true that I'm a piece up, but I'm not sure it'll do me much good.'

Peel interjected at this point, 'So we need to prolong the game as much as possible to allow more time to find Lake?'

'Correct,' replied "C".

Peel added nothing else. It was clear an idea was forming but "C" decided to give him time to articulate it. He continued in the meantime.

'I think making any direct link in your newspaper between the match and the possible assassination of the King and Queen would be unwise, Mr Peel. Do you agree?'

Peel nodded ruefully, 'And the link with Russia?'

'I see no reason not to continue, Mr Peel,' said "C".

Kit looked askance at "C", 'Is that wise, sir? This will create a lot of ill feeling in the country and tension between the governments.'

'I think we've long since passed the point of worrying about that. The Russians are up in arms already if you'll pardon the expression. They're denying any involvement with these murders. The Foreign Office is still too angry over the Forbes-Trefusis murder to believe them. All in all, it's a bit of a mess. So, if anything, I'd rather welcome it.'

"C" did not elaborate on why, so Kit left this question unasked. He had long since given up trying to understand the rules of the diplomatic game and he knew better than to expect "C" to open up unless he chose to.

'Mr Peel, you've met Serov now. Do you believe him to be implicated in these acts?'

'Honestly, I don't believe so, but I can't say for certain,' replied Peel. 'What happens now?'

'I'll see that Jellicoe hears of your suspicions, Kit. In the meantime, Mr Peel, you should make your way over to Scotland Yard to give the good Chief Inspector descriptions of Bergmann and Daniels. You may also want to publish them in your paper,' said "C", his eyes twinkling.

Peel eyed "C". He was unsurprised by the shrewdness of the man and, partly, reassured in this knowledge. The years spent in France had only hardened his hatred of the upper classes who had led men like him into a slaughter. There were rare occasions when he met more credible examples of the breed; all too rarely, sadly. The man before him was one such man. Aston also, if what he'd heard was true.

The chance to lead with this story was impossible to turn down. Even Lansbury, as sympathetic as he was to Russia, would agree. At their heart, both were newsmen, both wanted the truth, both abhorred suppression. This was uppermost in his mind.

It was disappointing not being able to break the news about the connection to the chess match, but he accepted the rationale. He consoled himself with the thought of how his close involvement with the case would eventually force the truth out, whatever it might be.

For the next half hour, "C" went through the situation in forensic detail. Both Kit and Peel were impressed by his immediate grasp of the facts and his ability to translate them into implications for national security, diplomacy, and politics. By the end of this session, the stakes were very clear, and they went beyond the immediate risk to the life of Lord Oliver Lake.

The actions of the self-proclaimed "Sword of Light" added weight to the faction in His Majesty's Government lobbying for more troops on the ground in Russia. The objective was partly to defend the existing British armaments stockpiled in Arkhangelsk but for many in this faction, it was also seen as a precursor to a Western alliance to fight and defeat the Bolsheviks.

'I can't believe we would seriously consider war with Russia. Have these people no idea what we went through?' said Kit, when "C" had finished.

Peel glanced at Kit in surprise. This was unexpected. He was aware of some of Kit's actions during the War. Unlike many people of rank who had taken mainly ceremonial roles, Kit had fought alongside people like him. Peel had viewed these heroics as merely the actions of some Boy's Own fantasist. The reality seemed different. Rather than a totem of British imperialistic interests he saw a man bitterly opposed to further war.

'You'd be surprised Kit,' said "C", but his tone of voice did not suggest either shock or dismay. Instead, Kit saw a man who was resigned to the follies of political machinations and interested in mitigating their impact when and where he could.

The meeting seemed to be ending, when "C" turned to Peel and asked what, to Kit, seemed like a strange question.

'Have you any thoughts on how Kit can keep Mr Serov occupied longer than he would like, Mr Peel?'

Peel looked at "C", and not for the first time during the meeting found himself in awe of his insight. He smiled in recognition of this and nodded his head, 'Would you believe, yes?

26

Olly Lake lay on his bed. It was night. Sleep had been fitful. He rolled over and eventually his breathing became more rhythmic. The dream returned. The one where he had met her.

The first time he had seen Kristina was with Roger Ratcliff and Colin Cornell. Ratcliff had spoken about this ravishing girl working in Kerensky's secretariat. He wondered if he had designs on her himself, the dirty devil. His first view of her in the summer of 1917 had, for once, put him in the unusual position of agreeing with Ratcliff about something. She was the most exquisite looking girl he had ever seen, and he had spent time with his fair share.

Her frazzled fair hair could not be contained by the red band. It spilled everywhere. It was all he could do to stop himself pushing the strand of hair that had fallen out from the hair band, back into place. Watching her finally push it back with those long, elegant fingers was a quasi-spiritual experience. Although seated at a desk behind a typewriter, Lake could see a pair of large blue eyes full of curiosity and unable to hide their amusement at Ratcliff.

It made Lake laugh to see Ratcliff and Cornell attempting small talk with the girl as they waited for Kerensky. Lake contented himself by looking at Ratcliff with a half-smile and smoking, aware of her interest in him. Unlike Ratcliff and Cornell, he knew women. He could play the game, for that's what it was. That was the big secret women hid from fools like Ratcliff and Cornell.

When Kerensky had finally invited them into his office, Lake elected to stay outside.

'Do you really want me in this meeting Roger?'

'Please yourself,' growled Ratcliff in response, glancing at Kristina. He knew what Lake was up to and if any man could succeed where Cornell had failed, it was him.

Lake sat down again and finally looked at the girl, he had studiously avoided gazing at, except via his peripheral vision. He smiled and said in perfect Russian, 'I'm sorry, my friend didn't introduce us. My name is Lake, Olly Lake.'

It surprised her to be addressed by the man in front of her. She saw someone younger than the other two men. There was something indefinable about him, a disinterestedness that stopped short of cold reserve, resolving itself instead as something more fascinating, almost predatory. Dislike was her first reaction.

She merely nodded in response and returned to her work. Frustratingly, he said nothing more, but she sensed his eyes on her. Normally, she was used to attention from men. It was flattering but no longer pleased her as it once might have. She glanced up from her work at long last. His eyes were still shamelessly on her. This time he cocked his head slightly and his grin widened.

'Can I help you, sir?'

'You could tell me your name,' replied Lake.

She remained silent for a moment as she considered how to react. It did not occur to her the likelihood of his knowing anyway. He raised his eyebrows as a prompt. This amused her, much to her irritation.

'Kristina.'

*

Lake awoke and shielded his eyes from the sunlight streaming onto his face. The big Russian was in the room with him. He brought over a tray with a glass of clear liquid. Moments later Lake spat the contents out.

'Water? What the hell are you giving me water for? Have you no gin?' asked Lake in Russian.

This appeared to confuse the man. He shut his eyes again and tried to work out which was worse, the thumping headache or a throat that felt as if it was being rubbed by sandpaper every time he swallowed. He heard the door closing but could not be bothered to open his eyes. It was still too early. He hated mornings but gave in to the inevitable and rose from the bed. Time to dress.

*

Later the same morning, Serov walked through Highgate cemetery accompanied by Kopel. The chance to visit the grave of one of his heroes was one of the conditions he had insisted on at the outset. He was glad that Kopel had agreed so readily to the request, in the strange absence of Bergmann.

Serov had first read "The Communist Manifesto" as a student. Unsurprisingly, the ideas of Marx were not freely available in the orphanage he had grown up in. In fact, books were all too rare. It was a wonder he'd ever learned to read or write. If he'd believed in God, the idea of him becoming a chess grandmaster would have been nothing short of a miracle. Instead of God, the words of Marx became a Bible that he could quote from as freely as a Presbyterian from the Old Testament.

Although it was cold, the sun streamed through the trees providing dappled spotlights along the narrow path banked by the heavy memorials either side. If ever a place lacked spirituality, reflected Serov, it was this cemetery. All around, the bourgeoisie seemed to be in competition with one another to build the most vulgar monuments to their own memory.

The grave of Marx was out of the way along a side path. He was buried in the same plot as his wife. Its location and the lack of ostentation pleased Serov. It seemed a validation of the great man's principles that he should occupy a simple grave, in marked contrast to the tasteless tombs built by those who had spent their lifetime exploiting the masses.

Kopel looked on as Serov gazed down reverentially at the ground where Marx rested. Unusually for him, he felt moved by the profound spiritual reaction Serov was clearly undergoing. This was a surprise to him. He felt ashamed watching Serov's tears flow. He realised how deeply Serov believed in the ideas written over eighty years previously which were now changing the world. Of course, he'd never felt it himself.

Kopel had always taken a soldier's view of life and politics. His Bible was Clausewitz. He was an instrument of national policy. Or supra-national policy. It didn't matter who made the policies and whatever those policies were. Fundamentally, only one policy mattered where he was concerned.

In one sense, it was an area of common ground between he and Serov. The whole was more important than the individual parts. Like Marx, and like the chess player in front of him, he

206

understood how sacrifices were sometimes necessary to achieve the ultimate goal.

Serov said little as they returned to the hotel. Kopel wisely left him to his thoughts. The next few days were going to be a test for all of them. Even Serov seemed apprehensive, which surprised Kopel. His confidence had bordered on hubris throughout the couple of weeks they had been together. The prospect of finally facing Kit Aston seemed to be acting as a dose of reality.

In truth, Kopel no longer cared. Win, lose, or draw, the match result was immaterial. Serov had fulfilled his role. Soon he would be left to fend for himself. The taxi deposited Serov at the Waldorf. Kopel took his leave recognising Serov desired solitude following his time in the presence of his master. Or was it simply a desire to prepare, to leave nothing to chance against Aston?

*

The headline on the news stand caught Serov's eye as he entered the hotel. He made a small detour and bought the newspaper. His understanding of written English was not as strong, but he could read well enough to grasp what was being said. The rage in him grew as picked through the article by Billy Peel.

For the last week or more he had begun to feel more sympathy for Britain than he would have cared to admit. Parts of the country were beautiful; the weather was almost tropical compared to his homeland. The workers, far from being in chains, were much better off than his fellow countrymen. The level of antagonism to Russia was not as high as he'd expected. And then he read Peel's article.

'Liar,' he snarled causing a gentleman in a top hat to look up with a start. Serov ignored him as he strode angrily into the hotel.

'Lies,' he thundered. All around him, people in the lobby of the hotel stopped and looked at him. Serov's indignation made him oblivious to the stares. He sat down and continued reading the inside pages. Billy Peel became the sole object of his wrath as he poured forth a stream of curses aimed at the journalist, the so-called fellow socialist, who was a puppet of the ruling classes. Such was the intensity of the rant, several women moved away in obvious distress. This caused the duty manager of the hotel to come over. With some trepidation he approached the strange man uttering oaths in a foreign language and asked if there was anything he could do. Serov glared up at the man who had just interrupted his tirade.

'Yes?' asked Serov, still unconscious of the effect he had created around him.

'You seem to be agitated sir,' said the trembling manager.

'Agitated?' repeated Serov.

Unsure if he spoke English, or had misunderstood him, the manager made the mistake of repeating the word, only more slowly, followed by the raising of his eyebrows and a smile that was as pointless as it was patronising.

'I know what it means,' roared Serov, 'I'm not an idiot.'

The commotion had already attracted the attention of the doorman who had immediately run to a nearby policeman. Within a matter of minutes, Serov was gazing up at two policemen. At this point rationality broke through the red haze. He realised he had gone too far. Just as he was about to apologise, he spied Daniels arriving through the front entrance. The big man looked shocked as he saw the police

208

surrounding Serov. Unaccountably, to Serov, he turned and walked outside again without returning.

Serov looked at the gaggle of men in front of him. He held up his hands, palms facing outwards. This calmed proceedings slightly and gave Serov the opportunity to speak. He explained the reason for his highly visible displeasure. This served to appease both the duty manager and the police. In fact, the younger policeman was following the chess match and recognised the Russian grand master. The older policeman eyed his younger colleague with something beyond distaste at this revelation and made a mental note to speak to the young man. These new constables were having ideas above their station.

Having established his peaceful credentials, the crowd dispersed leaving Serov alone in the lobby of the hotel wondering about the strange behaviour of Daniels. A few minutes later, he saw the big Russian return. He went on the offensive immediately.

'Why did you disappear?' asked Serov, staring intently into the eyes of Daniels.

'I was looking for Georgy, he was in a taxi. I thought he could help. He'd left, so I came back.'

Serov nodded. It made some sense, but he remained sceptical. For reasons he could not quite articulate, there was something about the look on Daniels face that perturbed him. It had just been a moment.

'Where is Georgy anyway? I haven't seen him for a week or more.'

'I can't say comrade Serov,' replied Daniels. This served to stop any further questions from Serov but did not provide any reassurance. This was apparent to Daniels, but by now, he no longer cared. Their job was nearly done and his involvement with Serov at an end. He felt no ill will towards the grandmaster, but he wanted to finish this operation. Also, he was lying. He hadn't seen Bergmann either and the thought of this made him uncomfortable.

Daniels left him a few minutes later to go up to his room. Serov remained in the lobby. He felt on edge and walked into the bar. The anger had not subsided. And the intuition of Daniels was correct. He was far from reassured. The game was two days away. Whether it was the events of the last half hour or the prospect of facing Aston, he didn't know, but he felt a premonition. A wave of despair washed through him. A barman approached him.

'Vodka,' said Serov, not looking up.

The barman poured him a small vodka. Serov picked it up and then drained its contents before indicating to the barman he wanted more. Whatever was troubling him, Serov knew just how to address the issue. He would go about it with resolution.

Another vodka arrived and was dispatched with alacrity. As the barman poured another shot and went to take the bottle away, Serov tapped his hand.

'Leave. I'll take all of it.'

He made himself comfortable; it was going to be a long evening.

27

Harry Miller rushed along the Kings Cross concourse accompanied by Sam. He was late. The train had arrived five minutes ago. He'd been surprised by the afternoon traffic. As he jogged towards the platforms, it became clear the little terrier was struggling to keep up. Miller bent down and lifted him.

'You're getting lazier in your old age,' pointed out Miller.

Sam acknowledged the lift by licking Miller's cheek before settling in for the ride. Miller finally found the platform he was looking for. He could see two people standing there. They looked at him expectantly. Miller nodded, and they both came forward.

The older lady was around thirty, judged Miller, not unattractive even if her hat was not very fashionable and a smile wouldn't have killed her. He looked down at her companion. The girl looked up at Miller and smiled. She held out her hand, much to Miller's surprise, so he shook it.

'Fiona Lawrence,' said the young girl introducing herself.

'Harry Miller.'

'I'm Miss Upritchard,' said the older woman. Miller shook her hand also. He sensed a degree of irritation in her manner, possibly due to his being late. Or perhaps, judging by the disapproving set of her mouth, this was just her manner.

Fiona Lawrence looked at Sam and then back to Miller, expectantly. It was clear she was a dog lover. She's welcome to Sam, thought Miller.

'This is Sam,' explained Miller, 'Would you like to hold him? He's getting on a bit these days. Likes to be chauffeur driven. Bit like his owner.'

'Yes please,' beamed Fiona. The arrangement appeared to suit Sam also as he embarked on a frenzied amount of licking. Both Fiona and Miller ignored the unhappy reaction of her guardian for the trip and walked ahead.

'What's Lord Aston like?' asked Fiona.

Miller took an instant liking to the young Scottish girl. Her accent had a beautiful lilt and clarity which was in stark contrast to some of the men he had served with who hailed from Glasgow.

'Have you read much about him?'

'Everything. He is my hero. I'm so nervous.'

Miller looked down at the young girl who had already made Sam a friend for life.

'Why?' asked Miller, puzzled.

'I suppose I'm afraid he won't be as I've imagined him,' responded Fiona.

'How have you imagined him then?' inquired Miller.

'Tall, good-looking, cultured, highly intelligent, funny.'

Miller laughed and then answered, 'I think your expectations will be exceeded, Fiona. He's the very best of men.'

Fiona looked up at Miller as he said this. He could have sworn he saw tears form in her eyes. They reached the car moments later. The young girl gasped when she saw the Rolls Royce. She walked around it twice before getting in.

Once inside, Miller asked, 'Do you think you'll help him, Fiona? He's a bit nervous about the match. Don't say I told you, by the way.'

'Mum's the word,' confided Fiona before adding chirpily, 'And yes Harry, I can help him.'

Miller turned around sharply. Her voice no longer seemed that of a star struck young girl. The look on her face made Miller's heart leap. It combined resolution with certainty. As they drove away, Miller began to believe with this girl in his corner, Kit really did have a chance against the Russian. He certainly wouldn't lack for inspiration with this other little terrier beside him.

*

Kit had arranged for Fiona and Miss Upritchard to stay at the same hotel as Esther. After they had deposited their belongings, Miller took them to Kit's apartment. As he opened the door, he explained, 'They may be out but I'm sure they'll be back soon.'

If the Rolls Royce had made Fiona gasp, then the first look at Kit's apartment almost made her pass out. She walked around the main living room, mouth agape, drinking in the paintings and the sculptures. The part of the room dedicated to Kit's library caused her to scream with delight. She flew around the shelves trailing her finger along the titles. Miller looked at her with a broad grin. Miss Upritchard successfully conveyed how unimpressed she was.

After a few minutes examining the library, she turned to the rest of the living room and looked on the table at the two chess boards. Her eyes widened as she looked at them. Miller sensed this was no longer a little girl in awe of her surroundings. She was a huntress.

213

'This one is beautiful,' said Fiona, indicating the larger of the two boards.

'John Jack or something, I believe,' said Miller.

'Jacques,' corrected Fiona before pointing to the smaller of the two boards, 'I presume this is the board he plays on.'

'Correct,' said Miller. 'Can I bring either of you ladies something to drink?'

Miss Upritchard shook her head, but Fiona Lawrence was already lost. She sat down and gazed intently at the smaller board. Pouncing like a panther she moved a white piece followed by a black. She stopped and looked at the board for a minute before replacing the pieces. Then she burst out laughing, oblivious to the fascinated stare of Miller and the feigned indifference of Miss Upritchard. The young girl had transformed the atmosphere of the room and Miller judged, correctly, even Miss Upritchard could not be unaffected by this energy.

Slowly she moved white again and then black. Once more she sat back grinning. Rather than replace the pieces she had moved, she continued to play the game. Sam stood by the board, as fascinated by the intensity of the young girl's attention on the game as the other two. His head moved from board to Fiona and back again as the game progressed.

After a few minutes, the board which had once been arranged in neat groupings resembled a battlefield. As she reviewed her handiwork, she was unconscious of Miller leaving the room with a stage whisper to Miss Upritchard that he was to collect Kit.

*

The morning started off badly for Filip Serov and proceeded to get worse at an alarming speed. He woke up to

214

the realisation that he was lying, fully dressed, on top of his bed. There was a sickly smell in the room. As he was face down, he was able to locate the source very quickly because he was sleeping on it. This led to a string of oaths that increased in vehemence as the full extent of his headache became apparent. He briefly wondered if his companions had a gun. At a moment like this, he would happily have put it to good use.

It took several minutes, but he finally managed to rise from the bed. He removed his shoes and socks and padded over to the bathroom. He made it just in time as, once more, the effects of the impressive intake of vodka from the previous evening became manifest.

It was while he was arrayed over the toilet that he heard a key in the door. Unable to move, and frankly not caring anyway, he continued to decorate the commode. Outside the room he heard some men; they didn't sound like either Kopel or Daniels. Then the door to the bathroom opened and, from his kneeling position, he looked up to find two policemen looking down at him. They didn't look very impressed by what they saw. He couldn't blame them.

*

The cell where Serov found himself was a dark, unhappy place, which rather matched his mood. He'd spent the morning there, dividing his time between the bed and the bowl. No one had spoken to him since he had arrived. He had no idea why he was there. His memories of the previous evening were a fog. The vodka had not only desensitized him from his depressive mood of the previous evening it had rendered him senseless, too. He gave up trying to recall if he'd done anything untoward and settled down to awaiting his fate.

After a short period, the door opened and in walked a man in his fifties. He had a beard and his face looked mournful. He was not wearing a uniform. Serov guessed, correctly, this was a detective.

'Mr Serov, I understand you speak English?' said the man slowly, clearly trying to ensure Serov could comprehend.

Serov nodded his head but remained silent. This was less to do with anger than his desire to avoid further humiliation by being ill in front of the detective. He wasn't sure, either, if his breath might not knock out the man in front of him.

'Would you care to come with me please?'

Once more Serov said nothing but stood up and sullenly accompanied the detective outside. They walked down a corridor, with another policeman, into a small, windowless room. There was a wooden table and two chairs on either side. The man invited Serov to sit down.

'Mr Serov, may I introduce myself. I am Chief Inspector Jellicoe. No doubt you are wondering why you're in a police station.'

Serov nodded impassively. By now he felt too ill to be angry. Instead, his mind matched his body's lethargy. He just wanted the nightmare to be over. He concentrated partly on what the detective was saying and partly on not being sick again. Through the haze of self-pity, remorse, and residual anger, he was aware of the man's eyes on him. On any other day, he would have happily stared right back. Not today, though. Jellicoe placed two pieces of paper on the table in front of Serov. Each had a charcoal drawing of a man. Serov looked up at Jellicoe.

'Do you know these men?'

Too tired to be belligerent, Serov nodded yes.

'This one is Georgy Bergmann,' said Jellicoe pointing to the drawing of Bergmann, 'and this is Leon Daniels, correct?'

The question was greeted with another nod in the affirmative.

'Where are they now, Mr Serov?'

Serov finally spoke, his voice barely a whisper, 'I don't know. Why are you asking me this? Why am I here?'

'Your two friends have murdered at least three people to our knowledge and have kidnapped another. So, I will repeat Mr Serov, where are they now?'

The stupefied reaction of Serov seemed genuine to Jellicoe. It confirmed the suspicion of Peel, who he had met this morning, that Serov was an innocent dupe in the events of the last week.

'I don't believe you. This is a lie,' growled Serov, voice a little stronger, anger finally conquering his lassitude. He glared back at Jellicoe. 'I demand to speak to someone from my embassy. I want the Ambassador.'

'There hasn't been one in London for two years now, Mr Serov, so I suggest you calm down and start answering my questions.'

*

Leon Daniels had witnessed the police taking Serov away from across the road of the hotel. He hurried back to Kopel to update him on what had happened. Much to his surprise Kopel seemed unworried and continued to eat his breakfast.

'You're not concerned by this?'

'No Leon. I didn't intend for us to attend the match anyway, at least not in any formal sense. We have another job to do.'

217

Kopel didn't elaborate, much to the frustration of Daniels. It made no sense to him. If the police had made a connection between the murders and Serov, then it would only be a matter of time before they would be hunted down. In fact, this seemed to be Kopel's intention all along.

Daniels walked over to the window and pulled back the lace curtain. He felt on edge now. Many aspects of this operation had mystified him. Why they hadn't just killed the men quietly, made no sense. Using the chess match and, frankly, bizarre methods of execution, now seemed perverse. It was as if Kopel wanted them to be caught. He sensed Kopel looking at him and turned around. Another thought entered Daniels' mind once more. In quiet moments it would invade his conscience and take root. Why had they killed them at all?

'What's wrong Leon?' asked Kopel benignly.

Everything thought Daniels.

*

Kit walked into the apartment with Harry. His first view of Fiona was her back, hunched over the chess board. To her right he saw Miss Upritchard. She was just as Miller had described her, only less fun. Which was a pity, acknowledged Kit. Miller certainly had a good eye.

'Your Lordship, may I present Miss Upritchard and Fiona Lawrence,' said Miller with a smile. Fiona Lawrence spun around and greeted Kit with an enormous smile. Miss Upritchard maintained her grave, disapproving, demeanour.

Fiona leapt up from the seat with wide eyes. Kit walked forward grinning. He held out his hand.

'Fiona, I've heard an awful lot about you, young lady. I gather we're going to give Mr Serov a beating.'

218

'Oh yes we are sir,' said Fiona with a beaming smile, 'Can I show you something now?'

Kit's eyebrows raised at this announcement, and he laughed. He joined Fiona at the table.

'Absolutely young lady.'

The arrival back at the apartment of Kit took Fiona Lawrence to hitherto unexperienced levels of excitement. Her delight was evident and infectious, lifting the mood of Kit who was beginning to feel a little low without Mary.

'Mr Serov thinks he can take your Castle here,' explained Fiona.

'Yes, for a lot of reasons I don't want this to happen,' replied Kit.

'I know because it'll be mate in eight moves,' agreed Fiona.

Kit shot a look at Fiona, 'I made it ten.'

'Definitely eight, sir,' said Fiona with a certainty that Kit was not going to argue against.

'By the way, please call me Kit. My friends call me Kit, and I think we're going to be great friends, Fiona.'

Fiona was squealing with delight inside but thought better of making that apparent. She moved the pieces back to their original position.

'The thing I learned about Mr Serov is that he is easily rattled. He likes order, clean lines of attack and the slow constriction of his opponent.'

'Indeed,' laughed Kit, stroking his neck, 'I've been feeling it.'

'What you need to do is create complications. Make moves that are irrational and throw him off his pre-prepared approach.'

'Go on,' said Kit looking at the board.

Fiona made a few moves that included the sacrifice of Kit's Queen. Kit looked aghast at the board which, thanks to the pocket Boudicca beside him, resembled more of a war zone than a chess match.

'Good lord,' said Kit, struggling to make sense of the disarray. 'Are you sure Fiona? His Queen will be very difficult to counter in the end game.'

'He'll want a draw, trust me, Kit. There are some other tactics you may want to consider also.'

'Such as?' asked Kit looking at Fiona archly.

By the time Fiona had taken him through some of her favourite off the board moves, Kit and Miller were bent double laughing and even Miss Upritchard was observed to smile, albeit briefly, before returning to her normal, serious mien.

'Fiona I couldn't possibly do any of these,' laughed Kit.

'Why not? Chess is not a game on a board, it's war: psychological war. Have you read Sun Tzu, Kit?'

'I'm familiar with him but, no, I can't say that I have,' said Kit slowly, looking in astonishment at the little girl before him. He was becoming more in awe of her with each passing minute. A glance at Miller confirmed he was having a similar reaction.

'If your opponent is of choleric temper, irritate him,' quoted the young polymath.

This caused more amusement for the adults which made Fiona smile proudly.

'You may laugh, but I can tell you, Mr Serov has a foul temper. It doesn't take much to have him frothing like a rabid dog.'

Through his laughter Kit managed to say, 'Do you know, Billy Peel, who told us about you, said you'd pulled so many tricks on Serov, he felt sorry for the big man by the end. I think I understand better what he meant now.'

If anything, Fiona's smile grew wider. Being appreciated as a good chess player was one thing, having it come from Lord Kit Aston was quite another, but recognition for her skills in gamesmanship, seemed to represent the very pinnacle of praise.

Kit and Fiona resumed playing. This time they began to work through the implications of the moves suggested by Fiona. By the end of their session, Kit was feeling distinctly more optimistic than he had previously. However, he could not be sure the match would even take place. The context was so extraordinary, Kit half expected either Jellicoe or "C", to call a halt to proceedings.

28

Kit was sad to see Fiona leave for the hotel. She had been a tonic for him. For the three hours they had been together, he found his mind focused exclusively on chess rather than his oldest friend, Olly Lake. He sat alone gazing out of the window at a darkening sky. A knock at the door awoke him from the anguished trance. A moment later Miller appeared, 'Sir, there are a couple of men here to see you.'

Kit stood up and was greeted by two middle-aged men. One of them, he recognised vaguely. His hair was grey at the sides, but his clean-shaven face gave a more youthful appearance. This was the Commissioner of the Police for the Metropolis, Sir Nevil Macready.

'Sir Nevil,' said Kit before anyone could speak. He held his hand out.

'Your lordship, I'm flattered you remember me. May I introduce Chief Inspector Jellicoe from Scotland Yard.'

Kit and Jellicoe shook hands, 'Pleased to meet you Chief Inspector, I've heard many good things about you from mutual friends.'

'You're very kind,' replied the Chief Inspector. Despite his grave appearance, Kit's comment had pleased him, and he reddened slightly in embarrassment.

'I know this is a horrible time of night to call on anyone,' said Macready but would you care to join us for a meeting in Whitehall? I'm sure you can guess the subject.'

*

Twenty minutes later, their car drove along King Charles Street before pulling up outside a large grey-white building: Britain's Foreign Office. The three men walked up the steps and carried on through Dunbar Court with its impressive marble flooring and Doric columns. They went through a door that led to a small staircase. Moments later Kit found himself in a small reception area and then a large, wood-panelled office. Kit and Sir Nevil sat down after being introduced to the man behind the desk. Jellicoe was not introduced and remained standing, much to Kit's surprise.

The man behind the desk looked grave. On the few occasions Kit had met him previously, he had found George Curzon, 1st Earl Curzon of Kedleston, former Viceroy of India and now the, recently appointed, Foreign Secretary for His Majesty's Government, to be a pompous bore. For once, though, he had a good reason to be sombre. He rubbed the side of his temple and exhaled slowly.

'Thank you for giving us your time tonight and thank you also for helping us understand better the source of these vile murders. I don't have to tell you how serious this matter is.'

'No Foreign Secretary, I can see the potential ramifications.'

There was silence in the office for a few moments. Although barely on nodding acquaintance, Kit knew Curzon well enough to know that the Foreign Secretary liked long moments of reflection in his conversations before

223

pontificating. Often at length. Kit settled down for a long evening.

'The murder of British subjects by a foreign power on our own soil is clearly very serious. That this foreign power appears to be the Russian government adds an additional level of complication. They deny it of course, and we have no proof other than the letters and the possible identification of one Cheka agent. However, there are many aspects of these attacks that are, to say the least, odd.'

Kit nodded; this had been on his mind also. As arrogant as he found Curzon, Kit did not doubt for a moment that he had a first-class mind.

'I agree sir. It made no sense to me why they should choose such a public method for killing and then link it so obviously to the chess match.'

Curzon looked pointedly at the two policemen beside Kit and said sardonically, 'Not so obvious to the police.'

Kit felt sorry for the two policemen. He made a promise to himself to apologise to them afterwards and be more circumspect in his use of language on the handling of the case.

'What are your thoughts on this matter your Lordship?' asked Macready.

'Well, Sir Nevil, I think we need more proof before we should point the finger towards Russia. We need to communicate to the press on this to stop them creating a febrile atmosphere. On the specific matter of Russian involvement, I remember from my time in Russia before the revolution, Petrograd was chock-a-bloc with revolutionary factions. Groups would form, merge, disband, kill each other. It was chaos. My point is, there are still many groups in Russia and abroad who would happily see the Bolsheviks ousted.

You'll know more about this than I, but it could also be a new theatre in the Russian Civil War. The Russian theatre is nearing an end if what I hear is true. Perhaps Comintern are taking the attack to those who have overtly or tacitly supported the Whites.'

Curzon looked at Macready for a response.

'You believe these murders are an attempt to provoke His Majesty's Government into a response?' asked Macready.

'Possibly sir, if they really have been initiated by the Bolsheviks,' responded Kit.

'In which case they are a warning,' finished Curzon.

'Correct, Foreign Secretary, or perhaps, revenge for our involvement in Russia over the last few years,' said Kit.

'I think the less said about this, the better. As it stands, we need to find out the truth and soon. There are, shall we say, a few ministers in the government who favour a robust approach to this situation. The longer this matter remains unresolved, the stronger their hand in pushing through some form of renewed military intervention. This time it won't be by proxy. I think we all share a horror at this prospect.'

Kit and Macready, if not Jellicoe, recognised the reference to Curzon's former friend, Winston Churchill. Both nodded, Kit glanced at Macready. He knew Macready had seen active service during the War. He would understand.

Macready turned his attention to Jellicoe, who had remained silent during the meeting.

'Perhaps, Foreign Secretary, we should hear what Chief Inspector Jellicoe has to say. He is heading up the investigation of these horrible murders. What has your interrogation of Serov uncovered?'

225

Kit was shocked that Serov had been arrested, this was news to him. He looked at Jellicoe, fascinated to learn more about his opponent.

'Serov is either a very accomplished actor or he genuinely has no idea of what he's involved in.'

'Which is it, Jellicoe?' asked Curzon, rather curtly, to Kit's mind.

'The latter Foreign Secretary.'

'Why?'

'Firstly sir, our inquiries have shown that he was not in the vicinity of the murders when they are known to have taken place. In fact, he was not in the country when, we believe, Lord Lake was kidnapped. Secondly, I have it on good authority from people that we know who have more in-depth knowledge of the situation in Russia,' he glanced slyly at Kit, which brought a smile to both him and Macready, 'that Serov was not known to be an agent of Cheka. He is known to be a supporter of the Bolsheviks, but I understand he arrived somewhat late to the party, so to speak.'

Despite the situation, Kit found himself smiling at Jellicoe, and noted Macready's eyes twinkling also. He liked Jellicoe and all the more because he clearly was getting beneath the skin of portentous Foreign Secretary, who was obviously not amused. Jellicoe continued before Curzon could voice his disapproval.

'Finally, sir, I have over twenty years of experience in interviewing suspects. After a while, you develop a nose for it. I can't describe it exactly, but you have a sense if a man is capable of planning, commissioning, or undertaking personally, murder. This man isn't a murderer. He's a dupe. Plain and simple.'

Once again Kit found himself nodding in agreement. This was his opinion. Curzon noticed this also.

'You agree with this assessment?' he asked.

'Clearly, I do not have access to the evidence the Chief Inspector has, but I've met Serov before. He's a socialist, yes. He's certainly one of the most arrogant men I've met.'

Kit pondered for a moment if Serov was more arrogant than Curzon. It was close. On balance he had to give it to the British aristocrat as Serov could, at least, claim to be one of the top five exponents of the most cerebral game on earth.

'But I would concur with the Chief Inspector, he's no murderer,' added Kit quickly.

Curzon nodded unhappily.

'So, we release him then? And what of this chess match? You play tomorrow?'

It was Jellicoe who spoke.

'I believe it should continue,' said Jellicoe glancing at Macready. Kit noticed the exchange of looks and concluded they had agreed their answer.

Curzon appeared to ignore Jellicoe and looked at Macready, 'Why?'

A shadow of irritation passed over Macready's eyes but answered calmly, 'It will buy us more time to find Lord Lake, Foreign Secretary. In the meantime, we have circulated likenesses of the two men we believe responsible for these ghastly acts.'

Macready nodded to Jellicoe. The Chief Inspector fished out of his leather bag, two photostats. Each contained an artist's impression of the two men mentioned by Macready. This was the first time Kit had seen the two men. He looked intently at both. One of the men seemed familiar, he wore

227

glasses and had a moustache. Noticing his reaction, Jellicoe said, 'We believe this is Bergmann. Almost certainly an alias. According to Serov, he's not Russian but Latvian.'

'Has Serov told you much?'

'Not really, we've had more from Peel, frankly,' admitted Jellicoe. 'Serov is somewhat angry at his treatment and unhelpful, to say the least.'

This made Kit look up sharply at Jellicoe which, in turn, made Jellicoe smile.

'Mr Serov is not under any duress, but he's clearly displeased at being held in a cell. He was also somewhat hungover, sir. The hotel told us that he was on something of a bender the previous evening.'

Kit smiled, despite himself. It also made him wonder what would have prompted the usually serious-minded, Russian to cut loose in such a manner.

Macready added to Jellicoe's comments before the Foreign Secretary could weigh in, 'We'll release him tomorrow morning. We're not pressing charges.'

Kit smiled for a moment as Fiona Lawrence came into his mind. I can't believe I'm going to say this, he thought.

'Why not just keep him in the cell? Perhaps you could bring him to the venue tomorrow afternoon.'

Macready stared at Kit for a moment puzzled by this suggestion. Kit remained silent but with a half-smile.

'So, you wish him to remain in a prison cell up until you resume your match?'

Kit nodded.

'Not really cricket, is it?' said Macready, somewhat taken aback.

228

'Nor is murder, Commissioner,' interjected Curzon. 'I agree, lock him up and starve him if you wish. I don't care. Gentlemen, I think we're finished for this evening.'

'Have you any other photostats, Chief Inspector?' asked Kit as they left the Foreign Office building in Whitehall.

'Yes sir,' replied Jellicoe and handed Kit several more photostats. 'May I ask why you need them?'

'I know someone that can help us,' smiled Kit. His mood had lifted considerably since earlier in the evening. He felt reassured by the solid, straight-talking policeman. Jellicoe looked archly at Kit.

'Would you mind if I accompanied you to meet this person. It'd be better if our efforts are coordinated.'

Macready looked at the two men, 'I shall leave you gentlemen to the search. Good hunting.'

*

The police car took Kit and Jellicoe to an apartment building in South Kensington. The white walled apartments had a Palladian entrance. Kit looked with amusement at Jellicoe.

'How the other half live, Chief Inspector?'

Kit received an amused nod by way of reply. The door opened and an elderly man led Kit and Jellicoe up one flight of stairs to a wide corridor. The first door was already open, and Kit walked in followed by Jellicoe. A few minutes later the Chief Inspector was standing before the former Prime Minister of Russia, Alexander Kerensky.

After introductions were made, the three men sat down, and Kit briefly summarised the meeting he and Jellicoe had left with the Foreign Secretary and the Commissioner of Police. Kerensky looked grave as he listened to Kit's account of the murders and the kidnapping of their mutual friend, Lord Lake.

'I hate these men, Kit, with all my heart, but this is fantastical. Murders in Britain, kidnapping and all connected to a chess match? I've never heard of such things. Can we be sure it's the Bolsheviks?'

'It's highly likely, Alexander. Either this was a direct act by the Russian state against our country or the Russian government's lost control of its agents. Daniels has been,' said Kit indicating one of the Photostats, 'identified as Cheka. Bergmann, we know nothing of.'

Kerensky looked at the two Photostats. He spent a little more time scrutinising Bergmann.

'Yes,' said Kit, reading his mind, 'pity about the hat. There's something about him.'

Kerensky nodded, then regarded the two men, 'So what do you need from me, gentlemen?'

Jellicoe was happy to get down to business, 'I understand from his lordship that you've a great many contacts in the ex-patriot Russian community, particularly in North London.'

Kerensky smiled but only nodded.

Jellicoe continued, 'We lack the resource to go door to door with these artist impressions. Can we call on your help?'

'Of course, Chief Inspector. But do you really believe these men are likely to be found in Little Russia?' replied Kerensky.

'It's possible Prime Minister. We call it hiding in plain sight,' replied Jellicoe.

Kerensky smiled, 'Thank you Chief Inspector but I am no longer Prime Minister. You're probably aware but someone else is running my country now.'

230

The meeting concluded with Kerensky announcing his intention to leave right away to distribute the likenesses to friends in the ex-patriot community in Haringey.

'If they are in Little Russia, we'll know soon, gentlemen,' concluded Kerensky.

Kit was not sure if this raised his hopes but, in the absence of any other way forward, it gave him a sense of momentum.

'I hope so, Alexander, for Olly's sake.'

*

Around the same time as Kit and the Chief Inspector were meeting with Kerensky, a small lorry drove along Hampton Court Road. It stopped at a secluded mews at the side of the main entrance of the palace.

Kopel climbed out of the cabin and walked over to a security guard who had come out to greet them. Both Kopel and the security guard held clipboards. When dealing with petty officialdom, Kopel had two steadfast principles: take the high hand and carry a clip board. In an authoritative English accent, which impressed even Daniels, he quickly got to grips with the security guard blocking the entrance of the lorry.

Cedric Barnes was a twenty-seven-year veteran of security work. Tall but slight, his eyes were bovine brown. A smile was rarely near his face. This combination of seriousness and unapologetic stupidity had proved excellent credentials for the security work that had been his life.

'You're Barnes, aren't you?' said Kopel.

This took Barnes by surprise, for he was, indeed Barnes. In the twenty-seven years of employment in the security sector, no one had ever addressed him directly by name, or indeed, so peremptorily. He bristled but, at this moment, couldn't be sure of who he was dealing with.

231

'Yes sir,' replied Barnes, immediately regretting the use of sir.

'Good, good, come over here will you,' continued Kopel, affecting an impeccable English mien, somewhere between arrogance with and outright contempt for, the lower orders.

To the credit of Barnes, years of being a petty official meant he was not easily cowed, even by his superiors. It was one of the perks of an, otherwise, low paid job that he could use his position to stand up to authority.

'You can't bring this thing,' said Barnes, indicating the lorry, 'in here. Your name's not on the list.'

Barnes felt a stab in his stomach, as he realised, he had not actually checked the manifest. He hoped his assertion was true or the battle would be lost immediately. Kopel was unperturbed and said in an off-hand manner.

'Show me.'

Barnes handed him the manifest, praying he was right. Kopel made a great show of reading through the contents of the clipboard.

'This is ridiculous, we need to speak to Hesketh immediately, Barnes. I'm going to give him a piece of my mind. This is intolerable.'

To give someone a piece of your mind in England was the penultimate indication of dissatisfaction, just behind disembowelling your enemy. Barnes was now on the back foot, and he knew it. The man before him was clearly acquainted with Samuel Hesketh, the Palace manager. This man, he acknowledged, not only exuded authority there was also a growing rage discernible in his eyes, burning like an inferno. Barnes quickly concluded that Hesketh would not be overjoyed with him if he continued to block the delivery. He changed tack.

'Mr Hesketh left hours ago. I'm not sure I can disturb him at this time of night.'

Kopel glared at Barnes, causing him to cower internally. This was getting out of hand. He needed to regain some sort of control.

'What exactly, are you delivering?'

'What do you mean by exactly? Who do you think you are dealing with exactly, my man? I shall have a word with Hesketh about you.'

Daniels flinched. He was worried that Kopel was overplaying his hand. Daniels wasn't the only one flinching from the onslaught. Barnes was beginning to wilt under the impact also. He attempted one last sally.

'I need to check all deliveries,' said Barnes before adding, 'sir.'

Kopel could smell victory and mollified his tone. He nodded to Daniels, who also stepped down from the cabin. Daniels went around to the back of the lorry and opened it up. Inside was, to the eyes of the security man, a coffin.

'What does this box contain?' asked Barnes.

'A waxwork of Sir Thomas More,' responded Bergmann. He stepped over to the box and opened the lid. Barnes peered at it. It was difficult to see it properly as it was covered in straw, but it certainly looked lifelike to Barnes. Furthermore, he had no idea what the former Lord Chancellor looked like.

Barnes could think of no further objections and gave Kopel keys to the back entrance of the Palace. There was no thank you as Kopel and Daniels swept off into the Palace grounds.

Fifteen minutes later, the lorry returned. Kopel climbed out and returned the keys to the cowed security guard.

'It will be well for you, my man, if you forget this ever happened. I might consider not reporting my displeasure to Hesketh.'

Barnes nodded obsequiously, relieved that the matter might end there. Such was his state of discomposure he failed to notice that, oddly, it was Kopel who was driving. Furthermore, he was no longer accompanied by Daniels. Instead, Barnes returned to station and sat down with a thump. He took off his cap and threw it on the desk and prayed earnestly for a quiet night. This had been enough excitement for one evening.

29

London: 9th January 1920

Early next morning, Kit had arranged to meet up with Fiona Lawrence to go through some last-minute preparation in the afternoon and the completion of his match. While he waited for Fiona to arrive, he looked down again at the two photostat artist impressions of Bergmann and Daniels. He hoped against hope that the assistance of Kerensky would reap a reward. They badly needed a break.

An idea occurred to Kit as he gazed at the picture of Bergmann. He turned to Bright, who was finishing his breakfast.

'Richard, this chap Bergmann rings a bell with me from somewhere. Can you ask Esther to do me a favour?'

'Of course. Name it,' replied Bright.

Kit handed the photostat to Bright and said, 'Ask her if she can draw me a new version of the person in the photostat, only without either the glasses or the moustache. It's like a disguise out of some penny blood.'

Bright laughed, 'I know what you mean. I think that moustache fell out of fashion around 1892.'

'Thanks – it's really important. I'd love to see what he really looks like.'

Bright nodded, 'We'll bring it to Hampton Court for the match. How are you feeling about it?'

Kit smiled and replied, 'Well, since meeting Fiona Lawrence, a lot better. She's really quite something.'

Bright laughed, 'We both look forward to meeting this young prodigy. It's a pity she's not playing him.'

This was greeted with a laugh from Kit who nodded his head, 'I think she'd be a better opponent. She's already drawn with him. Didn't fancy him one bit. She's desperate for me to beat him. We worked through some interesting approaches, and when I say interesting, I mean it. I'll tell you after.'

As they were speaking the phone rang. Miller answered it. Moments later he said to Kit, 'Sir, it's the police.'

*

Fiona Lawrence stepped into the lift accompanied by Miss Upritchard. She looked up at the other woman in the lift. The young woman seemed like someone from a film or a magazine. Fiona could not stop looking at her. The young woman noticed this and smiled at the girl.

'I'm sorry. It's just, well, you're so beautiful,' admitted Fiona openly.

The young woman laughed, 'That's so kind of you, thank you. You've made my day and it's not even started.'

Even her voice, thought Fiona.

Miss Upritchard was having none of this, 'I'm so sorry madam. Fiona, I've told you before about disturbing people.'

The young woman immediately leapt to the Fiona's defence, 'Please don't, it was a lovely thing to say. I wouldn't ever change, Fiona.'

Fiona Lawrence beamed triumphantly.

'I'm Esther Cavendish,' said the young woman, holding out her hand, 'and perchance, are you Fiona Lawrence?'

It was difficult at that moment to decide whose mouth dropped further, Fiona or Miss Upritchard. Fiona could not speak and merely nodded. This brought a sympathetic smile from Esther.

'I believe we've a mutual friend in Lord Kit Aston.'

Fiona's head whirled in disbelief, 'You know Kit?'

Esther laughed, 'Very well. He's going to marry my sister, I hope. Are you both going to breakfast now?'

Both Fiona and Miss Upritchard were still finding speech difficult in the presence of this supernatural being. Both nodded.

'Well then, I insist you join me for breakfast. I want to hear all of what you've planned for Mr Serov.'

The next twenty minutes was entertaining for Esther and magical for Fiona Lawrence. Even the frosty disposition of Miss Upritchard melted in the face of Esther's serene charm. Fiona heard Miss Upritchard laugh with a spontaneity that she had never heard before. It seemed to transform her face and body into someone who Fiona could not recognise but wanted to know.

It was so fascinating that Fiona became quieter. Instead, she allowed Miss Upritchard and Esther to chat to one another. The naturalness of Esther coupled with her inner grace was working wonders in getting Miss Upritchard to talk. From the conversation, Fiona learned more about Miss Upritchard in a matter of minutes than she had in the last five years. Miss Upritchard seemed to be changing before her eyes.

Or maybe it was she who was changing. With more than a sense of guilt she realised how little effort she'd made to get to

237

know Miss Upritchard. Her life had been centred around chess, and education. The people around her had been treated like servants for her prodigious talent. She couldn't remember the last time she had thanked any of them for their help. The thought of how much she had taken Miss Upritchard, and the rest of the parish community, for granted over the years brought a wave of self-reproach in the young girl. With a dawning realisation she was learning who this person was and who she should be.

Tears formed in her eyes. She fought hard to control her emotions. To cry now, she understood, would be yet another act of selfishness. Instead, she forced herself to listen to the two women talk to one another. They spoke of Esther's upcoming nuptials. Love radiated out of Esther.

No, there was no one special in her life, admitted Miss Upritchard. This surprised Esther who pointed out what Fiona Lawrence had just seen for the first time; Miss Upritchard was a very attractive woman. A glance at Fiona caused Miss Upritchard to redden and nothing more was said.

The conversation was interrupted by the arrival of Bright. This caused Fiona to gasp as she was introduced.

'My goodness, you're all so glamorous down here,' said Fiona. Bright laughed as did Esther. 'I mean it. You're even better looking than Kit.'

'Fiona,' said the old Miss Upritchard, but perhaps with less intensity. He was very handsome.

'I wouldn't go that far, Fiona,' said Bright modestly.

'I would,' laughed Esther conspiratorially.

*

Jellicoe walked through the flat and into the room where, he presumed, Lake had been held. There were two beds, both

238

of which had been left unmade. The room smelled of stale sweat and cigarettes. He looked at the window but a nearby policeman shook his head. The windows were nailed shut.

'Fingerprints?' asked Jellicoe to a nearby officer.

'Someone is on their way, sir.'

Jellicoe nodded and escaped from the room. His inspection, as brief as it had been, told him that there was no sign of obvious violence. If Lake was dead then he had been killed elsewhere. Hopefully, he was still alive. Jellicoe found this prospect increasingly difficult to believe. The release of the pictures to the newspapers had always risked hastening the death of the captive. Their one chance was the kidnappers would still be playing by their own rules and waiting for the chess game to progress further.

Outside, he saw the newest member of Scotland Yard, albeit on a temporary basis. Alexander Kerensky was talking to star struck dwellers of the apartment block, on behalf of the police. His involvement had been a coup for the police. It guaranteed the support of many ex-patriot Russians in the Haringey area, and it delivered a swift result. Sadly, not swift enough, reflected Jellicoe.

Jellicoe approached the former Prime Minister. He was speaking to a man wearing a vest and with an unshaven, jowly face. Kerensky was unshaven too. Jellicoe wondered if he had been up all night. His next thought was around what kind of debt Kerensky owed Kit or Lord Lake.

'Chief Inspector, may I introduce Pavel Rodchenko. He lives next door to this flat.'

Jellicoe shook hands with Rodchenko.

'Mr Rodchenko has identified Daniels and Olly. He hasn't seen Bergmann. In fact, no one I've spoken to has seen him.'

239

'How was Lord Lake?' asked Jellicoe.

'He only saw him once, a few days ago. But he seemed well. He mentions another man, too. Quite young, same age as Olly. He was also in the flat, but he hasn't seen him since.'

'When was this?'

'Just before new year,' responded Kerensky.

Jellicoe nodded. This was a development, the possibility of yet another gang member. He looked at Rodchenko and then back to Kerensky.

'Would he be able to describe this man to a police artist?'

Kerensky spoke in Russian to the neighbour and then turned to Jellicoe.

'He could try but it was dark and quite a few days ago.'

'I understand but it's vital. I'll have someone come to you.'

The Russian seemed to understand and nodded his head. Kerensky and Jellicoe left the man and walked out of the building. The neighbour was the prime witness as few other people had seen the men.

'I'll let his lordship know what's happened. I'm sure he's very concerned about his friend,' said Jellicoe.

Kerensky looked sombre, 'We all are.'

'You knew him,' said Jellicoe before correcting himself, 'sorry, know him well?'

'Yes. He was, how shall I put it, dating my secretary, Kristina.'

Jellicoe was shocked by this revelation and asked, 'You were happy about this arrangement?'

It was Kerensky's turn to smile now, 'You mean a British agent dating the secretary to the Russian Prime Minister?'

'Well, yes, as a matter of fact. I'm not sure if it would be tolerated here,' laughed Jellicoe.

'True and ordinarily, I suppose, I would have stopped it. Or, perhaps, asked Kristina to leave. But those were not ordinary times. We had common enemies, and, in truth, British money was propping up our government and war effort. Kit, Olly, and the others were a support for me and even saved my life. A story for another day, however.'

The two men parted: Kerensky to his bed and Jellicoe to bring a man to a chess match.

*

The morning at the police station was proving no more amenable to Serov's mood than his first evening. Thankfully, the hangover was nothing more than an unpleasant memory and a warning to future excess. However, incarceration was a desolate experience. It reminded him of his childhood, assaulted his senses and worst of all, disturbed his preparations for the match. He felt in no mood to play. By now, he was hoping the chaos around the murder investigation would mean a cancellation or, at the very least, a postponement.

A knock at the door caused Serov to sit upright in his bed. Into the cell walked Jellicoe. Oddly, Serov quite liked Jellicoe. There was something about the seriousness of the policeman, a quiet dignity which made him seem more trustworthy than most. He sensed also that Jellicoe knew he wasn't connected to the murders although it scarcely seemed credible that either Bergmann or Kopel were either. Daniels and Fechin he was less sure of.

'Mr Serov, would you mind accompanying me to the interview room?'

Rather than answer, Serov rose to his feet and trooped out of the cell behind the Chief Inspector. They returned to the same room and Serov took his old seat. A new, even younger

241

policeman stood in the room with them. Jellicoe introduced him as Sergeant Ryan.

'Mr Serov, we've found a flat in the part of London known as Little Russia. Are you familiar with this flat?'

'No,' said Serov. He knew better now than to ask questions. The quicker he answered, the quicker the interview would conclude.

'When did you arrive in Britain?'

'Your New Year's Day.'

It took Jellicoe a moment to register that the Russian calendar differed from Britain's.

'In Edinburgh.'

'Correct.'

This effectively discounted Serov from being the other man identified by Rodchenko, although he would still have this checked by his team. It had only been a faint possibility anyway for Jellicoe as he was convinced Serov had no knowledge of the activities of his companions.

'One final thing before we bring you to your appointment with Lord Kit Aston,' said Jellicoe, noting the look of dismay on Serov's face, 'We really would appreciate if you could supply a description of Mr Kopel. You must appreciate Mr Serov, these men you were with are implicated in very serious crimes.'

Serov nodded but could not hide his consternation. He just wanted to go home, wherever that was. If his country was really murdering citizens of another country then it depressed him to think of returning, having been a dupe for these crimes.

'What do you want me to do?' asked Serov. His heart was heavy, his spirit exhausted and entropy inhabited his very core.

Jellicoe nodded to the young policeman. He opened the door and moments later another man walked in, carrying a sketch pad. He seemed a flamboyant character, with long hair and a, distinctly, colourful waistcoat.

'This is Mr Watts. Would you mind describing Kopel to him and he will draw a likeness which we can circulate to other police officers who are looking for him?'

Jellicoe stood up and Watts walked over, moving the seat around to be beside Serov.

'I'll come back in twenty minutes and then, perhaps we'll look to head to Hampton Court. I'm sorry about all this Mr Serov. I imagine you're feeling angry about having spent a night in a police cell. We felt it was for the best. These men are very dangerous. It was actually for your protection,' said Jellicoe, reddening at the outrageous lie he was telling.

The look on Serov's face told Jellicoe it had worked. He had turned white as the realisation hit him. Aston will be delighted, thought Jellicoe, although he harboured a slight sympathy for the hapless grandmaster.

'Right,' said Watts, placing the drawing pad on his knee, forming his hands into a steeple and fixing Serov with an unnerving stare, 'Tell me what this naughty man looks like.'

30

Early afternoon, Hampton Court Great Hall had witnessed many great events of state over the centuries. This was surely not one of them, reflected Kit as he looked around. The Hall was filling up with people who filed around its edge. In the middle, roped off from the audience, was a small table with a chess board atop. A large mirror was suspended over the table enabling the audience to view proceedings. They could have been in a Parisian bordello. At the far end of the Hall, also roped off, were some waxwork models of Henry VIII with his advisors.

Kit was standing inside the roped off area. He looked up at the tapestries adorning the Great Hall. They showed ten scenes from the life of the prophet Abraham. This was not the first time Kit had gazed at the series. As ever, he was impressed not just by the intricate workmanship containing dozens of figures but also by their scale.

Looking at each of them, Kit wondered if Henry had commissioned them to make a point to the world. Perhaps he wanted the world to believe that the three Abrahamic religions of the world, Judaism, Christianity, and Islam, now had a fourth branch, the Church of England. He smiled to himself at the ridiculousness of the idea.

The hum in the Hall was gradually becoming louder as excitement grew amongst the onlookers. Serov was still to arrive. Esther, Bright and Fiona were also absent, noted Kit dolefully. He felt as if he were in the lion's den. The sight of his friends and coach would be a lift. He did see Billy Peel arrive and the two men nodded to one another. Peel moved through the audience to a position where he would be facing Kit.

Beside Kit stood Sir John Ormerod Scarlett Thursby, long time President of the British Chess Federation. Kit had known Thursby for many years and considered him a friend. Around sixty years old, Thursby had been a leading light in British Chess for many years, helping found the Federation of which he had been President for fifteen years. Thursby glanced up at Kit and smiled. The dimples on the side of his face deepened.

'How are you feeling old boy?'

'Like Isaac, John,' said Kit nodding up to the tapestry showing Abraham about to take a knife to his son, Isaac, before being stopped by an angel.

Thursby laughed at the Biblical allusion before pointing out, 'It worked out well in the end, Kit. Have faith.'

Kit raised his eyebrows doubtfully. He was tired and in no mood to play. His mind was caught in its own No Man's Land between missing Mary on one side and Serov and the murders related to the chess match on the other. As his mood darkened, the commotion in the Hall rose a number of levels.

'I think your man is here,' said Thursby.

'I'm missing my angel,' smiled Kit sadly.

Serov had indeed arrived, flanked by Jellicoe and another police officer. His face looked like murder. Kit flinched, not a little guiltily. However, Serov seemed none the worse for his trials. In fact, the sympathetic Jellicoe, uncomfortable at the gamesmanship employed by Kit, had allowed Serov to return to his hotel to wash, shave and generally tidy himself up.

The two men shook hands but not before Serov, through gritted teeth said, 'So much for English fair play.'

Kit smiled in response, there was little point in being in denial about it. Thursby could sense the antagonism between the two men and decided not to delay any further the finish of the match.

'Let's make it a clean fight, gentlemen,' said Thursby in a stage whisper. This made Kit's grin grow bigger and even Serov face softened momentarily.

'Ladies, gentlemen, children and members of the press,' said Thursby, which provoked an amused titter, 'The Great Hall at Hampton Court is now almost four hundred years old. Let us for a moment ponder the many great personages who have walked in this room. Henry VIII, Elizabeth I, Cromwell, perhaps even the Bard, himself. It now gives host to two of the foremost chess players in the world, Filip Serov and, our own, Lord Kit Aston. As many of you will have read, these gentlemen have been engaged in a correspondence match which has gripped the nation.'

Kit glanced at Thursby archly, causing the President to smile.

'Well, certainly, the British Chess Federation, anyway.' More laughter in the Hall before Thursby continued, 'We will now witness the conclusion of this fascinating encounter. Gentlemen, if you will take your seats. May I request, though I realise I hardly need do so, that we have silence for the duration of this match. White to move.'

Kit and Serov walked slowly, like condemned men, towards the table. It was clear to Kit that Serov was as nervous as he was, or perhaps it was the trauma of the last twenty-four hours. Both paused for a moment at the seats waiting for the other to sit first. A moment's confusion passed and then both sat down. Kit was gratified to see the table sides were covered, remembering something Fiona Lawrence had said. Just as he was thinking this, he saw Esther and Bright arrive in the company of the young genius and her guardian. Kit waved at the new arrivals. He felt better for seeing them.

The black mood of Serov had not lifted since arriving at the venue. As he suspected, Jellicoe was fundamentally a decent man, and he was grateful to have had the chance to return to the hotel. But a lingering anger remained over his treatment. Seeing the big crowd gathered within a grand monument to the oppression of the poor aggravated the Russian further. He would have preferred to dispatch Aston within the confines of a small room with knowledgeable onlookers bearing witness to his humiliation. Instead, the alleged crimes committed by his companions, the possibility of his having been deceived and used as a dupe in their plan had cast a gloom over his enthusiasm for what lay ahead. He fought to regain his motivation and focus. Then he saw Aston waving gaily at someone.

*

Reproducing the artist impression had taken Esther longer than anticipated. Her preference in her own work was for landscape. She hadn't tried portraiture since childhood. Thankfully, Bright found Fiona Lawrence delightful company, and the time passed quickly for them. For Esther, it went too quickly. Acutely aware of the need to finish the drawing in

247

time for the match, and make it useful for Kit, put her under a great deal of pressure.

Finally, after an hour and half struggling with the likeness, Esther felt satisfied with what she had accomplished. She brought the completed drawing over to Bright and Fiona Lawrence who, noted Esther with a smile, gave every impression of having developed an enormous crush on her fiancé. Miss Upritchard also seemed very much taken with Bright. Join the club, thought Esther.

As was her habit, Fiona reacted excitedly and with great enthusiasm for Esther's efforts. Miss Upritchard was more guarded approval. Bright gave a more romantic demonstration of his approbation, which had Fiona grinning broadly and Miss Upritchard reprimanding her with a look.

Esther looked at Bright with concern and said, 'He looks familiar, doesn't he?'

Bright nodded grimly, 'He does. Kit won't be happy.'

'Time to go, we'll have to take a taxi,' said Esther, picking up her coat. 'Let's hope traffic is not too bad.'

It was.

They arrived at Hampton Court just as the match was scheduled to start. All four ran towards the Great Hall, as the clock struck two. Outside the Palace were a handful of tourists and, thankfully, a small queue to get in. The drizzly weather had probably deterred people from coming. An ambulance pulled up at the entrance also, just as the four entered the Palace.

*

Serov turned around to see who had attracted Kit's attention. If his mood had been one of resentment before, it

248

turned volcanic when he spied Fiona Lawrence. The young demon had been helping Aston!

Serov spun around and glared at Kit, who simply shrugged his shoulders and smiled off-handily. He turned around again and glared at the hell cat, who returned his glare, before sticking her tongue out at him.

Unsure if returning this gesture would be becoming of the dignity of a grandmaster or indeed an adult, for that matter, Serov returned his focus onto the game. The only way to answer this kind of provocation, he decided, was to put the man in front of him, metaphorically given the circumstances, to the sword.

And then Kit made his first move.

He sacrificed his Queen.

There was an audible intake of breath, and that was just from Serov. A whispered clamour was quickly shushed by Sir John. Serov stared first at what Kit had done and then turned around to Fiona Lawrence. She looked as innocent as Satan. Glaring at Kit, Serov responded, as he had no choice, by taking the Queen off the board. Kit quickly made his next move, which took Serov's Castle.

Fiona Lawrence's eyes never left Serov. At twelve years old, she had developed an acute sense of people. She had heard tell of a card game called poker which intrigued her as it seemed to be as much about reading your opponents as strict probability. One day, she would learn how to play, go to America, into a saloon, where it was played, according to the penny westerns she read, and make a lot of money. Her reading of Serov now was highly accurate.

Serov was angry, very angry. This made him more prone to make mistakes, but she also sensed the rage in him was cold

249

rather than hot. This could spell trouble as, for all her confidence in her own ability, she had to acknowledge Serov's great skills at chess would likely uncover different lines of attack than she and Kit had considered. This would be a risk. Her only hope was the certainty that Serov had never prepared this end game.

In this she was right. Serov gaped at the bloodbath in front of him. It was unsettling partly because he was certain Aston and the she-devil would have prepared it and, mainly, because they could be certain he hadn't. Serov hated uncertainty. He hated untidiness. He hated chaos. This is what he gazed down at, aware of Aston, smiling at him. The rage swelled further. As Fiona had surmised, it was cold.

Serov began to focus on what he saw. As he collected his thoughts, he took stock of his situation. He was a Queen up. Over time this advantage would surely tell. Unless the sprite had another trick up Aston's sleeve, he would surely triumph if he stayed calm and remained patient. Just as he was about to make a move, he felt a sharp pain in his shin.

Kit had kicked him under the table!

Incredulous he glowered at Aston. When the witch had done this to him previously, an innate decency had stopped him from responding. This time he had no such compunction. He kicked Aston back.

Incredulity turned to astonishment and then doubt as his foot met something that felt like wood. He'd kicked Kit's prosthetic limb. The look on Serov's face made Kit grin broadly. Meanwhile Serov was resisting the urge to look under the table. Kit smiled back at him and whispered, 'The War.'

While all of this was going on, the audience was blissfully unaware of what was happening. All except one. Fiona

Lawrence recognised the exchange of blows. She was surprised that Serov had responded in kind. Much to her surprise, she felt a grudging respect for the Russian for his reaction. He's learning, she thought.

Returning his focus to the match, Serov considered his options. He felt that whatever had been planned was academic. The plain fact of the matter was that black had the advantage and his skills would be enough to carry the day. An inspiration struck him. His two opponents would have banked on his hatred of disorder, his remorseless logic based on percentage play. What if he raised the stakes? He moved his Castle to take Kit's remaining Bishop.

Another audible gasp erupted from the audience. Serov was sacrificing his Castle. Peel, Bright and Esther looked around at the shocked faces of the onlookers, many of whom were Federation members. Peel leaned down to Fiona Lawrence.

'What just happened?'

But Fiona couldn't answer. She was in a state of shock also. Neither she nor Kit had anticipated this. She looked at Kit. Kit looked back at her; his eyes widened. She shook her head. He was on his own now.

Serov had noted with satisfaction the look on Kit's face. His gamble had paid off insofar as it had clearly isolated Kit from his preparations. However, it diluted his advantage significantly. Despite his belief in his superior ability, he was not going to underestimate the English lord. He was a fine player. The memory of his first match, and defeat by Aston, acted as a cautionary reminder to stay concentrated on his task. The match was already complicated enough without hubris influencing his strategy as it had before.

Fiona Lawrence turned to Billy Peel. Beside Peel, Miller, Esther, Bright and Jellicoe leaned in to hear what she had to say.

'We didn't prepare for Serov to sacrifice his Castle,' admitted Fiona.

'What does this mean, Fiona?' asked Esther, looking concerned.

Fiona was silent for a moment. She chewed her bottom lip.

'Kit will have to play the game of his, and his friend's, life.'

*

31

The move by Serov had taken by Kit by surprise. He reprimanded himself for making this so obvious. The smile on Serov's face was enough to tell him he scented blood. It had been too long since he'd played competitively. He wasn't just playing the game; he was playing the man too. Serov now knew that he was in uncharted territory. Kit's only comfort was knowing this was the case for Serov, too. It wasn't much comfort though. He was at a material disadvantage against one of the best players in the world. Frankly, he thought, it would take a miracle for this to result in anything but defeat.

But fortune was to smile on Kit.

The Hall seemed to pulsate with excitement at the first series of moves. Sir John felt compelled, from time to time, to gesticulate to the audience to remain quiet. This was a losing battle. Watching two masters of the game locked in mortal-ish combat was the very stuff of chess boy's own stories. Even Sir John was absorbed in the encounter. Like Fiona Lawrence, he saw Kit's situation as desperately difficult, although not impossible. One look at some of his fellow members told him they were not optimistic about British success.

Nor was Kit. In his assessment, there were less than a dozen moves remaining. Worse, his two Castles, were vulnerable. Sitting in the Great Hall at Hampton Court, he had no idea what this meant for his friend Olly Lake.

Remembering the advice of Fiona Lawrence, he studied the board with a view to disrupting Serov's strategy. He moved his King to attack Serov's remaining Knight. It was Serov's turn to look surprised, which Kit noted with grim satisfaction. A glance at Fiona Lawrence showed she was surprised also, but not in a despondent way.

And then it happened.

At the back of the Hall behind the audience, there was a muffled thump. It was audible because just before, Sir John had quietened the room down again with a movement of his hand. The sound of the thump was greeted with cries of distress.

Kit glanced up to see what was happening. He saw Jellicoe, who had been standing in his line of sight move towards the disturbance. The crowd seemed to be gathered in a circle around something. Kit stood up from his seat and made his way over towards Jellicoe. Making his way through the crowd, Kit arrived to see Jellicoe and the other policeman kneeling over a prone body.

Jellicoe put his hand on the neck of the man lying on the ground. He looked up as Kit emerged from the crowd.

'What happened?' exclaimed Kit.

Jellicoe shook his head, and shouted over the hubbub, 'Search me. He's still alive, thank God.'

Kit knelt beside the man and looked at his face.

'Is this Lord Lake?' asked Jellicoe.

'No,' replied Kit, 'I think this is Adam Walsh.'

Jellicoe looked none the wiser.

'Lord Walsh of Trent. I thought he was off travelling in the Far East or somewhere,' explained Kit.

'He needs a hospital. It looks like he might've been drugged.'

Kit looked up and saw Esther standing with Bright and Miss Upritchard. He stood up gingerly and went over to his friends.

'What happened Kit?' asked Esther.

Kit quickly explained who the man was. As he did so, he looked over to the chess table. Fiona Lawrence was standing near the table looking at the board intently. Serov was on his feet, glaring at her. Clearly there was little love lost between the two of them. He saw Fiona Lawrence look up from the table and return Serov's gaze.

Serov sensed Kit was looking at him. Both were unsure about what to do. Kit walked over to Serov and Fiona Lawrence.

'It looks like your comrades have struck again.'

'I knew nothing,' replied Serov angrily.

Kit held his hands up, 'I believe you Filip. We've both been made fools off, I'm afraid.'

Serov glared at Kit and then his features softened a little. He nodded and then looked at the board, before returning his gaze to Kit. Serov shrugged a question.

'Draw?' suggested Kit, holding his hand out.

'Draw,' replied Serov, not without some relief. He turned to Fiona Lawrence. They looked at one another for a few moments and then Serov held out his hand to her also.

This surprised Fiona and she took a quick look at Kit. She could see he was smiling.

'Let's be honest, Fiona, it took the two of us to reach this point,' acknowledged Kit.

She shook Serov's hand. They looked at one another, impassively, like two warriors after battle, with peace declared and respect won on both sides.

Over by the crowd, it was apparent that Lord Walsh was being removed by the ambulance men. Jellicoe was walking towards Kit accompanied by Esther, Bright and Miss Upritchard.

'That was quick,' said Kit indicating the ambulance men.

Jellicoe seemed not to notice, instead he said, 'Miss Esther Cavendish has shown me a sketch you asked her to do of this chap Bergmann.'

Kit exclaimed, 'Of course.' He slapped his forehead with the palm of his hand. 'Did you bring the drawing with you Esther?'

Esther nodded and handed her work over to Kit. Over Kit's shoulder, Serov glanced at the drawing, with a puzzled frown.

Taking the drawing in his hands Kit stared at it in disbelief. Jellicoe registered the reaction and said, 'What's wrong Kit?'

'I know who Bergmann is.'

*

The ride in the police car was a grim affair. Kit looked out of the window unwilling to say much. Outside dark clouds ushered in the evening and the prospect of rain. Jellicoe sensed Kit's troubled mood and remained quiet for the duration of the journey across the centre of London. The situation was now clearer, but some things remained frustratingly opaque. His mind raced around the possibilities. One thought disturbed him. He tried to cast it from his mind, but it remained. It infected his mood tossing him into a stormy sea of doubt and fear.

256

Twenty minutes later they had arrived at their destination. Jellicoe looked around and realised they were the first.

'We should wait until we have more officers,' advised Jellicoe.

Kit nodded sullenly. He didn't believe the officers would be needed but was too downhearted to argue. Although it had barely gone five, the skies were dark and brooding. The icy air licked against Kit's face, invaded his pores, and enveloped his bones. He felt profoundly sad.

Finally, at the top of the road he could see several police cars arriving. He wasn't sure if he should feel relief. He returned his gaze to the apartment block. Something was wrong. He had missed a connection. It was there in front of him. He could almost touch it.

Three cars pulled up. There were around ten policemen in all. Jellicoe assembled them quickly and briefly summarised the situation. Kit was to follow them up to the apartment, but the police officers would enter first. Kit could see they were armed. He turned to Jellicoe.

'I understand the need to be careful Chief Inspector, but I'm not sure about all of this,' said Kit, indicating the weaponry.

The police ran up the steps and banged on the front door. No answer. Several of the larger men used a wooden battering ram to force open the front door to the apartments. They ascended the first flight of stairs, followed by Kit and Jellicoe. The door was partly open when they arrived.

Kit and Jellicoe arrived at the top of the stairs. The other policemen looked at them expectantly. Stepping forward, with Kit, Jellicoe peered inside to an unlit corridor. He looked at Kit, and then wrapped the knocker on the door.

257

*

Roger Ratcliff sat at the table. On the table was a bottle of Chivas Regal, some pills, and the Daily Herald. His eyes were red, but no tears could fall. He looked down at the front page. Dominating the cover were police artist impressions of two men.

The room was dark save for a table lamp on the bureau behind him. He took a sip of the whisky and let it gently glide down his throat. He shut his eyes. It tasted of ripe, honeyed apples. He would miss this. Ratcliff became aware of Colin Cornell beside him. He looked up at Cornell and saw him gazing at the front page.

'Quite a good likeness, don't you think,' said Cornell.

'Yes, to be fair to them, they've done a good job,' replied Ratcliff

'How long do you think it will be?' asked Cornell.

Ratcliff looked up at his friend then shook his head.

'I thought they'd be here by now. Perhaps they had to play the game first. I don't know.' Ratcliff took another sip of the whisky. He lifted the glass up to the light and then set it down. Reaching over to the bottle, he poured a generous measure into his tumbler. He lifted the bottle towards Cornell. His friend didn't look interested and rubbed the back of his head again.

'Are you sure, Colin? It'll do wonders for that headache of yours.'

'And the next morning?' responded Cornell sardonically.

'What next morning Colin?'

As Ratcliff said this, they heard a door crash open downstairs. Footsteps followed up the stairs. Moments later they heard their front door knocker.

A voice he did not recognise shouted 'Police.'

Ratcliff looked up once more to Cornell then said in a voice just audible enough to be heard, 'In here. I'm unarmed.'

*

Hearing Ratcliff's voice, the policemen took out and readied their revolvers. Kit stepped in front of them and Jellicoe, holding his hand up.

'No. Let me.'

Jellicoe looked unhappy and said, 'Your lordship, I must insist. He may be armed. There may be others in there armed. We can't take a chance.'

'No Chief Inspector. I know this man. Follow me. No guns please.'

Not waiting for a response Kit walked through the door followed by an unhappy Jellicoe. He walked along a short corridor and through to the main living room. It was dark save for a small table lamp lit behind Ratcliff. Kit's eyes went straight to Ratcliff sitting at the table. He could see the half-drunk bottle of whisky and the newspaper, with the pictures of Bergmann and Daniels on the front. Jellicoe stood beside Kit and for a moment there was silence in the room.

'What have you done Roger?' asked Kit, his voice barely a whisper.

'You have to believe me Kit, I knew nothing of what was happening,' replied Ratcliff. The tears began to stream down his face. He lifted his hand to wipe his cheek. It was then Kit saw the pills on the table.

'What are those?' Kit asked in a stronger voice.

'It's too late Kit,' rasped Ratcliff, 'but you must believe me. I knew nothing of the murders until I saw the newspaper. He used me. He betrayed us, Kit. I see that now.

259

'Who Ratcliff?' interjected Jellicoe, 'Kopel?'

Ratcliff nodded but looked up at Kit, 'He used me to get to you Kit. I'm so sorry Kit.'

'Roger, what's their plan? Tell me quickly,' said Kit, now over by the table standing over Ratcliff.

'Ask Colin, he'll tell you Kit,' said Ratcliff weakly, 'I knew nothing.'

'Who is Colin?' demanded Jellicoe loudly, 'Tell me man.'

But it was too late. Ratcliff's face fell forward, his lifeless still eyes open.

Jellicoe turned wildly to Kit, 'What did he mean, ask Colin?'

Kit turned to Jellicoe. His face was desolate but there was something else. Jellicoe looked at Kit. The tall lord was shaking his head in puzzlement.

'I don't understand,' said Kit, 'Colin Cornell?'

Part 3: End Game

32

Petrograd, Russia: 11th November 1917 (November 23rd, 1917) - Early morning

'We've been betrayed,' said Ratcliff to the assembled men in the room. Kit, Olly Lake and Colin Cornell looked at their commanding officer. None of them seemed surprised by this announcement.

'It's been coming,' said Cornell, 'Too many people know us now.'

'Somewhat defeated the notion of the Far-Reaching System, don't you think?' said Lake sourly. This brought a sharp look from Ratcliff to Lake, who merely shrugged nonchalantly.

'You may think this a time for your brand of humour, Olly, I don't,' admonished Ratcliff, although not too strongly, 'The plain fact is we have to leave Petrograd until we're in a position to return. We'll need to create new identities. I'm fairly certain Hoare's team will also have to leave.'

Kit finally spoke up, 'So what are our instructions? Who stays, who goes?'

Ratcliff nodded to Kit, thankful to return to the reason for the meeting.

'Kit, you and Colin will make your way to Helsingfors. A launch will take you to Kronstadt. It leaves tonight at six. At midnight, a boat is leaving Kronstadt bound for Helsingfors. This is the bit you won't like. The secret police are watching all ports for British agents. You'll meet the boat out on the Gulf itself. The captain can't risk taking you before then. Rebrov is in Kronstadt, he'll meet you there and take you to a rowing boat at Fort Rif. You'll row out from there and get picked up by the boat.'

Cornell and Kit looked at one another, each with the same thought.

'Roger, can we be sure Rebrov has not sold us out?' asked Cornell.

'I'd stake my life on it, Colin,' replied Ratcliff firmly.

'Strictly speaking, it's our lives that are being staked,' said Cornell, smiling grimly. Ratcliff smiled back and nodded. It was difficult to argue against this.

Ratcliff turned his attention to Olly Lake, 'You'll stay on if that's your wish.'

'It is,' said Lake.

'Where's Kristina?' asked Kit.

'Safe. I'll join her soon. We'll make our way to Moscow in the next day or two,' replied Lake.

'They'll be after her too, won't they? They'll think she can lead them to Kerensky,' pointed out Kit.

'True, but these people are, fundamentally, idiots. When I'm in Moscow I'll be joining the Secret Police along with Roger, here.'

Kit looked askance at Ratcliff.

'It's true, Kit,' said Ratcliff, 'We've been planning for this contingency for a while now. We still have some friends there, that's how we received this tip off.'

'Do they know who betrayed us?' asked Kit.

'No but it goes all the way up to Felix Dzerzhinsky'

Mention of Dzerzhinsky quietened the room. He had been a central figure in the Revolution. Currently he headed the Bolshevik security but was rumoured to be reforming the Russian secret police. If he was involved in the search for British agents, then they were up against a formidable opponent.

Kit felt relieved to be going. The atmosphere since the end of the Revolution was, if anything, even more febrile than before. Already food was becoming scarcer than dogs or horses on the streets. Kit was sure the two were linked. He looked at his old friend Olly Lake. Staying in Russia would be dangerous, but his friend was suicidally attracted to danger in a way he could not understand. But it was more than just the danger. It was Kristina. This made more sense, but Kit suspected he would have stayed anyway.

Lake caught Kit looking at him. He smiled and nodded his head to reassure Kit. Ratcliff turned towards Kit and Cornell.

'From Helsingfors you're to make your way directly to Stockholm. "C" is moving our centre of operations there. I understand you'll receive further instructions in Stockholm.'

Kit and Cornell both nodded, neither said anything else. The four men looked at one another in silence. Finally, Ratcliff ended the meeting.

'Well gentlemen, this is it. I hope we shall meet up again one day in London, soon, when this ghastly business in Europe is over.'

The four men shook hands and wished each other luck. Kit and Cornell each grabbed a small bag. Kit turned to Lake and smiled.

'See you in the library at Sheldon's.'

264

*

For what seemed like the thirtieth time that night, Cornell cursed the moonlight as he and Kit trudged their way along the coastline of Kotlin Island. Behind them the town of Kronstadt was brightly lit, but it was the light of the moon overhead that concerned them.

'You lack a sense of romance Colin,' said Kit, although he was worried. Their companion Rebrov was uncommunicative. He was clearly unhappy at having to accompany these men. This worried both Kit and Cornell. The sense of treachery hung heavy in the air. Neither knew Rebrov. He was Ratcliff's contact. His demeanour suggested he would rather be anywhere else than with them. Kit couldn't blame him for this, but would he go so far as to betray them?

The three men kept up a good pace. They needed to; such was the cold. Kit wore several layers of underclothes and a heavy leather coat. It was barely enough against the icy chill. Cornell had long since abandoned his bag, but Kit had kept his backpack for reasons that even he found scarcely credible. He was carrying a first edition of 'Anna Karenina' to add to his Tolstoy collection. It was clearly a folly, but walking along the coast, near midnight, with the secret police on their tail was madness anyway.

Suddenly, Rebrov dived to the ground behind some scrub. Kit and Cornell did likewise. Rebrov pointed ahead. They could see several torches and several men. Cornell glanced nervously at Kit.

Kit shrugged. He wasn't sure if it was just a patrol or whether they were searching for them. Instinctively his hand moved down to the revolver in his pocket. Cornell was of a similar mind. His revolver was out of his pocket, and it was

265

clear he was ready to shoot Rebrov should their companion do anything to give away their position.

The patrol walked inexorably towards where they were hidden. Quietly, Kit removed the revolver from his pocket. His breathing became shallower and the sound of his heart, thumped like a tympanum against his chest. How could they not hear this?

Closer came the patrol. Kit tensed. His revolver, like Cornell's, was pointed through the scrub, directly at the patrol. A light breeze caused the scrub to tickle Kit's face. It was freezing cold, but a bead of sweat developed on his forehead.

Closer.

There were four men. The problem wasn't killing them. Both he and Cornell were expert marksmen. It was the noise. It would give them away and there was nowhere to run. It was also the idea of cold-blooded murder. The slaughter of France seemed less intimate than what they faced here. Kit recoiled at the thought.

The four men passed to within a few yards of Kit and his companions. They were laughing and joking. Was this a diversion or were they really not on the lookout for anyone? Kit held his breath. And then they were past. Walking ahead, oblivious to the presence of the men huddled behind the scrub.

The three men eyed the patrol all the way to the crest of the hill, and then they were gone. They waited another two minutes and then Rebrov stood up and marched ahead. Cornell and Kit replaced their guns and glanced at one another in shared relief. Just over the next knoll, they could see Gulf open out in front of them. A few minutes later they were on the beach. In the distance was a small rowing boat tied to a jetty.

Rather than walk onto the sand, they picked their way along the edge of the beach, fearful of the exposure. Finally, they reached the jetty and climbed into the rowing boat. They had ten minutes to row out to the point at which the boat could rendezvous with them. Rebrov helped them push the boat out onto the water. Each took an oar and began to row at a steady pace. They could see Rebrov wave to them and then turn to walk away.

The breeze was stronger once they had escaped the immediate confines of the beach. The water chopped up over the sides. A glance back told Kit that Rebrov was away from the beach safely. He turned back and focused on rowing away from the shore.

Just in time, they saw the lights of the fishing boat sailing towards them. Kit stopped rowing for a moment and shone a torch to indicate their position. On board the boat, they saw someone hold a torch up in reply. They continued to row.

'Bloody hell,' rasped Cornell, 'Look.'

Kit turned around. On the headland at Fort Rif, they could see several men holding torches. Moments later they came under fire. Both ducked low. The rowing boat was struck half a dozen times but was well made. The bullets could penetrate no further.

The fishing boat was now alongside them. A rope ladder was thrown down over the side. Cornell arched his head towards the ladder to indicate that Kit go first.

Kit let go of the oar and scrambled towards the bow of the rowing boat. Grabbing hold of the ladder he hoisted himself off the boat and onto the second rung. He felt something thud into him. No pain. He continued climbing. Within seconds he was grabbed by several hands and hauled onto the deck of the fishing boat.

Cornell was onto the ladder quickly. Unencumbered by the backpack, he made swift progress. Kit, sensing his arrival, stood up to help him onto the boat. He grasped the arm of Cornell as it appeared over the side and hauled with all his might. As Cornell appeared, his head jerked back suddenly.

Kit pulled him onto the boat. But Cornell was already dead. Kit stared down at the body of Cornell lying on the deck. His head encircled by a halo of blood.

'Oh God, Colin.'

Kit felt himself being pulled roughly down onto the deck. He nodded to the seaman who had, in all probability, saved his life. Shots were still being fired, but Kit could not hear them. He stared into the eyes of his dead companion. The boat tilted in the waves. Kit looked down as the blood ran slowly along the deck onto his hand.

33

Jellicoe stared at Kit then shook his head in disbelief. Their chief suspect was dead and the only lead he could give them was a man who was also dead. It was clear Kit was caught between grief for his old commanding officer and anger for having been used. He put his hand on Kit's arm.

More police had arrived on the scene. The lights in the room were on. Kit glanced once more at Ratcliff. A wave of pity overcame him. It didn't have to be this way, he thought. The guilt must have been unbearable. If Ratcliff was telling the truth, it meant someone else was responsible for the murders. Not only this, but also for the original betrayal back in Petrograd. An image of Colin Cornell swam into view. Another image followed it: a book with a bullet embedded in it. He looked down at his hands. There was no blood on them.

'Search the flat' ordered Jellicoe to the other policemen. Find something that can tell us who Ratcliff has been in contact with. Find me someone.'

From the pit of his stomach, Kit felt a cold fear grip him again. It had started in the car journey and returned, this time more strongly. He knew Ratcliff was telling them the truth, and he knew who was responsible and he knew why.

He turned to Jellicoe.

'It's Olly.'

Jellicoe glanced back at Kit, confused. Olly?

'Olly Lake is Kopel,' said Kit in a voice that mixed certainty with anguish and something else: anger.

'How can you be so sure? Shouldn't we wait for the artist impression?' replied the astounded Jellicoe.

Kit walked absently over to the sofa and sat down. He needed to think. The commotion in the room was distracting. He rose to his feet slowly and walked out of the flat, somewhere quiet. The corridor was cold, but it acted to sharpen his senses. Out of the corner of his eye he saw Jellicoe follow him. The Chief Inspector remained quiet, thankfully, and left Kit to his thoughts.

Why hadn't they killed Adam Walsh? Kit walked up the corridor outside Ratcliff's apartment. It made no sense. Yet this was key. They hadn't killed him for a reason. It was important he lived. It was even more important he was found, saved even. Kit's mind raced furiously. They needed him to live.

'Why didn't they kill Walsh?' asked Kit but more to himself than anyone else.

'Perhaps they thought they had,' suggested Jellicoe.

Kit shook his head, 'No. They wanted him alive. Olly wouldn't make that kind of mistake.'

Then a thought struck Kit. It reared in front of his eyes like a phantom, a silent scream in the night.

'What hospital did they take him to?' asked Kit, his eyes widened by the knowledge of the answer he expected to receive.

Jellicoe thought for a moment, 'I think I heard them say the hospital at...'

'Teddington,' finished Kit.

270

'Yes, that's the one,' replied Jellicoe, unsure of what Kit was driving at.

'We have to go to the hospital immediately,' said Kit with urgency.

'I don't understand, Kit, why?'

'You remember how we thought the ambulance was very quick in arriving? It was Olly. He's the one who took Adam to the hospital, I'm sure of it.'

'But why? I'm still not with you.'

Kit was already moving down the stairs, forcing Jellicoe to follow him. The Chief Inspector gesticulated to other officers to follow.

'The King and the Queen are visiting the hospital today. He's going to kill them. It's all been leading to this.'

*

The Teddington and Hampton Wick Cottage Hospital was nearly fifty years old and resembled a well-to-do suburban villa. In fact, the name of the building was Elfin Villas. The hospital had expanded, slowly, from its original four beds to twenty-four. But there were high hopes in the community of it growing further. Such was the pride in the hospital, many thousands of pounds were being raised to develop a nearby site to extend the hospital's capacity. The presence of the Royal couple set the seal on its undeniable place in the healthcare of the community.

Hundreds of locals were lined along Elfin Grove as Kit and the police drew up in several cars. All were waiting to see King George V and Queen Mary, the Queen Consort. Elfin Grove was a very narrow road. The combination of the crowd of locals as well as the police meant progress was slow. Jellicoe ordered the car to stop and he, Kit and another officer

271

hopped out and made their way on foot to the hospital. Police presence was not heavy, noted Jellicoe sourly. He made his way towards an older officer he knew.

'Hello sir,' said the officer, recognising Jellicoe.

'Hello Johnson, who's in charge here?'

Johnson pointed to a man dressed in plain, dark clothes, called Macintyre. He was clearly military. Ramrod straight back, and shiny black shoes. It was early evening, and the sky overhead was black. It felt like a storm was coming. Jellicoe glanced upwards at the sky and then at the crowds, amazed so many people could be bothered to stay out on such an evening. He made his way through several large policemen towards Macintyre, followed by Kit.

'Are you Macintyre?' said Jellicoe.

Macintyre looked at Jellicoe suspiciously, 'Yes, and you are?' He had a Scottish brogue and clearly was in no mood for time wasters.

'I'm Jellicoe from Scotland Yard,' said the Chief Inspector, showing his identification. 'We believe an attempt may be made to assassinate the King and Queen Consort today.'

'Good lord! Why wasn't I told of this?' demanded Macintyre.

'It's only just come to light, sir. Where are they now?' pressed Jellicoe.

'Inside the main ward having afternoon tea with some patients and staff,' replied Macintyre, with just a hint of a curl on his lip. His tone was less abrupt, however as the implications became clear. He took Jellicoe's arm and moved him indoors, taking a quick glance at Kit and the other police officers.

'They're with me,' said Jellicoe indicating Kit and the other men.

'What are we looking for?' said Macintyre heading through the entrance doors.

'Ambulance men. They brought in someone three quarters of an hour ago.'

Macintyre stopped and stared at Jellicoe and Kit. He then looked at the other policemen, 'Can they check at the back, where the ambulance would've arrived.'

Jellicoe nodded to the men, 'Four of you go. These men are armed and dangerous. Be careful.'

The men nodded and headed off in the direction indicated by Macintyre. Jellicoe looked at Kit. He could see a look of consternation on his face. He hadn't known Kit long, but he recognised the look.

'What's wrong?'

Kit looked at Jellicoe, then Macintyre before replying.

'They're dressed as policemen.'

        *

Daniels had observed the arrival of Kit and the police with alarm. He followed them as they went over to Macintyre and then through the hospital entrance. As Kit had surmised, Daniels was now dressed as a policeman. He was standing with other policemen outside, with the crowds. This presented a problem. A big problem. Kopel was inside waiting for the Royals to leave their appointment. He had no way of warning him, and Aston would immediately recognise his friend.

The question he was wrestling with was how to get inside without attracting the attention of the other policemen. Fortune smiled.

'Hey, you,' called out a policeman at the front entrance.

Daniels nodded in response.

'Come here, we need some men.'

Daniels did as he was instructed. Moments later he was inside with five other policemen.

'I want you all to go inside the ward where the Royals are. For God's sake do it quietly, don't draw too much attention to yourselves. I don't want to spook everyone. They'll be finished shortly.'

'What's happening sarge?' asked one of the men.

'Not sure exactly, but there's a possibility someone might be trying to kill them. Nonsense if you ask me. Now off you go.'

*

On the second floor, in a small office overlooking the front entrance sat Olly Lake / Kopel. He, too, had seen the arrival of Kit with the police and with a similar degree of alarm. There could be no doubt as to why they had come. Then he smiled. It was a smile of admiration for his old friend. He had underestimated him, yet he felt oddly reassured by this. A wave of affection passed through him, a reminder of another time. A happier time. Perhaps, a less enlightened time. He was a different person now. The image of Kristina swam before his eyes.

Sitting back from the window, he checked on what was happening outside while he considered his options. It was clear the operation was compromised. They would conduct a thorough search of the hospital. Upstairs, where the front windows overlooked the entrance, would be an obvious starting point.

The room was small and easy to defend, but not indefinitely. They could smoke him out. He had two hostages.

274

The thought of them made him glance down at a nurse and a doctor. They were lying on the floor. Both were tied up, both looking at him fearfully.

As he was lighting a cigarette, he saw Daniels being approached by another policeman. At first, he thought Daniels was about to be arrested, then it became apparent he was going to join the other police officers in the search. Putting a cigarette to his lips, he dragged slowly. Outside the office he could hear shouting and footsteps. Then he heard people trying to enter. From the muffled shouts he knew they were about to ram the door. He stubbed out his cigarette. It was time to move.

*

In the reception area, Kit, Jellicoe, and Macintyre watched the police officers deploy. A group headed off towards the ward where the Royal couple were situated. Another group went upstairs on Macintyre's order to check the front offices. The final group went to check the area where the ambulance had been left.

Macintyre looked at Kit and Jellicoe, 'What do you suggest we do now?'

'I think we should be near the couple. Are there any other entrances to the ward?'

'No, we chose it for that reason. Just through the front. We've two men stationed there and now a few men have joined them inside as well.'

Kit nodded and then a thought struck him, 'Did you recognise all of the men who went into the room?'

'I didn't recognise any of them. I'm in charge of palace security, I briefed a group of officers two hours ago, wouldn't

275

know any of them from Adam. You don't think one of them is an impostor?'

'I don't think we can take that risk,' pointed out Kit, 'I'll follow your men upstairs. You should check inside the ward itself.'

Macintyre nodded and watched Kit head upstairs. He turned to Jellicoe and said, 'This way.'

Both men began to move towards the ward. As they reached the doors of the ward, they could see the Royal couple on their feet shaking hands with the doctors and patients. The tea had obviously finished. Moments later they heard screams from outside. A quick glance at one another and they changed direction, the door through which they had entered. As they exited, Jellicoe could see the crowd outside looking up and pointing.

34

Kit made his way up the stairs as quickly as was possible. By the time he arrived on the first floor, the police had already searched the first few rooms on the right. Turning to his left, Kit made his way towards the last room on the corridor. He tried the door.

It was locked.

'This one's locked, help me open it,' shouted Kit. In a matter of seconds two policemen were ramming the door with their shoulders. The door burst open. Kit followed the policemen. His eyes were drawn immediately to the window and someone shouting outside. He ran over and looked out.

Meanwhile, Lake opened the window. He stared at his rifle for a moment and then set it down. A few seconds later he had hooked his leg outside and hoisted himself through the window and onto the ledge. Ignoring the shouts of the crowd, he inched his way along the ledge. At the corner he could see part of the roof straight ahead.

He heard the door inside crash open. Down below, the crowd below was screaming, and he could now hear shouts from the police. As he was dressed as a policeman, he guessed they were thinking he was chasing someone.

'He's escaping, get help,' shouted Lake.

Someone responded, but Lake was a little too preoccupied to care what they said. From behind he heard a familiar voice.

'Olly!'

He turned around and saw Kit looking out of the window.

'Sorry old boy can't hang around to chat, so long,' replied Lake with a smile and a mock salute.

Turning away from Kit, he fixed his eyes on the roof on front. Tensing his leg muscles, he tried to crouch as much as was possible in the tight space. He leapt forward towards the roof of the side building.

*

Daniels stared straight ahead. Less than twenty feet away, drinking tea with a few doctors, nurses and patients were King George V and Mary, the Queen Consort. He could feel the gun in his pocket. It would be so easy.

Two shots. It would be over.

Therein lay his problem. What then? The officers beside him were, in all probability, armed. He'd be dead by the time the second shot had been fired. Like Princip he would go down in history for this notorious act of regicide. Perhaps he would become a hero of the Revolution. Perhaps he would start another war.

Two shots. It would be so easy.

The Royal couple did not seem particularly relaxed in the company. It all felt artificial. Forced smiles. Nervous laughter. He wondered if anyone was enjoying the experience. He certainly wasn't. Daniels could see the flecks of grey on the King's beard. His hand caressed the cold metal of the revolver. A finger hooked around the trigger. Did he want to become a martyr of the Revolution?

The Royal couple were standing up now, everyone, except a couple of the patients did likewise. They walked over towards where he and the other newly arrived policemen were

278

stood. Daniels eyes widened in terror. George was coming directly to him.

And then they heard the shouts outside. Seconds later the doors of the ward burst open.

*

Macintyre ran forward to see what the crowd were looking at. He caught sight of a policeman jumping onto the roof and disappearing over the crest. It was impossible to tell if he was giving chase or the quarry. Macintyre turned back to Jellicoe and shouted, 'Check the Royal couple.'

Jellicoe raced inside and towards the ward and ordered the two men standing guard, 'Open the doors.'

Jellicoe ran through the door, followed by the two guards. The Royal couple stopped and stared at the intruder. Jellicoe removed his hat and said, 'Forgive me your highness, we've reason to believe an intruder is on the premises. Please follow me.'

Macintyre appeared at the door. This persuaded the couple. Jellicoe had to admire their calm reaction to his announcement. He allowed them to walk past, flanked by the two guards and out of the ward, following Macintyre.

Jellicoe stopped at the door as they left and turned around. He looked directly at Daniels and pointed towards the big Russian.

'Arrest this man.'

As he said this, Daniels pulled out a gun and levelled it straight at the Chief Inspector.

*

Lake landed on the edge of the roof. For a moment, his balance was off, and he leaned backwards. However, this was momentary. Re-steadying himself, he crouched forward and

279

made his way up the roof tiles and levered himself over the crest of the roof. He slid down the other side on his back.

Down below, he could see other policemen milling around. They still had not seen him and, in fact, seemed blissfully unaware of the commotion at the front. Taking a chance, he jumped down from the roof, startling a few of them.

'Where did he go?' he demanded of a young policeman.

'Where did who go?'

'The man I was chasing you fool. Weren't any of you paying attention?' Lake's tone of voice and natural command had all the policemen jumping to attention.

Pointing to two of the policemen, he ordered them to go around the other side of the hospital in case the intruder had managed to make his way across the back of the hospital roof. Turning to the young policeman he said, 'He may have escaped on foot. Is there a car?'

The young policeman pointed to a police vehicle parked a few yards away.

'Come with me.'

The young man accompanied lake to the car.

'I'll drive,' announced Lake.

*

Kit arrived at the bottom of the stairs, just as George V and Mary were exiting the ward behind Macintyre. The Scotsman looked at Kit who shook his head grimly. Kit glanced at the Royals, who were too preoccupied to notice him. Accompanied by the two police guards they continued to walk down the corridor, away from the entrance. Kit watched them go.

There was no sign of Jellicoe. He had either gone to the back or was in the ward recently vacated by the Royals. Kit decided to head towards the back of the hospital as this was the direction Lake would probably have taken. Followed by two of the policemen he turned down a different corridor and walked towards the back entrance. They were met by two policemen rushing through the doors.

Kit was confused by their arrival.

'Why are you coming this way? He went your direction,' said Kit, pointing out towards the back.

'The Sergeant told us he might've come this way,' said one officer.

'What sergeant?' asked Kit.

'He was chasing the intruder on the roof.'

Kit was alarmed by this, 'Where did this sergeant go?'

'He took the car.'

Kit exhaled slowly and shook his head. He investigated the faces of the policemen, who were slowly realising what had happened.

'He's with young Thomson,' said one of the policemen.

'Are there any other cars out back?'

But Kit already knew the answer.

*

Jellicoe slowly put his hands in the air, to indicate he had no weapon. He looked at Daniels and then lowered his gaze. The gun was pointed right at his chest. Daniels stared at Jellicoe, unsure of what to do next. He could hear his own breathing such was the silence in the room.

With his eyes, Jellicoe indicated for Daniels to look around him. Daniels did so. Four guns were trained on him. He returned his gaze to Jellicoe, a half-smile appeared on his face.

281

Jellicoe saw Daniels's smile. He wasn't sure how to interpret it. The man before him was a killer. He had killed at least four people in this country. There was nothing left for him except either death now, thanks to the several revolvers pointed at him, or the hangman's noose.

Daniels looked at the middle-aged man with the heavy moustache. He wondered if he had a wife. Children. A dog. The man seemed oddly at peace with his fate. Daniels could see no obvious signs of fear in the man's eyes. Either he did not believe he was about to die, or he was an exceptionally brave man. Daniels believed it was the latter. The man spoke in a steady voice.

'Put the gun down Mr Daniels. As you can see, there's no escape.'

Daniels glanced at the other policemen before returning his gaze to Jellicoe. It was true, there was no escape now. He was glad there was no false promises of a fair trial, British justice. One way or another, Daniels would not have much longer to live.

But the man before him would.

Daniels lowered his arm and dropped the pistol. He nodded to Jellicoe and allowed the policemen to come forward and take his arms.

Jellicoe watched the big Russian being marched out of the ward. He slowly exhaled. Moments later, a doctor came over to him.

'Would you like a cup of tea?'

Jellicoe was too astonished to say anything other than, 'Yes please.'

*

Kit rushed back towards the entrance. As he did so, he could see Daniels being led away in handcuffs by three policemen. Kit changed direction and walked into the ward. Sat with the doctors was Jellicoe, taking a sip of tea. He had removed his hat Perspiration matted his hair. Jellicoe looked up at the arrival of Kit.

'Lake?'

Kit shook his head, 'He escaped. In a police car. He has one of your men.'

'Good Lord,' said Jellicoe.

'Indeed,' said Kit, clearly unhappy, 'Your men at the front have been told. They're looking for him now.'

'Will he kill our man, Kit?'

Kit did not answer immediately. A vision of four boys sitting by a pond came to mind. On the pond was a toy boat. A schoolmaster came to join them. The sun was shining, all were in shirts, ties removed.

Will he kill the policeman? Kit shook his head, his eyes faraway.

Jellicoe didn't know if this were an assurance he would not, or if Kit could no longer tell how his friend might act.

*

Lake and the young constable were moving steadily along Church Road. The young man turned to Lake.

'Who are we looking for sarge?'

Lake glanced at his companion and remained silent for a moment. Finally, he replied, 'Chap's dressed in dark clothing, couldn't make out his hair that well.'

They continued along the road with Lake making a show of looking around at the pavements either side of the car. 'Been in the job long, son? I'm Lake by the way.'

283

'Thomson, sir. No, just six weeks since I left training,' replied Thomson.

Lake smiled, 'Family?'

'No plenty of time for that, sir. I live with my mum in Shoreditch.'

'Dad?'

The young man's voice caught a little, 'Lost him in fourteen, sir.'

Lake looked at Thomson, he could see the young constable's eyes redden. He smiled sympathetically, 'Sorry son. Ghastly business.'

Thomson saw a man straight ahead, dressed in dark clothing, entering Teddington Cemetery. He pointed towards the man. Lake looked ahead and saw who Thomson was pointing to.

'You could be right, son,' said Lake pulling over. 'You follow him on foot, don't engage him. He could be armed. 'I'll drive around to the other side of the cemetery, maybe we can take him by surprise.'

'Yes sarge.'

Thomson hopped out of the car and ran towards the cemetery. The man in the dark coat was fifty yards ahead of him. Suddenly, the man stopped and moved over towards one of the graves. Thomson dived behind a nearby tree. As he did so, a thought struck Thomson: why didn't Sergeant Lake come with him? The man was now kneeling by the grave. He gently left a bouquet of flowers by the gravestone.

Moving away from the cover of the tree, Thomson approached the man. The man turned and looked up at him. He was probably no older than thirty. There were tears in his eyes.

284

'Sorry constable, I didn't know it was time to leave,' said the man.

Thomson looked at the headstone. It read "Sarah Ogden, 1894–1918".

'Don't worry, sir, stay as long as you wish. I'm sorry for disturbing you,' said Thomson to the man. He turned and walked towards the exit.

35

London: 11th January 1920

Early morning, two days later, Kit sat in the office of "C" in Holland Park. "C" looked across the table at Kit, Spunky Stevens, and Billy Peel. Removing his monocle, he polished it for a moment. The office was particularly gloomy, and this was not solely because of "C's" penchant for low lighting. "C" started summing up for the benefit of the others in the room.

'There have been no sightings of Lord Lake, I'm afraid. He's gone to ground and, as we know, he has a lot of experience in doing this. I'm not hopeful of finding him. The ports have been alerted of course. Kit, you knew him best, was there no indication, at all, he'd gone rogue?'

'None, sir. Since he came back, he seemed to be in a depression. He said Kristina had been captured and shot. I believed him. His drinking became worse, and he became abusive. I saw less of him as a result.'

'I understand. His behaviour in Russia has been somewhat erratic. It was one of the reasons we pulled him in the end. He may have been mixed up in that Reilly business, and afterwards he seemed to spiral out of control,' said "C".

Kit nodded, remembering the attempt to assassinate Lenin by Sidney Reilly and launch a coup to take over Russia. It was news to him that Olly had been involved.

'Is this when Kristina was taken?' asked Kit.

'We simply don't know, Kit. We only have Olly's confirmation of this,' replied "C".

'What of Daniels? Has he said anything yet?' asked Peel.

'Not surprisingly, Daniels is refusing to speak. I understand there's been various attempts to persuade and, shall we say, coerce him. Nothing is working. He's quite a strong individual. I gather our people do not have great expectations of success,' responded "C".

'So, we've no idea why Olly did all this?' asked Kit disconsolately.

'I'm afraid not, and we can only speculate as to why Roger became involved. I'm inclined to your view Kit that Roger was duped into persuading you to play the match by Lake on the prisoner pretext, which is entirely true by the way. Roger told us about the idea for the match and we were supportive. We must conclude that it was Lake who planted the idea of the match initially with Roger before faking his descent into alcoholism and depression. Along the way he used Roger as his dupe to bring us and you, Kit, into the fold.'

'I'm convinced of this sir,' said Kit, 'I think somewhere along the way Roger lost his mind. He believed Colin was still alive. Perhaps Olly knew this and used him accordingly. I think Roger really believed he was working with us again.'

One other thing had been on Kit's mind since the night at the hospital. He said, 'We've been assuming that Olly was working with the Russians, sir, but what if it was someone else?'

Kit glanced at Peel and then back at "C".

"C" nodded and said, 'I take your meaning. I think it would be fair to say that if Olly is working with ORCA, then

287

Daniels would be too. A body search of Daniels revealed no tattoo and, furthermore, our interrogators reported that he seemed confused by any reference to this group. My feeling is he was duped by Lake also. He may genuinely be a Cheka agent doing his country's bidding. But, to your point Kit, this doesn't mean Lake isn't with ORCA.'

'ORCA?' asked Billy Peel.

'I hope I need not remind you that you've signed the Official Secrets Act, Billy,' said "C".

Peel nodded.

'ORCA is the Organisation des Révolutionnaires, des Communistes et des Anarchistes. I'm sure, even in French the name is self-explanatory,' replied Kit.

ORCA was a mysterious international organisation that Kit had come up against once before. Yet, its aims and ideology were unclear other than to instigate conflict between nations.

'So that's the end of it then?' asked Peel.

'For the moment, yes Billy. Their mission failed, thanks to Kit, and Lake is on the run. To return to the chess theme, we shall have to await their next move.'

'What will happen to Daniels?' asked Kit.

'Unless he's prepared to talk, he'll hang.'

Peel asked the next question.

'And if he turns?'

'It would be a pity to lose such a source of information and capability,' said "C" enigmatically.

This brought the meeting to a close. Kit and Peel followed Spunky out of the office. When they reached the bottom, Kit bid adieu to Spunky and walked out into the cold January air.

'You have your story then,' said Kit.

'Not the one I wanted,' said Peel sourly.

288

Kit looked at him strangely, 'Surely you didn't want...'

'No don't be an ass. I'm no royalist but I certainly wouldn't want to see them assassinated,' said Peel laughing, before adding, 'Exiled maybe.'

It was Kit's turn to laugh. Outside the gate, Kit could see Harry Miller waiting for him.

'Can I give you a lift?'

Peel reluctantly gave way and climbed into the Rolls Royce. Kit instructed Miller on where to go. As they left Peel said ruefully, 'I hope no one sees me getting out of this damn car. My career will be over.'

*

Olly Lake pulled up the collar of his blue pea coat and pushed his woollen cap down. Walking towards a small trawler, he climbed aboard and waved at the captain, who had just arrived on deck.

'Ezeras,' beamed the Latvian captain. It was a smile only a mother could love. Half a dozen rotten teeth remained; their life expectancy matched that of the captain's liver.

'Where have you been, you old dog?'

'Here and there Lukas, here and there.'

They both spoke Russian. Lake was gratified to see how welcome he was. A few other members of the crew appeared, and he received some pretty hefty slaps on the back. He occasionally joined their boat, worked hard, never took any pay and then left. No questions were ever asked.

'How long do you want to stay with us, Ezeras?' asked the captain.

'A month?'

'A month it is. Get yourself downstairs and changed.'

289

Lake didn't need to be shown the way. He walked over to a hatch and gingerly climbed down. He took the second door and found himself in a communal cabin. Two other men were there playing cards. It took a few moments for them to register the arrival of Lake and then both stood up to greet him.

'Ezeras! Where have you been up to?'

Lake laughed and swung his bag onto the top bunk. He took off his cap and the pea coat and lay them on the bunk also. He looked down at their game and said, 'Room for one more?'

Both men assented, and Lake sat down to join them. As one of the men dealt the cards, Lake rolled his shirt sleeves up. The dealer looked down at his forearm, shook his head and smiled.

'You need to get a better tattoo than that, my friend. I can bring you to the best tattooist in Riga. What's it supposed to be anyway?'

Lake smiled and looked at the tattoo.

'It's a killer whale. An Orca.'

36

The short journey to the Daily Herald took place in a surprisingly cordial atmosphere. Kit found Peel more good-humoured than their initial meeting had suggested. Despite this, he kindly declined a tour of the offices and a chance to be interviewed for the paper.

After they parted, Kit said to Miller, 'Let's go to back to the flat.'

'Yes sir,' responded Miller before adding, 'Wasn't a bad sort, Mr Peel.'

'Indeed, he helped a lot. Complicated chap, not what I was expecting.'

They set off on the short journey to Belgravia. Along the way they passed the telegraph office that Miller had been using to communicate the chess moves. Kit asked Miller to pull over. This caught Miller somewhat by surprise, but he found a space immediately outside.

'I think I'll send Mary a telegram.'

They climbed out of the car and marched into the office. There was no queue but there was the young lady that Miller had been dealing with over the last few days.

They walked straight over. If the young woman recognised him, she gave no indication. Kit glanced wryly at Miller who was a picture of innocence. He quickly scribbled a note and handed it to the young woman. She glanced at the name of the person sending it which caused her eyes to shoot up. Kit pretended not to notice.

Barely looking up she held out her hand to receive the message to be sent. She looked over the message and seemed to redden slightly. It read: My friend would like to take you out to dinner. Are you free this Saturday at 7pm? Dinner at Café de Paris. My friend is called Harry Miller.

She looked up at Kit and then Miller who was looking a little confused by what was happening. She smiled and wrote something at the bottom. A few people were now standing behind Miller. There were two words written underneath Miller's message: Yes. Sarah.

Kit handed the note to Miller and walked away leaving the two of them in an embarrassed silence.

'How did you guess?' asked Miller when they were back at the car.

Kit laughed before replying, 'I'd noticed you were rather keen on going to the office and even waiting for a reply. One morning I went to send Mary and surprise telegram and I saw the young lady. It didn't take a great deal of deductive effort on my part believe me.'

A few minutes later they were back at Kit's flat in Belgrave Square. As he arrived outside his flat, he heard Esther crying. He stopped in the corridor, his heart crashing to the pit of his stomach. What had happened? With an effort of will he pushed forward and opened the door.

Mary turned around at his sudden entrance. She smiled.

Kit stopped in the doorway unable to believe his eyes. He stared at her for what seemed like an eternity, taking in her hair, her eyes, and that smile. Then he raced forward. As he reached her, he stopped, unsure if he could hold her or not.

He compromised and took hold of her hand. At last, he regained the power of speech.

'Mary, you're back,' he exclaimed delightedly.

Mary smiled at him. She said, 'Lord Christopher, I can't leave you a week or two and you're off solving other cases. What am I to do with you?'

Kit glanced at Esther and Bright before replying, 'I've some thoughts on that topic.'

Mary's eyes narrowed, 'Sounds ominous.'

'I'm glad you mentioned this,' replied Kit, 'There's something I've been meaning to ask you.'

Esther turned away for a few moments, or was it minutes, while Kit acted on an impulse that was, happily, one that Mary shared too.

*

Filip Serov took an early morning stroll through the park. It was Saturday and the rain beat steadily on his umbrella. He didn't mind. Long winters in Russia made him impervious to all elements except heat. He preferred the cold. Summer in Petrograd could be unbearable at times.

The park was quiet. This surprised Serov, but he accepted that people in Britain had no conception of what winter could do. They could not comprehend how it felt to be so cold that your skin hurt, when the moisture in your eyes could freeze. He was disappointed, nonetheless. Large puddles lay ahead of him, but he did not change direction. He wondered at what point he had stopped walking through puddles.

The pitter pattering on his umbrella seemed to be diminishing, so he pulled it down. He removed his hat and allowed the sprinkling of rain, to fall on his cheek. The traffic to his left created a ceaseless hum but he could still hear birds nearby in the trees singing. They seemed as happy with the weather as he was.

He continued walking through the park until the end, then he slid left and walked up some steps onto the street. Following the road down the hill, he reached his destination. It still looked no more attractive than before, but he found it reassuring all the same.

Unknown to him, his arrival had been noticed. A woman watched him as he walked past the house into the hall. Slightly alarmed she rushed to finish dressing, stopping momentarily to check her hair. She wondered what would happen if she ever wore make up. The thought passed, and she rushed out.

Serov walked through the double door entrance of the hall. Inside the hall, seated at a table with a chess set atop, was a young girl. Not yet observed, Serov gazed at Fiona Lawrence, lost as she was, in concentration. Finally, she raised her head.

If she was surprised to see Serov, she didn't show it. Instead, she merely stared back at him as he approached the table. When he reached her, he looked from Fiona to the chess board and then back again.

'Excelsior?' asked Serov

Fiona nodded, returning her gaze to the table.

'You know the solution?' probed Serov.

Another nod and then she spoke, 'I'm trying to stop it.'

Serov nodded and sat down beside her. As he did so, Miss Upritchard entered the hall. She stopped at the doorway and looked at the two chess players. Unsure of what to do next, she remained silent as neither of them observed her arrival.

'Shouldn't you be out playing with your friends?' asked Serov.

Fiona looked at Serov, anger flashed in her eyes.

'I'm a twelve-year-old maths prodigy. What friends?'

Serov nodded sympathetically, 'Where are your parents?'

Miss Upritchard heard this question, her fists tightened. She watched her ward, desperate to go over to her, but reluctant to interrupt. Serov didn't seem to have ill intentions. In fact, for once, his demeanour seemed compassionate rather than angry.

'They didn't want me. I'm an orphan.'

She was glaring at Serov now. Her eyes were burning, not with anger but with tears. Serov looked away and nodded. He knew about this. He glanced up and saw Miss Upritchard standing at the door. Their eyes met for a moment. Then he looked at Fiona Lawrence.

'Mine didn't want me either.'

Coda

Belgrave Square, London: 11th January 1920

Later that day, Mary sat with Esther, Bright and Miller. Mary and Kit had been allowed some time to catch up on their week apart although Esther had remained nearby to ensure that propriety and Kit's virtue had been maintained.

'Right, let's hear the rest of the story, darling,' said Mary looking up at her fiancé.

'Must we?' asked Kit dolefully.

Yes, chorused everyone except Miller. He, too, knew what was coming. Kit glanced at him, and the two men shifted uncomfortably.

'From where you left off, poor Mr Cornell has been shot and you're on the boat. What happened then?'

Kit sighed audibly and began once more.

*

I made it to Helsingfors and then from there to Stockholm, without incident. In Stockholm I received new instructions, which I think poor Roger must have been aware of, that I was to go to Germany.

As you can imagine, this was far from happy news, but it was important. Our High Command were naturally concerned about the prospect of the Russians pulling out of the War. Doing so would release a lot of German soldiers onto the

Western Front. They needed information about German positions, numbers, and movements in the region of Cambrai. They also needed an idea of the strength of German reserves. I had a couple of weeks to reach Cambrai, assess the situation and contact one of our agents in the area who could radio the information to Allied High Command. But, as Von Moltke once observed, 'No plan survives contact with the enemy.'

Two covers were developed for me. I was given papers, military uniform, the lot. The first one you'll be familiar with Mary, Klaus Adler, I had faked instructions attaching me to a unit right at the front in Cambrai. My second cover was Michael Fischer, an Austrian, returning from Russia to be re-assigned. In both cases I was to be a Colonel, would you believe? I was pleased with my promotion, pity it was in the German army.

I returned to Russia. First to Petrograd and then a town to the south, Pskov. We knew the Germans were pulling some of the Austrian Fourth Army, or what was left of it, back to be reintegrated for the big Spring push we believed the Germans were planning in 1918.

I joined the army in Pskov, no easy matter I can tell you. The German secret police were on the lookout for spies, and I had a few hairy moments as they checked my papers.

After that it was a simple matter of joining some of their men in a local bar. Our intelligence proved correct, and my division was shipped out with me on a train to Germany and then France. I should add that I was sporting a dashing moustache and a monocle. Rather a low rent disguise. I switched between Adler and Fischer when I was in the Cambrai area, depending on which corps of the 3rd Army I was gathering information on.

It was fairly chaotic; the battle was nearing its end. Lots of people were cut off in the fighting which meant I was able to move freely as no one knew who anyone was. On December 5th, I was meant to contact one of our men at a farmhouse in Marcoing, just south of Cambrai. I waited a couple of hours, but he never showed. I heard later that the poor blighter had been caught and executed.

Then I made the fateful resolution to try and make my own way across to our lines myself. The information I had on German movements and reserve strength was time critical. I made my decision in the early evening when it was dark. As luck would have it, I spotted some cavalry up ahead watering their horses near the farmhouse. I crept over and climbed up onto one of the horses, which was separate from the pack and unattended. I shouted, 'Quick he's getting away!'

The men quickly returned to their horses, and we gave chase to some unknown and completely non-existent British spy. It would've been funny had I not been so scared. At an opportune moment, I peeled away from the group and rode through the lines to a point where I could go no further. I dismounted and handed my reins to a soldier standing guard and ordered him to water my horse. The poor fool took one look at my rank and obeyed when he really should've been checking my papers.

From there I strolled along the trenches, guts churning, I may tell you. I finally came across a couple of chaps one was a sniper the other an officer. He was the only one to stop and ask for papers. After that we started chatting, it turned out he'd been to Heidelberg University before me. Would you believe we had acquaintances in common? This helped, I can tell you, because it was touch and go for a moment.

My accent was passably from Heidelberg. Anyway, we had a coffee and then I continued my 'patrol' along the front line. I was looking for the shortest stretch to pass in No Man's Land, also with enough craters for me to dive into if need be. Luckily for me there was a lot of cloud cover that night. It was very dark out there which I was banking on.

After ten minutes chatting about our time at the University, I said auf wiedersehen and moved along the trench. I was happy to get away from them at this point. I didn't like the way the other chap was looking at me. He seemed a lot more suspicious than his commanding officer.

My next stroke of good fortune was the way they had designed the trench. It turned at an angle, a bit like a turret you would say. The reason for this was to provide covering fire to other parts of front line if they were about to be breached. It meant that the chaps I'd just spoken to would not have such a good view of me, at least until I'd made some progress into the middle. I came to a group of Berliners about thirty yards up the line. One of them went to make a coffee and I joined him, on the pretext of being shown around. I slipped a 'mickey' into the coffee pot, a generous amount of it I should add, and stayed with them for a few minutes.

I moved down to the next post and repeated the trick, there was only one man there, so I think that some of the other fellows had left him to join the Berliners. Do you know, if we'd launched an attack at that moment, we'd have inflicted, considerable damage? I waited for ten or fifteen minutes. It felt like hours, believe me. Then I slipped over the top about midway between the two posts. Every so often a flare would go up and I was scrambling into a crater. I'll never forget how cold it was. My hands were numb, my bones were frozen, and my heart was beating like a steam engine. I knew I was making good progress and then...

And then I don't know what happened. An explosion I suppose. I kept slipping in and out of consciousness. I accepted I was a goner. Then, through the ringing in my ears, I heard some damn fool speaking to me.

'Don't worry, we'll have you back soon.'

The End

I hope you enjoyed the second Kit Aston book. **Please consider leaving a review so that others may find it and, hopefully, enjoy also**

A Note from the Author

I have made every effort to ensure historical authenticity within the context of a piece of fiction. Similarly, every effort has been made to ensure that the book has been edited and carefully proofread. Given that the US Constitution contained around 65 punctuation errors until 1847, I hope you will forgive any errors of grammar, spelling and continuity. Regarding spelling, please note I have followed the convention of using English, as opposed to US, spellings. This means, in practice, the use of 's' rather than a 'z', for example in words such as 'realised'.

This is a work of fiction. However, it references events that happened and real-life individuals. Gore Vidal, in his introduction to Lincoln, writes that placing history in fiction or fiction in history has been unfashionable since Tolstoy and that the result can be accused of being neither. He defends the practice, pointing out that writers from Aeschylus to Shakespeare to Tolstoy have done so with not inconsiderable success and merit.

I have mentioned a few key real-life individuals in this novel. My intention, in the following section, is to explain a little more about their connection to this period and this story.

Winston Churchill

Churchill was Secretary of State for War between 1919-21. He sent a naval British military intervention in mid-1919 to protect British supplies and equipment held at Arkhangelsk and other Russian ports. Britain's involvement went further due to Churchill's passionate opposition to and fear of communism.

British troops were fighting the Soviets far into the Russian interior using the most modern aircraft, tanks and even poison gas. British forces were also in against the German 'Iron Division' in the Baltic. The last British troops killed by the German Army in the First World War were killed in the Baltic in late 1919.

Alexander Kerensky

Kerensky was a lawyer and revolutionary. A brilliant orator and, at first, a vastly popular figure, he became Prime Minister of Russia from July 1917 up to the Revolution when he was toppled by the Bolsheviks. It is entirely true that he escaped on the day of the Revolution from the Winter Palace in an American Embassy car. He fled to France then went to Britain before spending the rest of his life in the US.

Captain Sir Mansfield George Smith Cumming

Cumming helped found the British Secret Service in 1909, then known as Special Intelligence Bureau. Over the next few years, he became known as "C". Like Kit Aston, he lost part of his leg following a motoring accident before the War.

Oswald Rayner

Rayner's role as the final assassin of Rasputin may never be known. A BBC documentary, 'Who Killed Rasputin: The British Plot' from 2004 points the finger at him as being one of the conspirators and perhaps the deliverer of the coup de grace. Rayner was part of the 'Far-Reaching System' a clandestine group working in Russia, separately from the official agents working under Sir Samuel Hoare.

George Lansbury

British politician and social reformer who in early thirties led the Labour Party. He was editor of the Daily Herald between 1914-21. Campaigned against Britain's involvement in the Great War and the Russian Civil war.

Sir Nevil Macready

British Army officer who became Commissioner of police for the Metropolis in 1918. He took over the police at a time when morale was low, and they were on strike over pay. Instituted changes that proved popular with the force. A popular leader he was transferred to Ireland in 1920 to command troops in the counterinsurgency against the IRA.

Acknowledgements

It is not possible to write a book on your own. There is a contribution from so many people either directly or indirectly over many years. Listing them all would be an impossible task. First, a mention for key references used in this novel. I have been lucky to have access to great research material such as Giles Merton's 'Russian Roulette: A Deadly Game: How British Spies Thwarted Lenin's Global Plot. Highly recommended for anyone who wants to read of the extraordinary men who were the original MI6, including Reilly 'Ace of Spies'.

Another excellent source was the 2004 BBC documentary, 'Who Killed Rasputin: The British Plot'.

Other sources included: F.M. Bailey's 'Mission to Tashkent' and Edwin Thomas Woodhall's 'Spies of the Great War'. Extraordinary accounts of extraordinary men and women.

Special mention therefore should be made to my wife and family who have been patient and put up with my occasional grumpiness when working on this project.

My brother and Clare Trowbridge have also helped in proofreading which has been a great help.

My late father and mother both loved books. They encouraged a love of reading in me also. They liked detective books, so I must tip my hat to the two greatest writers of this genre, Sir Arthur, and Dame Agatha.

Following writing, comes the business of marketing. My thanks to Mark Hodgson and Sophia Shaikh for their advice on this important area.

Finally, my thanks to the teachers who taught and nurtured a love of writing.

About the Author

Jack Murray was born in Northern Ireland but has spent over half his life living just outside London, except for some periods spent in Australia, Monte Carlo, and the US.

An artist, as well as a writer, Jack's work features in collections around the world and he has exhibited in Britain, Ireland, and Monte Carlo.

There are now seven books in the Kit Aston series.

A spin off series from the Kit Aston novels was published in 2020 featuring Aunt Agatha as a young woman solving mysterious murders.

Another spin off series is features Inspector Jellicoe. It is set in the late 1950's/early 1960's.

Jack has just finished work on a World War II trilogy. The three books look at the war from both the British and the German side. Jack has just signed with Lume Books who will now publish the war trilogy. The three books will all have been published by end October 2022.

Printed in Great Britain
by Amazon